THE HALFADAY CREEK SERIES BY
JAMES B. HENDRYX

Strange Doings on Halfaday Creek
Skullduggery on Halfaday Creek
The Saga of Halfaday Creek
Badmen on Halfaday Creek
Murder on Halfaday Creek
Adventures on Halfaday Creek
Hell's-a-Poppin' on Halfaday Creek

Visit www.jamesbhendryx.com for more information on
forthcoming installments in the Halfaday Creek
uniform matching series.

MURDER ON HALFADAY CREEK

James B. Hendryx

MURDER ON HALFADAY CREEK

JAMES B. HENDRYX

ILLUSTRATIONS BY
PETE KUHLHOFF

ALTUS PRESS • 2016

© 2016 Altus Press • First Edition—2016

EDITED AND DESIGNED BY
Matthew Moring

SERIES EXECUTIVE CONSULTANT
Richard Hall

PUBLISHING HISTORY

"Black John Turns a Trick" originally appeared in the April 25, 1946 issue of *Short Stories* magazine (vol. 195, no. 2). Reprinted by arrangement with the Estate of James B. Hendryx.

"Black John Wins a Bet" originally appeared in the September 10, 1948 issue of *Short Stories* magazine (vol. 205, no. 5). Reprinted by arrangement with the Estate of James B. Hendryx.

"Skin Game" originally appeared in the June 10, 1948 issue of *Short Stories* magazine (vol. 204, no. 4). Reprinted by arrangement with the Estate of James B. Hendryx.

"Miner's Meetin'" originally appeared in the July 10, 1948 issue of *Short Stories* magazine (vol. 205, no. 1). Reprinted by arrangement with the Estate of James B. Hendryx.

"Permanent Resident on Halfaday" originally appeared in the November 25, 1948 issue of *Short Stories* magazine (vol. 206, no. 4). Reprinted by arrangement with the Estate of James B. Hendryx.

"Willie Shows Up on Halfaday" originally appeared in the November 10, 1948 issue of *Short Stories* magazine (vol. 206, no. 3). Reprinted by arrangement with the Estate of James B. Hendryx.

THANKS TO

Everard P. Digges LaTouche, Robert Loomis, Richard Moore, Rick Ollerman, Cynthia Whyte, & the Leelanau Historical Society

TABLE OF CONTENTS

BLACK JOHN TURNS A TRICK 1

BLACK JOHN WINS A BET 38

SKIN GAME 79

MINER'S MEETIN' 114

PERMANENT RESIDENT ON HALFADAY 146

WILLIE SHOWS UP ON HALFADAY 188

BLACK JOHN TURNS A TRICK

OLD CUSH PROPRIETOR of Cushing's Fort, the combined trading post and saloon that served the little community of outlawed men that had sprung up on Halfaday Creek hard against the Yukon-Alaska border, set out a bottle and two glasses as Black John Smith strolled into the room and crossed to the bar.

"Where's the box?" the big man asked, as he noted the absence of the inevitable leather dice box.

"Out in the kitchen. I dropped it in the rinse tub an' told the *klooch* to stick it in the oven an' dry it out."

"Shove out the dice, then. We can hand-roll 'em."

"Listen—I've be'n a lot of kinds of damn fool in my time—but not that kind."

Black John grinned. "So you think there's tricks in hand-rollin', eh?"

"I don't know if there is, er if there ain't. But I know damn well, if there is, you'd know 'em all. Fill up. I'll buy a drink—but I won't git beat out of one. An' what's more," he added, as the glasses were filled, "I want you should git them damn counterfeit bills out of the safe—them ones you got on that there Frisco Nell, that time."

"Hell, Cush—there's plenty room in the safe for them bills. I just took a batch of dust down to Dawson. I saved 'em because a man can't never tell when some sech stray chattel might come in handy. I used part of 'em to good advantage, didn't I, when

1

I bought the dust that Whitey an' that damn female procuress stole off old Bill Ames? An' I shore hope that woman got what was comin' to her, when the secret service guys nailed her with them bills."

"It ain't the room that's botherin' me—it's them damn bills." Picking up a folded newspaper from the back bar, he spread it before the other, and indicated an item with his forefinger. "Read that there piece," he said. "It tells about where some guy in Chicago got ten years when the police ketched him with ten thousan' dollars in counterfeit bills hid in his house—not fer passin' 'em, jest fer havin' 'em. When I read that piece I got them bills out an' counted 'em, an' there's twenty-five thousan' dollars of 'em, an' accordin' to what they done to that fella, I'd git twenty-five years if Downey'd come along an' find 'em there."

"You know damn well that Downey ain't goin' to come snoopin' around in the safe."

"I don't know no sech a thing—an' you don't, neither. I told you to burn them damn bills when you got 'em—er turn 'em over to Downey. An' now, by God, if you don't burn 'em, I will!"

As Cush spoke, he reached into the safe and tossed a package onto the bar. "An' what's more I ain't goin' to do no time fer havin' them bills in my safe. So there they be—an' if you've got any sense, you'll shove 'em in the stove an touch a match to 'em."

Black John picked up the package and riffled the edges of the bills with his thumb. "Pretty good job of printin', at that," he said. "Seems too bad to waste 'em. You know, Cush, it's always be'n my thesis that jestice should triumph—in other words, that a man should get just about what's comin' to him—if not in one way, then in some other. An' you know as well as I do that plenty of damn skulldugs foists themselves onto us here on the crick that are practically immune—"

"You'd ort to be'n a preacher, like yer pa," Cush grunted.

"No, the theologians content themselves with warning folks that their crimes an' irregularities will be punished in the here-after—a mere theoretical concept, at best, and manifestly not amenable to proof. Me, I prefer a more concrete brand of jestice—one that you can see work. I believe that one stone prison, with good stout iron bars that you can see, an' feel is far more effective in deterring inherent criminal proclivities than half a dozen hells that you can't see an' feel."

"Good God!" Cush snorted in disgust. "Is them real words? Er do you make 'em up as you go along?"

"What I mean—if a man commits a crime on this earth he ort to pay for it on this earth—an' not some other place. An' the

law holds a sim'lar view. But, owin' to its crudities an' technicalities, in many instances the law is powerless to act, an' thus jestice is left blindly holdin' her scales.

"Havin' observed this fact, it is my firm belief that it is the end that counts—an' not the means. An' even if it's in some roundabout or irregular manner that I can serve justice, I hold it my duty to do so. That's why I've hung onto this queer currency. It's an ace in the hole fer jestice—with of course jest a bare possibility of derivin' some slight profit for myself."

CUSH, WHO had been perfunctorily arranging the bottles and glasses on the back bar, turned, filled his glass, and shoved the bottle forward.

"Be you through?" he asked.

Black John filled his glass, as Cush made an entry in his day book. "Well—yes. I believe I've exhausted the subject."

"Yeah—an' me along with it, if I'd be'n listenin'. If that there oration means you want to leave them bills in my safe, it didn't git you nothin'. They're out—an' they're goin' to stay out."

The big man sighed heavily. "I might have known I was castin' my pearls before swine, as the Biblical sayin' goes."

"Yeah? They ain't nothin' kin happen that you ain't got one of them bibulous sayin's to fit it. But them bills don't go back in this safe."

"You're a stubborn man, Cush, onct your mind's made up. You won't listen to reason."

"Reason, hell! Listen—I didn't know anyone could git sent up fer havin' queer money in their possession. I thought they had to git ketched passin' it. But accordin' to that there piece in the paper, one's as bad as the other. An' there ain't enough big words be'n invented—even if you know'd 'em all—to auger me into puttin' them bills back in the safe. An' that ain't stubborn. It's common sense."

Black John grinned. "I'm forced to the conclusion that you decline further custody of this spurious currency. I had hoped to, in some manner, further the ends of jestice by passin' it on to some onworthy person, thereby givin' the law somethin' to set its teeth into."

"If yer hell-bent on hangin' onto them bills, why don't you take 'em over to yer cabin?"

The big man shook his head. "I already have quite a collection of knickknacks there—odd bits of property that I've acquired here an' there, and have at times found useful. I deem it inadvisable, however, to add these bills to the museum, although they're a sort of work of art, at that. So I'll just take 'em down to Dawson an' turn 'em over to Downey. I'll tell him I found 'em in a cache that some miscreant abandoned when we hung him. That way, he'll get whatever credit police gets for recoverin' counterfeit money, an' we'll be shet of it. I've be'n figgerin' on runnin' down to Dawson, anyway."

"Hell—you was jest down there last month!"

"Yeah—but that was a business trip. I had to take the dust down an' bank it for the boys. But with Doc operatin' on the crick, an' that damn cuss that called himself John Jones located in Olson's old shack, I deemed it best to get back here as quick as I could. I had to forgo my usual fling at frivolity. Besides that, by goin' down there I can inform Downey of Doc's ontimely end."

Cush eyed him sourly across the bar. "If I was you I wouldn't go makin' no business trip outa this one—like workin' off them there queer bills."

The big man scowled. "You don't s'pose I'd be damn fool enough to try to spread no queer money around Dawson, do you?"

Cush shrugged. "Mebbe not. But neither you ain't goin down there jest to hand over them bills to Downey, an' tell him about Doc—both of which you could do the next time he showed up here on the crick. There's a stud game goin' on here damn near every night, and likewise I've got plenty of licker on hand, so you ain't got to go to Dawson to do no frivolin'."

Black John's grin widened, as he picked up the package and turned toward the door. "There's food for thought in what you say. Mebbe by the time I get to Dawson you'll have it figger out. So long, Cush. I'll be seein' you anon."

II

THE DAY WAS warm. Bright sunlight flooded the valley of the Yukon and streamed through the open door of the Klondike Palace where a man stood drinking at the bar. Suddenly he stiffened as his glance encountered a large man who passed on the sidewalk.

Cuter Malone, the saturnine, paunch-bellied proprietor, noting the incident, leaned forward, his elbows on the bar. "Know him, Jones?" he asked, with a jerk of the head toward the empty doorway.

The other scowled. "I'll say I know him! He's Black John Smith. I hate his guts. He done me out of a hundred an' thirty-five thousan', an' then run me off'n Halfaday Crick."

Malone rolled the inevitable black cigar from one corner of his thick lips to the other, and regarded the man skeptically. "A hundred an' thirty-five thousan is quite a piece of change fer a man to have—'specially a *chechako*, like you."

"I had it, all right. I trailed a dirty, two-timin' skunk, name of Doc Sampson clean up from the States, which he'd double-crossed a pal of mine an' then knocked him off, an' lammed out with eighty thousan'. Time I ketched up with him on this here Halfaday Crick, he'd somehow run the eighty thousan' up to one-thirty-five. I slipped up to his cabin, one night, an' tied him up, an' fried his feet with a candle till he buzzed. Then I brained him an' fetched the one-thirty-five down to the shack where I was stayin' an' cached it, figgerin' to hit out with it next day. But when I went to git the stuff it was gone, an' the cache was empty. So I hits up the crick to put up a squawk to Black John, him havin' told me a while back how they hung cache-robbers on Halfaday.

"He'd already found out about Doc bein' dead, an' I meets him on the trail an' he says, okey he'll git the guy that robbed my cache an' hang him—but first he's got to investigate a murder, an' I've got to help him.

"I'll say! I didn't want to go back there to Doc's cabin—an' him layin' dead there on the floor, like I'd left him. So I tried to stall. But it worn't no use—Black John claimin' that if I don't help him with this here murder, then he won't help me git my one-thirty-five back. So I goes along with him—an' when I seen Doc layin' there, all messed up, I got the shakes, an' Black John talkin' along about how the boys would torture the one that done it instead of hangin' him, an' all to onct, he says 'What did you kill him fer?' an' I claimed I didn't—an' then he picks up the hatchet I'd brained Doc with, an' p'ints out the fingerprints on the handle." The man paused and shrugged. "I ain't no damn fool. I know when they got the fingerprints on you, the jig is up. So I sung my song, tellin' him about Doc robbin' an' murderin' pore old Jack Brower, an' he says how mebbe Doc got what was comin' to him, at that. But he claimed the boys on the crick would hang me for the murder anyhow even if they wouldn't torture me, on account they liked Doc, so he give me a pack sack of grub an' told me to scram.

"I know damn well he got that one-thirty-five—but what the hell could I do? If I stick around there I git hung—an' I don't git the one-thirty-five, neither."

CUTER NODDED. "He's a slick article, all right. He took me fer a hundred thousan' a while back. I'd shore give plenty to see him git his!"

"You mean that?" Jones asked.

"Yer damn right I mean it!"

"How much is 'plenty'?"

Cuter mouthed his cigar, his little swinish eyes meeting the cold stare of the pale blue ones.

"Well—er—that's accordin'. What's on yer mind?"

"The main thing on my mind is that I'm broke. I set in a game, last night, over to the Tivoli, an' them damn sourdoughs took me for what little I had left. I've got to get a stake."

"Yeah? An' what's that got to do with Black John?"

It might have a lot to do with him. Like you said, he's a slick article, all right. But hell, Cuter, there's two of us an' only one of him. What would you be willin' to put out—in case he was to get his—like you said."

"You mean—knock him off?"

"Hell, no! Don't play me for a damn fool, Cuter. I faced one murder rap—up there on Halfaday. An' I ain't facin' another—not with the Mounted on the job, I ain't. S'pecially with you bein' in a position to sing, if they put the bug on you. It's like this—if a guy's on the make, like he is, there's always some way he can be got."

"Yeah? Well, there's plenty of wise guys tried to git Black John—but no one's ever did."

"That ain't sayin' no one ever will."

"How would you figger on gittin' him if you didn't knock him off?" Malone asked skeptically.

"Them boys has got a sweet proposition up there on Halfaday Crick—an' this here Black John is the brain. I've be'n there, an' I know. Jest s'pose somethin' was to happen to him that would hold him off'n the crick fer five, ten yeah, an' two er three smart guys was to sort of horn in an' take over—an' you was one of them guys? It would look pretty good, wouldn't it?"

"How the hell would you hold him off'n Halfaday?"

"I couldn't. But the police could—give 'em the right set-up."

Cuter pondered the idea, then whispered huskily, more to himself than to the other, "If he could be kep' off'n Halfaday fer even a couple of years—er even one—"

HALF A dozen men entered and approached the bar. Motioning to a bartender to serve them, Cuter picked up a bottle and glasses, and with a jerk of the head motioning the other to follow, led the way to a small back room provided with chairs and a table. He placed bottle and glasses upon the table. "Fill up," he invited, and locking the door behind him, seated himself and filled his own glass. "An' now, Jones, what's this here set-up that would make the police hold Black John off'n Halfaday fer five, ten years?"

The pale blue eyes fixed the speaker with a cold stare. "You ain't answered my question?"

"What question?"

"How much is 'plenty'?"

Malone tossed off his drink, and refilled his glass. "Well—like I said—that's accordin'. Accordin' to what I'd git out of it."

"Okay—let's figger it out. First off—if he was behind the bars, you'd be kind of gittin' even with him fer that hundred thousan' he done you out of. An' I'd be gittin' even fer that one-thirty-five, It wouldn't git our money back—but it would add up to a hell of a lot of satisfaction. We ain't got no way of knowin' what his annual take is up there—but believe me, it must be plenty. Jest look at it—you an' me settin' here, an' he's took the two of us fer two hundred an' thirty-five thousan'. That ain't chicken feed, in no man's language. That's only two jobs, mind you—an' believe me, he wasn't sleepin' the rest of the time."

Cuter nodded slowly. "Cripes, if we could git control of Halfaday Crick—me workin' from here, an' you up there—there ain't no limit to what we could do!"

"That's right. But we'd have to take one more guy in. We'd have to have a go-between so we could keep in touch with one another. He'd have to be someone that's good on the trail, an' yet be someone we could trust, too."

Malone nodded. "I know jest the guy. Stanton his name is. He knows the country all right. An' he'll play square, 'cause I've got enough on him to hang him higher than hell. Wait, I'll fetch him. He rooms upstairs."

Returning with Stanton, to whom he briefly outlined the plan, he continued. "As we was sayin', with you up there, an' me here, an' Stanton as a sort of go-between, keepin' each one in touch with the other, it would be the sweetest racket in the hull damn North!" As Malone talked, his little eyes gleamed avariciously above his fat cheeks. "I could spot the *chechakos* that had enough on 'em to make it worthwhile, an' steer 'em up there, an' you an' the boys up there could knock 'em off. Safe, too. No one here in the Yukon would miss a damn *chechako* nohow. An' by the time their folks back in the States would begin to git worried, an' set the Mounted to tracin' 'em, it would be too late to find out anything. Even if the police should show up on Halfaday, you boys could step acrost into Alasky an thumb yer nose at 'em."

Jones nodded, his cold eyes on the other's face. "You've got the picture, Cuter. So, talk turkey. What would a set-up like that be worth to you?"

Malone stalled, rolling the black cigar from one corner of his mouth to the other, and back again. "The way I see it, it would be a percentage proposition. You'd git forty percent of the take, an' I'd git forty, an' Stanton here, we'd cut him in on twenty percent."

"Me an' you don't see it alike, by a damn sight!" Stanton interrupted.

"Listen," Cuter scowled. "I find the guys an' steer 'em up there, an' Jones does the rest. All you do is—"

"Yeah—all I do it all the work. It's a couple hundred mile to Halfaday Crick—an' every damn foot of it is upstream paddlin'. An' if I'm the go-between, I'm either goin' up to Halfaday er comin' back practically all the time."

"There's a short-cut through the hills somewheres. I've heard about it."

"Okay—call it a hundred an' fifty mile. A hundred-an'-fifty mile hike through them damn mountains packin' a pack, ain't no picnic at no price. An' buckin' Black John ain't no healthy practice, neither! No sir, by God, she cuts three ways equal, or there ain't no deal! An' don't go figgerin' on two-timin' me, neither. 'Cause, believe me, what I could blow into a cop's ear in two minutes would chivvy yer racket fer good an' all."

Malone sneered, "An' what I could blow into a cop's ear would hang you."

Stanton grinned. "Mebbe. But you won't blow, Cuter. Morocco put me wise to a little deal back in New Orleans that would git you the rope, er the hot squat—er whatever they use down there. So seem' we're all pals together, s'pose we git down to business."

Jones' thin lips compressed into a tight smile. "Looks like he's got somethin' there, Cuter," he admitted. "She looks like a three-way split. No sense in playin' hog amongst ourselves. We'll go equal pardners—an' there'll be plenty in it fer all of us. So, havin' settled that part, we'll take up the matter of cash outlay."

Cuter blinked. "What d'you mean—cash outlay?"

"Like I told you back there at the bar, I'm broke. Seein' how I'm the one that's figgerin' out the scheme fer puttin' Black John out of the way, how about you layin' a little cash on the barrel head?"

"I don't know what yer scheme is. How do I know it'll work?"

"You don't know. But when you hear it, I'll bet you'll figger it's worth tryin'."

"It better be good—damn good. Go ahead an' spill it."

"Fer how much?"

MALONE'S FACE flushed. "Listen here, Jones. I wasn't made in a minute. I ain't sucker enough to come accost with any cash, an' then have you come out with some damn fool scheme that wouldn't have a chant of workin' out. Believe me, I ain't payin' out no good money fer no bedtime story."

"I ain't askin' you to, neither. Here's my proposition—take it er leave it. I'll explain the scheme. You don't pay me a damn cent till you hear it. If you figger it's okay—then you slip me the change, an' we'll go ahead."

"Okay. Let's hear it."

"Fer how much—in case it's good."

"Well, if it's good—if I figger it's good enough to pull on Black John, how's five hundred dollars?"

"You've got to sing louder than that, Cuter. About ten times louder."

"Five thousan'! Not by a damn sight!"

Jones shrugged, and rose from his chair. "Okay. Let's jest ferget the whole thing. Of course, what we'd take in in a year's time would make a measly five thousan' look like a thin dime. But it's your money." He swallowed his liquor and returned the glass to the table. "I'll be trottin along. Good luck, Cuter—an' thanks fer the drink."

"Set down," Malone said, shoving the bottle toward the other. "Fill up. I was jest sort of feelin' you out. Like you say, this racket will pay off big, if we can work it. I won't hold out on five thousan'—pervidin' yer scheme looks good. Let's have it."

As Jones resumed his seat and refilled his glass, Stanton downed his liquor and reached for the bottle. "Yeah, an' there's me, too. I'm jest as broke as what Jones is! I ain't had nothin' but some loose change in my pocket fer a hell of a while. We're all equal pardners. I gotta have five thousan', too."

Malone scowled. "Okay—okay! If the set-up'll stand five thousan' it'll stand ten. Go ahead, Jones, spill it."

"It's like this—we all know Black John's an outlaw—the police, an' everyone else. An' him robbin' my cache, we know he's a cache robber. Okay. What I claim, anyone that'll rob one cache an' git away with it'll rob another."

"I'll say he will," growled Malone. "Hell, he's robbed a hundred of 'em! Plenty of guys has hit fer Halfaday after puffin some job down here along the river, but they don't none of 'em ever git off'n Halfaday with their dust. Black John waits till he kin locate their cache, an' robs it, an' then he calls a miner's meetin' an' hangs 'em. Er else he runs 'em off'n the crick, like he done you."

Jones nodded agreement. "That's right. So we'll jest give him a chanct lo rob another cache."

"How do you mean—rob another cache?" Malone asked.

"It's like this—everyone knows about that twenty-five-thousan' dollar payroll the Amalgamated lost a while back— where they found the messenger with his head bashed in—an' everyone knows the police is runnin' around in circles to find the one that done it. All right—s'pose I was to slip the word to Black John that I know where that payroll is cached. I'll tell him I'm grateful to him fer savin' my life up there on Halfaday by slippin' me that grub an canoe so I could pull out before the boys hung me. I won't let on I know damn well it was him that got that one-thirty-five outa my cache. I'll tell him I hate this guy that knocked off the Amalgamated messenger, an' cached the dust, on account of him beatin' me out of five thousan' in a crooked card game, but I ain't got the guts to go after the cache myself—but if he'll slip me the five thousan' I lost, he kin keep the other twenty thousan'.

"We'll get quick action, too, because I'll tell him I heard this guy say he was pullin' out on the steamboat tomorrow for Seattle. An' that he aims to get the dough out of his cache jest before daylight. An' that'll give Black John plenty of time to slip to the cache. An' when he does, Downey'll be waitin' there for him, because, in the meantime Stanton here, will go to Downey an' tell him he overheard a couple of fellas in a booth in here talkin' about the cache—an' how they was goin' to get the stuff out of it along towards mornin', an' how when the two left the booth, he seen Black John come out of the next booth, with a grin on his face. He'll tell Downey he figgers that Black John aims to git that dough. Stanton'll claim he's after the five thousan' reward the Amalgamated has posted fer information leadin' to the recovery of the payroll, er the arrest of the robber. Then Downey'll hit for the spot an' be waitin' when Black John visits the cache.

"In the meantime, I'll slip up an plant the dough in the cache, about suppertime."

"The dough? What dough?" Cuter asked.

"Why—the twenty-five thousan' that Black John will lift out of the cache, of course."

"Where's this here twenty-five thousan' comin' from?"

"You're puttin' it up. Hell, you'll get it right back. When Black John lifts it out of the cache, Downey'll be right there to nail him. As soon as Downey looks them bills over, as checks 'em with the numbers on the Amalgamated payroll bills, he'll know they ain't the ones, because he's got the numbers of 'em. Hell, the newspaper has carried a list of them numbers ever sence the robbery. Then you an' me'll slip over to headquarters an' you claim the money, tellin' Downey it was money you give me to make a part payment on a claim—an' I'll back you up, claimin' I cached it there till tomorrow."

"Not by a damn sight!" Malone growled. "We'll rig up a dummy package to put in the cache."

Jones sneered. "An' how much time would Black John do fer liftin' a dummy out of a cache? Don't be a damn fool, Cuter. We want to get Black John—an' get him good."

"Black John'll know it's a frame-up, when he finds that money belongs to me, an' not to the Amalgamated," Cuter said.

"What do you give a damn what he knows? He'll do jest as much time fer stealin' your money as the Amalgamated's—an' believe me he'll do plenty. By the time he gits out, we'll have milked the Halfaday Crick racket dry, an' we'll be to hell an' gone out of here with plenty of dough to last us from now on."

As Malone pondered the proposition a slow grin twisted the thick lips. "By God, I believe yer right! An' it'll shore burn him up to know that I put one over on him, at last." He paused abruptly, and regarded the two men between narrowed lids. "An' jest by way of a warnin'—you two guys better not fergit who you're takin' on this deal."

"Why—what do you mean?" Stanton asked.

"Meanin' that that twenty-five thousan' goes into that cache, an' stays there till either Black John er Downey lifts it out. If the scheme works, Black John'll lift it. If it don't, Downey'll be the one to do it. An' in either case, I get it back—see? An, on top of that, you better make the play good, 'cause I ain't puttin' out no cash fer no failure. If it works, you'll get your five thousan' apiece out of that twenty-five thousan', when I get it back. If it don't work, I get my money back—an' you get nothin'. An' what's more, any idees you might git in yer heads about grabbing off the twenty-five thousan' had better be throw'd in the discards, 'cause I've got boys here that'll drop you in the river with a rock wired to yer necks the minute I give 'em the word."

"You don't need to he afraid we'll two-time you," Jones said. "Hell, that twenty-five thousan' wouldn't be nothin' to what we'll pull down off'n Halfaday."

Malone nodded. "Okay. Now, Stanton, you slip over an' sing yer song to Downey, an' come back here an' tell us what he says. If he falls fer it I'll slip Jones the money an' he kin plant it. But first off, we got to figger where to cache it, so you kin tell Downey."

"I be'n studyin' about that," Jones said, "an' I know jest the place. I be'n down there along the river bank where folks dumps their trash fer the last couple of days huntin' pieces of tin to patch my shack with, an I seen an old sheet iron worshtub there. It lays clost to the top of the bank, jest beyond the last lumber pile. I was goin' to take it along, but I didn't have nothin' to bust it up with. I'll cache the dough in under it."

"Git goin', Stanton, an' hurry back, so I kin plant the stuff before supper. No one won't pay no 'tention to me bein' down to the dump, 'cause like I says, I be'n foolin' around there fer a couple of days. I'll plant the stuff, an' then hustle over to the hotel, an' spill Black John an earful whilst he's eatin'."

III

CORPORAL DOWNEY GLANCED up from his desk and scowled as he recognized the man who stepped through the doorway of his office at detachment headquarters and sidled toward him, as one of the habitual hangers-on at the notorious Klondike Palace.

The man paused before the flat-topped desk and winked. "I come over here to give you a tip," he said.

"Yeah? What kind of a tip?"

"Well, rightly speakin', it's two tips. It's about this here Amalgamated robbery where the messenger got knocked off an' the payroll stole."

"What do you know about it?"

"I know where the guys that done it has got the dough cached. An' likewise I got a hell of a good idee that a certain party aims to rob that cache sometime tonight. What I claim, if you play yer cards right, not only you kin git that there twenty-five thousan' back, but you kin git this guy dead to rights whilst he's robbin the cache."

Reaching into a file Downey drew out a dossier and ran through its contents. Finally he looked up. "Your record ain't so hot, Stanton," he said. "You done sixty days on the woodpile last fall for stealin' goods from the wharf. Before that you was suspected of bein' in on the robbery of a couple of *chechakos* down to the Palace, an' you skipped out. Then along in the winter you was charged with breakin' an' enterin'. The charge was changed to drunk an' disorderly—an' you got off lucky."

"That's all it was, too," the other defended. "I got loaded that night, an' started fer home. I was livin' in one of them shacks down by the sawmill, an' it was darker'n hell, an I got lost an' come to a shack I figgered was mine, an' I couldn't shove the door open so I figgered it was stuck, an' kicked it in. An' next thing I know'd some woman was yellin' an' hollerin' like hell, an' lammin' me over the head with a stick of stovewood. Then a cop come along an' run me in. I'll say I was lucky! If that cop hadn't of heard the rookus an' come down there, drunk as I was, that damn skirt might of brained me."

Downey grunted. "An' that jest goes to show that sometimes this force is too damned efficient. But about this cache? If you know where that twenty-five thousan' is cached, why haven't you made a play for it, yourself?"

"Not me! By God, what I claim—if them birds knocked off one guy to git it, they'd shore as hell knock off another one to keep it! Them babies is plenty tough."

"How does it happen that you know where that money is cached?" the officer inquired.

"It's like this—I was playin' cards, last night down to the Palace, an' 'long about two o'clock I cashed in. Bein' as I was a little ahead, I an' some other guys got to buyin' drinks, till I got a load on, an' instead of goin' home I snuck into one of them there booths in the dance hall an' went to sleep.

"Come daylight, I woke up an' I heer'd some gays talkin' in the next booth. They says how the *Julia B* was due to pull out fer Whitehorse tomorrow, an' they aimed to be on her. One of 'em asks the other one if he'd cached the dough where they could pick it up handy jest before daylight tomorrow mornin', on account they didn't want to have it on 'em in case they was picked up. He claimed that, what with the five-thousan' dollar reward the Amalgamated has got posted, the police is liable to pick up anyone on suspicion an' frisk 'em.

"The other guy says yes he did, an' he tells where he'd cached it. They done a little more talkin' an' got up an' went out. I peeked out through the curtains an' seen 'em go out the door, an' then I started to git outa there when I seen the curtains of the next booth on the other side of where these guys was start to wiggle, an' then a man steps out onto the dance-hall floor. He's got a kind of a wise grin on his face, an' I know'd he'd be'n listenin' to them two guys, same as I had. After he'd went out I slips out, too, an' I goes to the bar. There ain't no one else in there, except the bartender, so I has me a couple of drinks, which I shore as hell needed 'em, the way I felt. Then I went over to the restaurant an' gits somethin' to eat.

"I kep' a-studyin' what to do, First off, I kinds figgered to make a play fer that dough. But hell—them guys might be watchin' that cache, an' like I said, they'd shore knock anyone off that tried to lift it. An' even if they didn't, this other guy that know'd where it was, shore as hell would. 'Cause, you kin bet he figgers on liftin' it hisself, an' believe me, he's plenty hard! So I kep' a-studyin' what to do all mornin', an' finally I figgers the best thing to do is come over here an' see if I couldn't make a deal with you."

"A deal? What kind of a deal?"

"It's like this—if you git that twenty-five thousan' back, you collect that there five-thousan' dollar reward. How about split-tin' it with me? That way, I git twenty-five hundred—an don't run no risk of gittin' knocked off."

"The police ain't interested in the reward," Downey said. "If I recover the money on any tip you give me, you can keep the reward."

"You mean the hull five thousan'?"

"That's right. Now, who were those two birds you heard talkin' in that booth?"

"Them? Hell, I don't know who they was!"

"What did they look like?"

"I never seen nothin' but their backs when they went out. I don't know what they look like. Their backs looked like anyone else's back."

"An' this other fellow—the one you said come out of the next booth? You must of seen his face. You said he had a grin on it."

"Yer damn right I seen his face. He's the damnedest outlaw there is in the hull Yukon. He's the king of them outlaws that hangs out up there on Halfaday Crick."

"You mean—?"

"I mean Black John Smith. That's who I mean!"

A full minute passed as Downey sat drumming softly on the desk with his fingers. "Do you know Black John? That is, personally, I mean?"

"I'll say I know him; I hate his guts! He run me off'n Halfaday, one time. It's last summer—that time you claimed I skipped out when them two *chechakos* was robbed. I didn't have nothin' to do with robbin' 'em, but I figgered I might git picked up fer it, on account I was saw with 'em that night they was robbed. So I lit out fer Halfaday. When I got to Cush's place, him an' Black John was shakin' dice fer the drinks, an' when Black John seen me, he told me to git to hell back where I come from. He claimed they didn't want no cheap trash that hung around Cuter Malone's Klondike Palace on Halfaday, an' if I was still there, come night, they'd hang me. So he give me grub enough to take me back. What right has he got to say who kin live on Halfaday Crick, an' who can't?"

"No right at all," Downey replied firmly. "You had a perfect right to stay there, if you'd wanted to."

"But—hell—they'd of hung me!"

"Well, of course, there's that angle, too."

"Yet damn right! An' so now, if you watch that cache tonight, you kin git the goods on Black John. Jest let him lift that dough outa that cache, then nail him. Not only that, but you could lay there an' nab the two that cached the stuff when they come to git it. Black John knows they don't aim to pick it up till jest before daylight, same as I do. So he'll git there ahead of 'em. Not only you git the money back, but you pick up the three damn crooks, to boot. An' what I claim—a tip like that is worth that five-thousan' reward."

Downey nodded. "Guess you're right, Stanton. An now—where is this cache?"

"It's down back of them lumber piles along the river bank jest above the wharf. There's a dump there, where folks has throw'd trash, an' the dough is hid in under an old busted sheet-iron washtub, which it lays on the edge of the bank, an' only a little ways from the end pile of lumber. If I was you I wouldn't go there till night, though. 'Cause them two that cached it, will prob'ly be keepin' an eye on it, an' Black John, too. 'Course, you could git the money, right now—but you'd miss yer chanct of pickin' up these guys. You wouldn't have a damn thing on 'em."

Downey nodded. "That's right, Stanton. Thanks for the tip. An' if I recover that money, I'll see that you get the reward."

After the man had gone Corporal Downey sat for a long time drumming thoughtfully on his desk with his fingers. "I don't believe Black John would stoop to cache robbin'," he muttered finally. "But—in this case it might fit into his peculiar code of ethics, at that. The money belongs to a big outfit—an' he'd be stealing it from a couple of crooks. The thing looks a bit fishy, somehow. But, anyhow, see it through—let the chips fall where they may, as the sayin' goes."

A few minutes later Stanton passed through the barroom of the Klondike Palace and entered the back room where he was quickly joined by Malone and Jones. "Everything's okay," he reported. "An' when Black John lifts that dough outa the cache, Downey'll be waitin' fer him behind that there last lumber pile." He paused and grinned. "Downey, he promised to give me the five thousan' reward fer the tip. He don't know that I'll draw down five thousan', whether that's the Amalgamated's money, er whether it ain't."

Malone stepped from the room and returned a few minutes later with a common tin dinner pail which he placed on the table. "There's the money," he said, eyeing Jones, "an' if yer interested in stayin' alive, it better be there till either Black John er Downey lifts it out."

Removing the lid, Jones withdrew the bills, counted them, and returned them to the box. "Jest in case you made a mistake an' might accuse me of liftin' a few of 'em," he explained. Then, picking up the pail, he left the room.

IV

ARRIVING IN DAWSON, Black John registered at the hotel, tossed his pack in a corner of his room, and strolled out onto Front Street. As he passed the open doorway of the Klondike Palace, he noticed Jones standing at the bar talking with Cuter Malone—noticed, too, that the man gave a perceptible start at sight of him. He grinned to himself as he passed down the street.

"Looked kind of surprised seein' me here in Dawson," he muttered. "Wonder if he figgers I got that hundred an' thirty-five thousan' he stole off of Doc? If he does, I'll bet he thinks I charged him a hell of a price to refrain from hangin' him."

Stepping into the Tivoli, he whiled away a couple of hours, then returning to his room, removed the packet of counterfeit bills from his pack, slipped them into his pocket, and sauntered toward police headquarters.

As he approached the lumber yard, he noticed a man some fifty yards ahead of him, turn abruptly and slip between two lumber piles. The man was carrying a dinner pail, and as he caught a fleeting glance at his profile, he recognized Jones.

"U-u-u-m, now what the hell would he be up to?" be mused. "Whatever it is, I'm bettin' it bodes no good fer someone. He shore popped in between them piles like he didn't want no one to see him. Guess I'll jest trail along. Any odd bit of lore a man could pick up concernin' a character like Jones, might not come amiss."

Stepping into an alley between the piles that ran parallel to the one into which Jones had disappeared, Black John proceeded swiftly toward the river bank, and climbing to the top of a tall pile of lumber, lay flat on his belly, removed his hat, and peered cautiously over the edge. At first he could see nothing of his man, but presently he saw him emerge from between two piles at the top of the bank, pause and glance furtively around, then proceed on past the last pile of lumber. Again he paused and glanced about him at a point where the steep river bank was littered with an unsightly collection of discarded junk. Apparently satisfied that he was unobserved, he stooped swiftly, and thrust the dinner pail beneath a battered and overturned sheet-iron wash tub, then with another hurried glance about him, he slipped back into the lumber yard. A few minutes later, from his point of vantage, Black John saw him emerge onto the street, and hurry toward the Klondike Palace.

Clambering swiftly to the ground, Black John hastened to the tub, slipped the dinner pail from beneath it, and lifted the lid. His eyes widened at the sight of the big roll of currency, and with hardly a moment's hesitation, he reached into his pocket, ripped the paper covering from his packet of counterfeit bills, slipped them into the pail and returned it to its place beneath the tub. Pocketing the roll he had taken from the pail, he slipped into the lumber yard, and passed out onto the street.

"I figger that damn cuss was bent on some nefarious enterprise," he muttered, as he turned toward the hotel. "It shore beats hell how these crooks carries on. Anyways, he saved me the trouble of botherin' Downey with them counterfeit bills. An' when Jones digs 'em out of there as starts passin' 'em, there's liable to be repercussions that'll be amusin' in the extreme."

Sauntering toward the hotel he again passed the open doorway of the Klondike Palace, and again he noted that Jones stood before the bar talking with Cuter Malone and another whom he recognized as one of the regular hangers-on at the Palace. "Birds of a feather, as the Good Book says, is all tarred by the same brush. It's too damn bad I couldn't of rung Cuter in on them counterfeit bills somehow. There's one damn cuss that the worst that could happen to him wouldn't be no more than an interest payment on what he's got comin'."

AS HE stepped into the hotel the clerk beckoned with a nod of the head. "Better slip into the dining room with the first bunch. The doors will be open in five minutes. The *Robert R. Kerr* come through the other day with fresh beef, an' there ain't but damn little of it left. Boy, them steaks just melts in your mouth!"

"Thanks for the tip," the big man grinned. "A thick juicy steak'll taste good."

Hardly had he seated himself at the table when Jones appeared in the doorway, glanced about at the dozen or more diners, and made straight for Black John's table. "By God, I thought it was you!" he exclaimed, as he seated himself in the opposite chair. "Yes sir, jest a few minutes ago I was standin' at the bar over to the Palace, an' I seen you walk past headin' for the *ho*tel. 'Damme, if I don't believe that's Black John,' I says to myself. An' bein's it's right around suppertime, I downs my drink an' come on over."

Black John grinned. "Sort of figger on talkin' over old times, eh? Like you murderin' Doc, there in One-Eyed John's cabin."

The other frowned. "I don't like that word—murder."

"Yeah, there's quite a few others that ain't liked it, too—when it was put up to 'em by a prosecutin' attorney, or a miners' meetin'."

"That damn Doc got jest what was comin' to him, at that, fer what he done to pore Jack Brower."

"You was actin' merely to avenge this pal of yours, I s'pose?" Black John said. "The hundred an' thirty-five thousan' you stole out of Doc's cache, had nothin' to do with it?"

"I didn't know he had no hundred an' thirty-five thousan'," Jones replied. "I figgered it would only be the eighty thousan' he stole off'n pore Jack. Where he got that extry fifty-five thousan' is more'n I know. Most likely he stoled that too. But that one-thirty-five never done me no good. Some damn cuss robbed my cache before I'd got a chanct to spend a nickel of it. An' that's one thing I wanted to ask you about. Did you ever ketch the one that done it? You claimed they couldn't no one pull off no cache robbery on Halfaday without he got hung. An' believe me, I could use that one-thirty-five, if I had it."

Black John shook his head. "Fact is, Jones, the boys up there on Halfaday liked Doc, on account of him fixin' 'em up when they got hurt, an' doctorin' 'em when they was ailin'. They know damn well you murdered Doc an' robbed his cache, an' they're sore as hell about it. Any investigation I might make as to who stole the money off 'n you wouldn't get to first base. The boys would figger you had it comin', an' even if they know'd who done it, they wouldn't come acrost with the information. It's just like I told you when I slipped you that grub to get off the crick with—they'd hang you in a minute, if they could lay hands on you. You're lucky to be alive."

Jones nodded. "Yeah, I guess that's right. But jest the same, it's hell to be broke—an' prices what they be."

"You can't be very broke—eatin' here at the hotel. There's lots of cheaper places to eat in Dawson."

"I ain't got a damn dime, except jest what I make workin' by the day—a job here, and another one there. An' what's more, I don't eat here. This here's the first time I ever be'n in the place. An' I ain't got the price to pay fer my supper if I'd eat it. An the only reason I come, was 'cause I figgered I'd get a chanct to talk with you. I figgered mebby you might of ketched that cache robber."

"Or even if I hadn't, maybe I'd pay for your supper, eh?"

"You won't never regret it, if you do pay fer it," the man said. "'Cause I shore kin tip you off to somethin' worthwhile."

"Yeah?"

"You bet I kin! How'd you like to lay hands on twenty-five thousan'—good cash money?"

"We-e-e-l-l—that depends. Takin' it by-an'-large, as the Good Book says, I ain't averse to pickin' up odd amounts here an' there, where circumstances permits. I'd say it would be owin' to how much effort the venture would entail, an' also on how legal it would be."

"You mean how much work it would be to git it? An' could you git pinched if you was ketched?"

"Yeah, that's the gist of my argument."

"They ain't no work at all. Hell, the stuff's cached not over five minutes walk from right here where we're settin'."

"You mean—rob a cache? Me! Right here in Dawson, right under the nose of the police! You must think I'm crazy."

"This here ain't like robbin' no reg'lar cache, John. It's different. This here money was stole. I don't know if you heer'd about the Amalgamated gittin' robbed of twenty-five thousan', er not."

"Yeah, seems to me I did hear a rumor to that effect a while back."

"It wasn't no roomer. It's the God's truth. An' it was a dirty play, besides. The damn cuss that done it waylaid the messenger an' smashed in his head with an iron bar, an' grabbed off the payroll he was takin' out to the works. What I claim, anyone that would pull off a play like that had ort to lose out on it."

Black John stifled a grin. "Yeah," he agreed, "the ethics of murderin' a man fer the purpose of robbery is open to question. But how come you know where this payroll money is cached?"

"It's like this—las' night, it was, an' I'm in the Klondike Palace, an' a lot of guys was drinkin' an' settin' 'em up to the house, an' I git a snootful an' I sneaks into one of them there booths in the dance hall to sleep it off. Well, 'long to'rds mornin' I wakes up, an' a couple of guys is talkin' in the next booth. They're talkin' kinda low, like they didn't want no one to hear 'em. But them partitions is thin an has got cracks into 'em, to boot, so I stuck my ear to a crack an' listened to 'em. Well sir, one of 'em was the guy that knocked off this here Amalgamated messenger, an the other one was the guy that tipped him off about when the messenger would hit out with the payroll, an' how much was in it. This last guy worked in the Amalgamated office, an' that's how he know'd. He claimed he got fired sense the robbery on account they figgered he might of did some talkin'.

"They had the payroll money on 'em, an' they figger on pullin' out fer the States on the steamboat tomorrow. But they was afraid the police might pick 'em up before the boat pulled out, so they agrees to cache the dough so if the police did pick 'em up they wouldn't find it on 'em. They says how the boat is due to pull out 'long about seven in the mornin', an' they'd cache it where they could pick it up an' git to the boat quick. One of 'em says how he know'd a damn good place to cache it—an' he up an told the other guy, an' then they lit out. I waited around so's they wouldn't see me come out of that booth, an' this after-noon, I slipped over to where they claimed they'd cached the stuff, an' damned if it ain't there, all right—in a common tin dinner pail."

"Why didn't you grab it off?"

"Who—me? Not by a damn sight! What I claim, if a man would knock off one guy to git that money—he'd knock off two! How'd I know one of them guys mightn't of be'n watchin' that cache? If they seen me pokin' around there, an' I didn't take the stuff, they wouldn't do nothin, except mebbe move it out— but if they seen me hist it, by God, they'd do plenty. What I claim it's enough if them Halfaday Crickers is layin' fer a chant to kill me, without someone down here wantin' to git me, too!"

"Mebbe they did see you go to the cache, an' mebbe they did move the stuff out," Black John suggested.

Jones shrugged. "They might of. I shore as hell didn't hang around there to see. It wouldn't take long to find out. Like I said, you kin walk there from here in five minutes. If they didn't, yer in twenty-five thousan'. You could slip over there, like around midnight an' find out. They don't aim to pick it up till jest before the boat pulls out."

"It shore would serve 'em right if someone did lift it," Black John observed. "Why don't you slip over there tonight, an get it yourself?"

"Fact is, John, I ain't got the guts to. I figgered on doin' it—be'n figgerin' on it ever sense I snuck over there an' seen the money right in that dinner pail. But I know damn well, when the time come to do it I'd renig. I'm a damn coward, I guess."

"Why are you lettin' me in on it?"

"They's two, three reasons. First off, I know you've got the guts to do anything. Another reason is that one of them guys is the damn cuss that beat me outa the last five thousan' I had to my name in a crooked poker game. An' the other reason is that I want to pay you back fer savin' my life, up there on Halfaday. Yes sir—that's what you done—you saved my life, by warnin' me that the boys up there would hang me shore, et mebbe even torture me, on account of what I done to Doc—an' then slippin' me the grub to git down here on. I ain't no one to go back on a friend. By God, if a man does me a good turn, I'll do him one, if I git the chant. 'Course, if you git the money, an' wanted to slip me that five thousan' I got beat out of fer tippin' you off, it would be okay with me, bein' I'm broke. If I wasn't broke, I wouldn't touch a damn cent of it. I'd want you to have it all—on account you done me that good turn."

"Yer sentiments does your credit, Jones. It's like the Good Book says about castin' yer bread upon the waters, an' some day it'll come home to roost. Anyhow, go ahead an' order anything you want to eat, an' I'll pay fer it. You'll be that much ahead— even if the cache is empty. If I get the money, I'll split with you, fifty-fifty. Where's this cache at?"

"You go down to the lumber yard, an' on past the last pile of lumber, an' there's a dump there where folks throws their trash. Right clost to the top of the river bank they's an old sheet-iron worshtub layin' bottom up. This here dinner pail with the money in it is under that tub."

Black John nodded. "Okay," he said. "I'll loaf over to the Tivoli after supper, an' set in the stud game, then 'long about midnight I'll cash in, an' slip over to the cache. I shore hope them guys ain't moved the stuff—both fer your sake as well as mine."

V

SUPPER OVER, THE two stepped out onto the street. Through the doorway of the Klondike Palace Black John saw Stanton standing at the bar talking with Cuter Malone. He turned in and strolled to the bar with Jones following. "Hello, Cuter," he greeted. "How's things goin' in the big camp? Shove out the bottle. I'll buy a drink."

"Oh, about like always," Malone replied, setting out bottle and glasses. "How's things on Halfaday?"

"We can't complain," the big man grinned. "Jest work hard on our claims, an' onct in a while I fetch down a little jag of dust an' stick it in the bank. Say, Cuter, how's yer friend Morocco, these days?"

Malone flushed and scowled. "If I never see that guy ag'in, it'll be too soon."

Black John paid for the drinks and turned toward the door. "Guess I'll slip over to the Tivoli," he said. "The boy'll be startin' a stud game pretty quick, an' I want to be shore of gettin a seat."

When he had passed out of sight Malone exploded. "Damn him! It ain't enough he should take me fer that hundred thousan', but he's got to stand there an rub it in! Well, by mornin' he'll be laughin' out of the other side of his mouth!" He paused and eyed Jones. "Did you tell him about that cache? Did he fall fer it?"

"Hell, yes! He swallered the bait—hook, line, an' sinker. He don't know I figger he got that one-thirty-five. Thinks I tipped him off on account I'm grateful to him fer savin' me from gittin' hung up there on Halfaday. He'll grab that cache off all right.

Hell play stud till midnight, then he'll cash in an' hit fer the cache."

"Okay, an' now you git right on his tail an' don't let him out of yer sight fer a minute between now an' the time he gits to the cache. Onct he gits there, Downey'll do the rest. But he's a damn slick article, an' there ain't nothin' in the book that says he couldn't hit fer there right now—er some other time before midnight, an' I don't aim to lose that twenty-five thousan' on top of what he's already took me fer!" He turned to the other. "An' you, Stanton, you hit out and tail Downey. In case Black John wouldn't show up at the cache fer some reason er other, an' Downey would lift that money, you hit fer here as quick as you kin, an' me an' Jones'll go over to the detachment an' claim it. I'll tell him I give it to Jones to make a payment on a claim with, an' he'll tell him how he cached it there overnight so he wouldn't lose it."

As Black John strolled up the street toward the Tivoli, he grinned to himself. "I don't know what the game is, but whatever it is, it's a safe bet that Cuter's mixed up in it, somehow. He liked to blow'd up when I kidded him about Morocco. Prob'ly them three has figgered out some kind of a play to get even with me. Well—good luck to 'em. I've got a hunch, though, when them queer bills shows up, Cuter's goin' to find that another one of his plays has backfired on him. He's one hombre that's got to learn the hard way that honesty is the best policy. The denouement, as the intelligentsia would say, is goin' to furnish me considerable amusement, to say nothin' of some slight pecuniary reward, as well."

In the Tivoli, Black John bought a stack of chips and joined the half-dozen sourdoughs at the stud table. He noted that Jones sauntered in, and joined the dozen or more kibitzers who rimmed the table behind the chairs. For a game between those Titans of stud, never faded to draw an audience.

AS THE evening wore on the onlookers came and went, but the big man noted that Jones stayed on. Midnight came, and as pot after pot was played, he noted a growing restlessness on Jones' part. The man shifted his position frequently, and time and again as he caught Black John's eye, he glanced swiftly and meaningly at the big clock on the side wall. Apparently absorbed in his game, the big man paid him no heed. Two o'clock came— three—And outside daylight broadened.

Stanton appeared suddenly, and frantically beckoned to Jones who followed him out the door. Shortly thereafter the game broke up, and the sourdoughs adjourned to the bar for a few parting drinks. Black John handed Curley, the head bartender, a huge roll of bills. "Thirty-eight thousan, accordin' to my count," he said. "Stick 'em in the safe. That's more loose change than a man ort to carry around on him. Some damn cuss might rob him." He turned to the sourdoughs with a grin. "If you boys shows up tonight, I'll give you a chant to get some of this back. So long, I'm goin' over to the hotel an' get me some sleep."

As he stepped out onto the street, he saw Cuter Malone and Jones hurrying toward the police detachment, and a slow grin showed behind the heavy black beard. "H-u-u-m," he muttered. "So that was their game, eh? Planted that cache an' tipped Downey off that someone was figurin' to rob it. An' now they're headin' over there hell-bent to get the money back. Guess I'll jest slip over an' see the fun."

VI

AS DARKNESS APPROACHED Corporal Downey slipped into the lumber yard, concealed himself behind the last pile of lumber close to the overturned washtub under which Stanton had tipped him the Amalgamated loot was cached, and settled himself for a long vigil.

Slowly the hours passed as he fought sleep and cursed under his breath. "If it was anyone but Black John that was s'posed to rob this cache, I'd detailed a constable on this job," he muttered under his breath. "But the way it is, I can't take no chances."

Faint streaks of daylight grayed the east. The false dawn broke in a blaze of glorious color, and in his hiding place Downey scowled. "Hell," he grumbled, "not only Black John didn't come, but neither did the ones that cached it. It's a cinch, they won't come now it's light—an' damned if I'm goin' to stick here all day. I'll take the money over to headquarters if it's there. An' if it ain't, that damn Stanton's goin' to have to do some fast talkin'. When the Amalgamated gets their payroll back they'll quit squawkin', anyway. An' mebbe I can pick up the thieves later."

Stepping to the washtub, he overturned it, and reaching down, picked up the dinner pail. Opening it, he glanced at the huge roll of bills, returned the cover, and proceeded to headquarters, entirely unaware that Stanton had slipped from behind another lumber pile and headed toward the street at a run.

In his office Downey placed the pail on his desk, removed its contents, reached for the list of numbers, prepared to check the numbers on the bills. One by one he held some half-dozen bills in his hand as he vainly ran his pencil down the column of numbers. "What the hell?" he muttered, his brow corrugated in deep furrows. "There ain't none of these numbers on the list! What comes off here, anyhow?"

Picking up one of the bills he studied it, then reaching into a drawer, he withdrew a magnifying glass and examined it closely. He examined other bills, also. Then he returned the glass to its place. "If that ain't queer money I'll eat it!" he exclaimed, at length. "Anyway, I'll know when the bank opens. Guess my friend Stanton's goin' to have a chant to do some fast talkin', at that!" Returning the money to the pail he set it on the floor beside him.

A FEW moments later the door opened and Cuter Malone burst into the room, closely followed by Jones. "Hey, Downey, I be'n robbed!" he cried, bringing up before the flat-topped desk.

The officer eyed the dive keeper sourly. "Well, now that's jest too damn bad, ain't it, Cuter? How much was you robbed of? An' who done it?"

"How the hell do I know who done it? That's fer you to find out! But whoever done it he got twenty-five thousan' dollars in bills."

"Get it out of your safe?"

"No. It's like this—I bought a claim off'n a guy. An' I got to make a twenty-five thousan' dollar payment on it, cash money. So I counts out the dough an' put it in a tin dinner pail an' gives it to Jones, here, to take to the guy, which he said he'd be in one of them shacks over in Louse Town, last evenin'. Well, Jones, he goes to this shack, an' the guy ain't there, but another guy says he'll be there, come mornin'. Jones, he didn't want to be carryin' that much money around all night, so he took it down to the dump back of the lumber yard an' caches it under an old worshtub that was layin' there. An' then, a few minutes ago, when he went to git it, by God, it was gone!"

Downey grinned. "Hell, Cuter that story is as full of holes as a sieve."

"How do you mean—full of holes?"

"Well, for instance, why didn't this guy that was sellin' you the claim go to the Palace an' collect the money himself, instead of havin' you deliver it to him in Louse Town?"

"That's what I wanted to know, an' he claimed he was mixed up with some woman over there, an' she was in on the money, somehow, an' she wouldn't trust him to go an' git it hisself—figgered he'd double-cross her, er somethin'. So that's why I had to send it over to him."

"When Jones found he wasn't there, why didn't he take the money back to you, instead of cachin' it in the dump?"

"He claims he was scairt to. He figgered I'd give him hell if he showed up without doin' like I told him to do."

Jones shot the burly saloon keeper a sidewise glance. "Yer damn right you would," he whined. "I've saw you knock hell outa guys that done like you didn't tell 'em to, 'fore now. I wasn't goin' to carry that dough back to the Palace an' git a punch in the jaw fer not findin' the guy—not when I could cache it, an' take it to him in the mornin'. So I cached it, an' hung around the Tivoli all night, waitin' fer daylight. An' when I went to git it, it was gone."

Reaching down, Downey lifted the dinner pail to the desktop, removed the bills, and laid them on the desk before him.

"By God, there's my money—buckit an' all!" Malone cried. "Where'd you git it, Downey? I'm shore lucky!"

"Yeah? Well, not so fast, Cuter. I ain't counted this yet. How much did you say there was?"

"Twenty-five thousan'. An' it better all be there, er Jones is goin' to git a punch in the jaw he won't be fergittin' very soon!"

Deliberately Downey counted the bills. "It's all here," he said, "right to a cent. But, how do I know it's yours?"

"How do you know! I jest got through tellin' you how it come to be cached there, didn't I? An' about it bein' in a tin dinner pail? An' on top of that, Jones here, an' Stanton, too, seen me take it outa my safe, right there in the Palace, an' put it in the pail, an' hand it over to Jones."

"So Stanton is in on it, too, eh?"

"In on it? What do you mean—in on it?"

"I mean that he came in here last evenin' with a cock-an'-bull story about overhearin' the Amalgamated robbers talkin' about cachin' their loot in a dinner pail under that old tub. He claimed that another party overheard 'em, too, an' prob'ly aimed to heist it. An' he figgered that if I'd watch that cache, last night, I'd get the chant to pick up this party, red-handed—an' mebbe the Amalgamated robbers, too. I watched the cache all night, an' after daylight, when no one had showed up, I brought the stuff here."

Malone twisted an end of his huge black mustache, and his thick lips broke into a grin. "So he come here an' told you that, eh? Well, sir, I've done him a lot of good turns, an' I s'pose he figgered on doin' me one. The only reason I can see why he'd tell you that is like this—he prob'ly tailed Jones with the dough—jest in case he might try to pull a fast one on me—an' when he seen Jones cache the stuff, he come an' told you that yarn, so you'd be watchin' it, an' no one could sneak it outa there. 'Course, Downey, he hadn't ort to done it—puttin' you to all that bother—an' I'll give him hell fer it. But that's the onliest reason I kin figger why he'd tell you a damn lie, like that. So, if you'll hand over the dough, I'll be gittin' back to the Palace an' give him hell."

Downey nodded. "I guess this is your money, all right, Cuter. But in a case like this we've got to be shore it's your money. You can identify it, can't you? This money here on the desk is the money you took out of your safe in the presence of two witnesses, an' placed in this dinner pail, and handed over to Jones?"

"Shore it is!" Malone agreed, glancing at the heap of currency.

"Okay." Downey reached into a drawer, drew out a printed form, and for some moments busied himself with a pen. Then he handed the paper to Malone who read it, and nodded agreement. "Amongst a lot of other duties we've got to perform, up here, is actin' as notary public. This is an affidavit, as you prob'ly know, statin' that this is the same money you took out of yer safe, an' that it is your own property, etc. I'll make out a couple of more, one fer Jones to sign, an' one fer Stanton, statin' that they seen you take the money out of your safe an' put it in the pail. You an' Jones can sign now, an' I'll have Stanton sign his, later."

Malone and Jones readily signed the two documents, and replacing the money in the pail, Downey handed it over to Malone, who took it, just as Black John stepped into the room.

"Mornin', Downey!" he said, then as his glance flashed to the saloon keeper. "Hello, Cuter! Cripes, I didn't know you an' Downey was sech pals! An' damned if here ain't Jones, too!" He glanced at the pail in Cuter's hand. "Come to spend the day, an' fetched yer lunch, eh? What's the purport of this festive gatherin'?"

Downey explained the situation in a few words.

White teeth flashed behind the black beard. "So Stanton tipped you off that a certain party might try to make a play fer that bucket of bills, eh? Take it, first an' last, it looks like there was quite a bit of tippin' off goin' on yesterday. Jones, here, he tipped me off at suppertime that them Amalgamated thieves had stuck their loot in a tin dinner pail an' cached it under that old washtub. Claimed he didn't have guts enough to make a play fer it, himself. Claimed he owed me a good turn, so he let me in on it. But shucks, I got interested in a stud game over to the Tivoli, last night, an' fergot all about it. It couldn't be jest barely possible, I s'pose, that this here party Stanton mentioned to you was me, was it?"

Downey nodded. "That's right, John. It was you he mentioned."

The grin behind the beard widened, and the big man eyed Malone. "So you put up the money fer this little scheme, eh? Well, well! I s'pose you boys figgered that Downey would nail me dead to rights when I copped off that cache—an' then you'd sort of work it somehow to get a holt up on Halfaday Crick. You'll have to think up a better one than that, Cuter. Anyhow, you got yer money back, an' I'm sorry about that. 'Cause, believe me, if there'd be'n any way fer me to grab it off, without playin' right into Downey's hand, I'd shore done it. Like I say—you got yer money back, an' yer lucky."

"Maybe not so lucky as you think, John," Downey said, a flinty tone an his voice. "It was a damned dirty trick, an' I'm glad it didn't work. At that, you're the lucky one. Even if you had managed to get hold of that money without my getting you, I'd have picked you up the minute you started spending it. Every damned one of those bills are counterfeit!"

"Counterfeit—hell!" Malone cried. "Them's all good bills, right outa my safe!"

Rising, Downey stepped to Malone's side and placed a hand on his shoulder. "That's your story," he said. "The bank will report on the validity of the bills. In the meantime, you are under arrest for the possession of counterfeit money. Constable Rickey will show you to a cell. Of course, if the bills are good, I'll turn you loose."

Malone's face reddened. His neck seemed to swell visibly, and a huge blue vein showed on his forehead. He turned on Black John and shook a fist in his face. "Damn you! This is your doin's! If them bills is counterfeit, you switched 'em on me! I can't see how you done it—but by God, you did!"

Black John laughed. "Don't be a fool, Cuter, Cripes I was in the Tivoli all night, from long before dark, till after daylight. An' there's plenty of witnesses to that fact. If there was any switchin' done, most likely Jones done it. Looks like he's the only one that had the chant to."

Malone whirled on Jones, who shrank back, protesting his innocence. "You done it, all right!" he bellowed. "Like John says, you're the only one that had the chance to! You wait till I git out—an' by God, you'll wisht you'd never double-crossed me!"

"I never done it!" Jones whimpered. "I'm in a hell of a for now! If I hit fer Halfaday I git hung. An' if I stay in Dawson Cuter'll turn his damn gorillas loose on me. An' I dasn't go back to the States, neither. Where in hell kin I go?"

Corporal Downey grinned. "Seems like I've heard of crawlin in a hole an' pullin' the hole in after you. Anyhow you might try it—an I'll have one less scoundrel to worry about."

Black John turned to Malone and shook his head sadly. "It's yer own fault, in a way, Cuter," he said. "It's like my old pa used to say. Pa, he was a preacher, you know—an' he used to take me on his knee, an' he'd say, 'Shun evil companions Johnny,' he'd say. I always remembered that—an' I've be'n shunnin''em ever sence."

BLACK JOHN WINS A BET

BLACK JOHN SMITH tossed a handful of tea into the pail suspended above a little fire on a gravel bar at the junction of Halfaday Creek and the White River, then straightened and stared in open mouthed astonishment at the frenzied efforts of two Indians to beach a canoe that swept into sight around a bend some hundred yards upriver. The scowl that wrinkled his forehead as he recognized the natives gave place to a broad grin as the canoe grounded and both Indians, with terrified glances in his direction, leaped ashore and disappeared into the bush on the opposite side of the river, leaving a lone white man seated amidship staring in bewilderment at the spot where the two had disappeared.

Black John called and beckoned to the man who shoved off in the canoe, paddled clumsily across the river, stepped ashore, and eyed the big man in bewilderment. "I—I don't understand," he said, passing his hand across his forehead. "The Indians—they were to take me to—to Dawson City—the priest said. Then suddenly, as we rounded the bend yonder, and they caught sight of you, they ran the canoe aground and scampered away as fast as their legs would carry them."

White teeth flashed beneath the heavy black beard as Black John smiled. "The explanation is simple, their disappearance into the bush bein' an act of self preservation. Joe an' Charley Shirttail, their name is. They're Chilkats—belong down on the coast—an as ornery, no account pair of Siwashes as there is in the country. They worked for Jack Dalton last year, trailin' cattle in from Haines, an' on the way out they robbed a couple of caches here on the White. They took fifty pounds of bacon an' a couple jugs of licker out of old man Hizer's cache, down to Fish Rapids, an the next day Solomon Albert caught 'em liftin' a bunch of fur he'd cached right here at the mouth of Halfaday. Him an' Pot Gutted John fetched 'em up to Cush's to be tried by miner's meetin' an' hung."

The man's eyes widened. "You mean—you would hang them for stealing?"

"Oh, shore. Murder, cache-robbin', an' in fact any other form of skullduggery, earns a man a hangin' on Halfaday an' contiguous territory—provided, of course, there ain't no mitigatin' circumstances."

"And they robbed these men of cash, besides the bacon and liquor, and fur you mentioned?"

The big man looked puzzled for a moment, then his grin widened. "No, no! In this country when we hide a thing, we cache it—an' the place where it's hid is a cache."

The other smiled. "I see I have a great deal to learn." He paused, and again he passed his hand across his forehead. "A very great deal to learn. But—manifestly you didn't hang those Indians. There must have been mitigating circumstances."

Black John chuckled. "Yeah, there was. You see, I sort of preside at these here miner's meetin's, an' I've got an' inherent dislike to hangin' Siwashes, they bein' born with two strikes on 'em to start out with, you might say.

"In this case the only mitigatin' circumstance I could think up was that they robbed old man Hizer, him bein' the ornesiest old coot this side of Vancouver. So I sort of balanced off the two robberies an' ordered a vote of acquittal, with however, the stipulation that if either one of 'em was ever caught in this vicinity again, they'd be shot on sight"

The man smiled. "No wonder they disappeared so abruptly on sight of you. But—that leaves me in a rather embarrassing situation. How far is it from here to Dawson City?"

"Oh, it's right around a couple of hundred miles. Are you used to handlin' a canoe?"

"No. I had never even been in a canoe until I met these Indians. I had no part in handling it. I presume, however, that a man is never too old to learn."

THE BIG man frowned. "Listen, brother," he said. "If you undertake to learn how to handle a canoe, alone, on the White, you're jest as old, right now, as you'll ever get. Of course, if you're hell-bent on gettin' to Dawson—that's your business. There's an empty cabin four, five miles up the crick. Fellow name of Olson located the claim a while back. You're welcome to hole up there, if you want to. Someone will be goin' down to Dawson within a month or so, an' you can ondoubtless arrange transportation with them."

"But this man—Olson? Won't he object?"

"He ain't apt to," replied the big man dryly. "We hung him."

"Why did you hang him?"

"Oh, damn if I remember. For somethin' he done, most likely."

"You say that someone will be going down to Dawson—is there a settlement hereabouts?"

"Well, not what you might say, a settlement. There's forty, fifty of us boys located here on Halfaday. Fella name of Lyme Cushing runs a tradin' post an saloon about ten mile above here. It's a right handy place—Cushing's Fort is. We can get our supplies there, an' do what drinkin' we're a mind to, an' there's generally a stud game goin' on of an evenin'."

"But—what do you men do, up here?"

"We're prospectors. We work our claims."

"You mean you're gold miners?"

"That's right."

THE MAN was silent for several moments. Black John noted a far-away look in his blue eyes, as he passed his hand back and forth across his forehead as though trying to remember something. "I haven't the least idea where I am—or why I am here. But if I must be here a month I may as well try to dig some gold. This claim you mentioned—Olson's—could gold be found on it? And would there be any objection to my locating there?"

"It might be at damn good claim. No one's ever lived on it long enough to find out. There ain't no one to object if a man wants to locate there. Some of the claims on the crick are payin' out big. A good many more are doin' fair. Any of 'em will pay better than wages if a man ain't afraid of hard work."

"I don't know why I should go any farther then," the man said. "I could probably do as well here as at Dawson City."

"I'd say your chances here are a damn sight better than around Dawson, what with the country fillin'up with *chechakos* like it is. There ain't one in a hundred of 'em down along the Yukon that'll make wages. But—how come you to be here on the White with them two Shirttail boys? Did you head into the country on the Dalton Trail?"

Again the man's hand passed across his brow. "The Dalton Trail? No. I don't remember any trail. There was the sea coast—innumerable rocks—and the waves splashing and gurgling among them with a continuous sound. In the night I wake up and hear that sound—the monotonous gurgling and splashing of waves. I was soaked to the skin, and so cold and stiff I could scarcely move. Finally I walked along the shore. There were dead men—bodies wedged among the rocks. There was one man who was alive. He had dragged himself back among the rocks and built had a fire out of twigs and driftwood. I tried to talk to him—ask him where we were—but the poor fellow was so far gone he could only mumble and mutter unintelligible words. Several times I caught the word Mariposa. Is there a place called Mariposa?"

Black John shook his head. "Not that I ever heard of," he said. "But—how come you to be there on the coast?"

The man's brow furrowed. "That is the question I have asked myself a thousand times. That name Mariposa sounds somehow vaguely familiar, though I can't for the life of me, place it. Why would I be going to a place called Mariposa? But there seems to be no answer. I found myself there on the seashore. I added wood to the injured man's fire, and dried out my clothing. Then I fell asleep, and when I awoke the man was dead. He had a sheath knife and a waterproof match box. Those I took with me and struck out, following the shore. I was very hungry. Presently I found some wild berries, and later I came upon a covey of birds, somewhat resembling grouse. They were very stupid and unafraid and I managed to kill two of them with stones. I built a fire and roasted them, and shortly after that I came to a river. It was a turbulent stream and being unable to cross it, I followed its course, day after day ascending higher and higher into the mountains. I didn't know where it would lead me—but it didn't seem to matter. At least it took me away from that damned sound—the thundering, splashing, gurgling sound of the waves among the rocks. I fared well enough. There were berries, and daily I came upon coveys of the stupid grouse which I became quite expert in killing with stones. Then in several places I killed fish that had been imprisoned in pools in rapids.

"Then, one day when I had only three or four matches left in my box, I came upon a priest and those two Indians. The priest, Father Cassatt, he said his name is, asked me innumerable questions, the most of which I could not answer. He asked me if I had any money, and I handed him sixty-seven dollars which was all I had in my pocket. I have more money in a belt, but of this I said nothing. He gave me a blanket and what food they had with them, handed the money to the two Indians, and told them to take me to Dawson City. He told them that if they did not take me there safely, he would tell Corporal Downey and Black John, and in case anything happened to me they would both surely be hanged.

"That was five days ago. Two days later we crossed a high divide, and the Indians drew a canoe from under some bushes, and we came down this river. Everything seemed to be going well until we came around the bend, yonder, and the one in the bow saw you here, and emitted a sort of a yelp, and the other one said something in the native tongue, and swerved the canoe ashore and both took to their heels and disappeared into the woods."

Black John nodded. "They done right, accordin' to their lights. Like I told you, we'd promised to shoot 'em on sight if they ever showed up around here again. I swung down this way afoot, hopin' to get a shot at a moose, but after we throw a little lunch into us, we'll get in the canoe an' shove on up to Olson's old shack. You ain't got no hell of a lot of grub here, but you can get all you want at Cush's. It's lucky for you that them two Siwashes didn't know you had any more money on you or they might have knocked you off, an' took a chanct on keepin' away from me or Corporal Downey."

"Then," the man smiled, "you must be this Black John that the priest mentioned."

"Yeah. It's a nickname that got fastened onto me on account of the color of my whiskers."

"And who is this Corporal Downey?"

"Oh, he's in charge of the Dawson detachment of the Mounted Police."

"Are you, too, connected with the police?"

"W-e-l-l—not what you could say, connected with 'em— except in a casual sort of a way. Come on—let s fly into this grub, an get goin'."

II

ONE MORNING, A month after the stranger had taken up his residence in Olson's old shack some four or five miles down the creek from Cushing's Fort, Black John stepped into the saloon, crossed the floor, and elevated a foot to the battered brass rail, as Old Cush shoved the newspaper he had been reading aside to set out a bottle, two glasses, and the leather dice box.

The big man won the drinks in straight horses, and as he filled his glass from the bottle, Cush shoved his square-framed, steel-rimmed spectacles from nose to forehead and indicated the newspaper with a jerk of his thumb. "I was readin' a piece in the paper there, where it claims a couple of fellas down in Afriky somwheres' name of MacArthur an' Forrest has invented what they call the cyanide process fer takin' out gold. Now what I claim—that's a hell of a note! It was bad enough when they invented dredges, but accordin' to the paper, this here cyanide process has got everythin' else beat all to hell."

"Ain't in favor of it, eh?"

"Cripes, no! I ain't in favor of it! Why the hell would I be? Look how the damn dredges is raisin' bell with the cricks down along the river. 'Fore they come in the boys got out their dust with a pick in' shovel, an' they was doin' all right at it. Every man had a chanct. Them that worked hardest got out the most dust. Every man had a chant to make a strike. An' what dust a man got was his own private dust an' most of 'em spent it right here in the Yukon, an' after they paid fer their supplies, they blow'd the rest in liberal.

"Then the dredges come along, an' scoops out more dust in a day than a man could in a year. An' where does that dust go? It goes into the safe of some company an' gits shipped off to the States, er England, er somewheres. The ones that owns the company don't live here—never even seen the Yukon—an they don't blow in a damn nickel around the saloons, an' don't spend much in the stores, neither. They buy their supplies down in the States where they git 'em cheap, an ship 'em in."

BLACK JOHN nodded. "That's right, Cush. But they hire quite a few men—pay 'em wages—an' those wages are spent here in the Yukon."

"Yeah—an ounce a day! What I claim with prices what they be, if a man only gits an ounce a day, how much has he got left over after he pays fer his grub an' lodgin', to play stud with, er blow in around the saloons an' dance halls?"

The big man grinned. "The system has its merits, in that it promulgates and fosters frugality and inculcates habits that would ondoubtless be denounced by theologists and moralests."

"Moralest—hell!" exclaimed Cush, in disgust. "Cripes, we're the moralest crick in the Yukon—an' we drink an' play stud! An all them big words can't change us none, neither. All I got to say, there hadn't better no company put no dredge, nor one of them new-fangled cyanide processes on Halfaday, er I'll set off enough dynamite in under it to blow it halfway up a mountain!"

"I fear you're a confirmed obstructionist."

"If that means some guy that don't want no dredges on Halfaday, yer right. You know jest as well as I do that the dredges is ruinin' the country—an' the only reason yer augerin' fer 'em is so's you kin rob 'em!"

"What! Why, you damned old badger—I never robbed a dredge company in my life—an you know it!"

"No, but plenty others has—an' somehow er other, the gold they git generally allus gits shoved in the safe, here, to your credick. I know damn well, John, yer honest as hell—an' there ain't a man on Halfaday that would claim you ain't. Cripes, yer the only man on the crick we'd trust to take our dust down to Dawson an' bank it fer us, when the safe gits full! But jest the same, like I said, when some damn crook does pull off a robbery, you allus manage to wangle around an' git holt of the gold, er dust, er bills, er whatever they got. An' if it's a pore man got robbed, like some prospector, you allus turn the stuff over to Downey to give back to him—but if it's a dredge company lost it, by God, they never do git it back!"

"While your thesis is more or less correct, in its broader aspects, you have overlooked, or purposely ignored one vital fact, and that is that whatever steps I may take to deprive those depraved miscreants of the fruits of their crimes, are taken primarily for the purpose of demonstrating to them, in the only terms they can comprehend, that honesty is the best policy, and that crime does not pay. If at times some slight profit happens to accrue to me in the process, I assure you it is merely incidental."

"Uh-huh," Cush replied dryly, "An' now, seein' how you must of jest about run out of big words, havin' spoke about all of 'em there is, would you mind tellin' me, usin' little words that means somethin' when you get 'em said, what this here cyanide process is? Looks to me like if they keep on inventin' more ways to git out the dust, gold will git so common an' so cheap that it won't pay the boys to dig it out, no more. Then where'd we be? This here cyanide process—does it work like a dredge?"

BLACK JOHN refilled his glass. "N-o-o-o, not exactly like a dredge, Cush. An' as a matter of fact, you are laboring under a misapprehension—"

Cush scowled and reached beneath the bar. "By God—one more big word an' you git this here bung-starter right between the eyes!"

The big man chuckled. "Okay. What I was about to say is that you don't need to worry that this cyanide process will add anything to the world's supply of gold. The fact is that no new gold is produced by it. It's like this—did you ever hear of potassium cyanide?"

Cush knitted his brow, and scratched at his ear with a gnarled thumb nail. "Potassium cyanide," he repeated slowly. "Yeah, seems like I've heard it spoke of, somewheres. Say—ain't it some kind of pizen?"

"It is. One of the quickest an' most deadly poisons known."

"By God, that's where I heard about it! A fella that worked in a drug store around the corner from where I was tendin' bar on Freeman Avenue in Cincinnati. He used to lock up along about eleven o'clock, an' he'd gen'ly stop in fer a couple of drinks er so before goin' home. An' one night he says, 'Cush,' he says, 'the rats must be pretty bad up there in the flat where yer livin', ain't they?'

" 'Rats?' I says. 'Hell, I ain't saw no rats. What makes you think they's rats there?'

" 'Why', he says, ' 'cause yer wife was in right after supper this evenin' an' wanted to buy some cyanide of potassium an' when I asks her what she wants it fer, she says to kill rats with. I told her she'd have to sign the pizen book, an' she wants to know if its all right with me if she'd sign some other name to it? I told her not by a damn sight, it ain't all right, an' she went out without buyin' no cyanide.'

"It was that damn third wife of mine! An' she went right over to the grocery store an' bought a couple dozen sheets of flypaper—them was the sheets I found next day soakin' in warm water in under the bed to git the pizen fer to feed me so she could git holt of them 'leven hundred an' sixty dollars I win on that there three-horse parlay at Latonia, that time. By Cripes, if that there clerk bad sold her that there pizen that night, chances is I'd be dead, 'cause I'd prob'ly got it in my coffee next mornin', on account she wouldn't have to stop an soak it offen no flypaper. Yes, sir, I figger that there drug clerk—Claude James, his name was, saved my life—an' if I ever run acrost him I'll buy him a drink! But I never seen him agin, on account, when I found that there flypaper soakin', I throw'd my stuff in my grip, an' hit fer the depot—an' I never got off'n the train, except to change cars at Chicago, till I hit Seattle.

"But what the hell has this here cyanide of potassium got to do with diggin' out gold?"

"Nothin' with *diggin'* it out, Cush. An' that's why you don't need to worry about the world's supply of gold bein' throw'd out of balance. The cyanide process is used solely for the purpose of gettin' holt of gold that's already be'n dug. Your third wife had the same idea when she figgered on gettin' that eleven-hundred an' sixty dollars off'n you—only she didn't advertise it, as claim credit for inventin' the process. The way it's worked, is to find someone that's got a bunch of gold put by, feed him a liberal dose of cyanide, an walk off with the gold."

"But hell's fire, John—that would be murder! If these here MacArthur an' Forrest aimed to pull off a job like that they wouldn't go ahead an' tell no noospaper about it. An' like if some noospaper did find out about it, they wouldn't print no piece claimin' it was a great discovery, an' how them two guys deserved a hell of a lot of credick fer figgerin' it out. Not by a damn sight! They'd tip the police off to 'em. That's what they'd do."

"You must remember, Cush," said Black John, loftily, "that your education, if you will pardon the use of the word, has been sadly localized. Here in the Yukon, and in the rest of Canada, in England, and I believe in most of the States, murder, as a means of livelihood, has come to be frowned on. But as you yourself mentioned, these two men perfected their cyanide process in Africa, where, owing to a more liberal viewpoint, murder for profit is not only condoned, but encouraged. Thus, when two likely lads like this MacArthur and Forrest succeed in perfecting an entirely new process, they are not only immediately acclaimed in the public print, but are highly honored by the Government."

"Cripes sakes! You mean that over there in Afriky, if some guy invents a new way to murder someone they figger he's quite a feller?"

"Only," replied Black John gravely, "if the murder shows a reasonable profit. Trivial or frivolous murders are rather looked down on socially."

"Well—what a hell of a place to live!"

"Oh, I don't know. You've got to remember, Cush, that the African ethics are diametrically opposed to ours. Lookin' at it from their angle it's all right an' proper."

"Yeah? Well by God, I wouldn't like to git murdered from no angle! Nor yet, I wouldn't want no credick if I murdered someone else. What I claim—to hell with a country like that! The Yukon's good enough fer me."

THE BIG man grinned. "Well yes, I'm inclined to favor the Yukon system, too. But even so, Cush, in a true democracy, the welfare of the few should be subserved to the welfare of the many. We are looking at it from the viewpoint of men of property. I'll admit that under the African system a man of property is taking more or less of a gamble on his life. But you must remember that there are a great many more have-nots than there are have-gots. The system was evolved to favor the many, rather than the few."

"Yeah? Well to hell with their system! If I want to gamble I'll gamble with cards, an' not with my life. An', speakin' of gamblin', that there fella that's livin' down to Olson's old shack— the one which he claimed he couldn't rec'lect what his name is, an draw'd the name of Jubal Custer outa the name-can—what with them long lean fingers of his'n, an' not no callouses on his bands, I figgered he must be some kind of a gambler. But Cripes, the way he plays stud, he couldn't hardly be no kind of a gambler, whatever! Except, mebbe, he's lettin' on like he's jest learnin' the game, an' layin back fer to make a killin' some night.

"Them fingers of his'n is shore supple enough to do anything he wanted to with a deck of cards.

"I don't believe he's a gambler," Black John said.

"He could be some kind of a con man, mebbe."

The big man grinned. "Why not give him the benefit of the doubt, and figger him as an honest citizen?"

"Honest citizen—hell!" Cush scoffed. "Barrin' the Derelick, how many honest citizens has even lived in Olson's shack? Not a damn one—that's how many! Everyone that's ever moved in there has either got knocked off by some other damn crook, er Downey picked 'em up fer some crime er other, er else we thing 'em fer somethin' they done after they got here."

"It does seem, like an onlucky abode," the big man admitted. "Seems like everyone that moves in there is open to suspicion."

"Yeah, an' they'd ort to be! Most of 'em's only about two jumps ahead of the law. If they was an honest citizen, like a prospector, er someone, they wouldn't fool around with no abandoned claim, nohow. They'd go out an' locate 'em a location of their own."

"Well, Olson's claim ain't never be'n really abandoned. No one ever relinquished it."

"No one ever had time to before they was hung er shot er arrested. Them few shallow prospect holes punched in the gavel don't mean nothin'. That might be a damn good claim, for all anyone knows."

"It might be, at that. Maybe Jube Custer will find out. He seems different from the general run of folks that drifts in on us."

"YEAH, HE'S different, all right. But he ain't no prospector, noways you look at him. He's on the run fer somethin'. You kin bet on that. Prob'ly skipped outa the States fer somethin' he done, an hit fer the Klondike, an' then heard some damn fool say how we're all outlaws on Halfaday, an' how the police don't dast to show up here, so he figgered it would be a good place to hide out. You take a crick like Halfaday an' give it a bad name, an' all the bums heads fer it, an' the good ones stays a-way."

Black John nodded. "An the fact that we're the moralest crick in the Yukon don't mean a damn thing to 'em till after they get here—an' then it's too late. But speakin' of Jube Custer—I wasn't thinkin' so much of his hands when I said he seemed different. It's his eyes—an' his manner of speech. He talks like a man of education."

"Hell, you can't go nothin' on that! So do you—when you want to!"

Black John scowled. "What do you mean by that?"

"You know what I mean. If a man's eggicated he's liable to be a damn sight smarter crook than the ones that ain't. An' them eyes of Jube's—somehow they kinda give me the creeps. Even when he's lookin' right at you, it's like he ain't seein' you—like he was lookin' right through you at somethin' that ain't there— an' sometimes it seems like he's lookin' right inside yer head to see what yer thinkin' about. An' drawin' them long lean fingers acrost his forehead like he does now an' then—like he's tryin' to rec'lect somethin' he's forgot—er like he's tryin' to bresh somethin' away—only there ain't nothin' there to bresh. But them eyes—they're hard, an' blue, like a gambler's eyes—only, somehow, they're different."

"Yeah, they're different," the big man agreed. "They ain't like a gambler's eyes. There's no ice in 'em. It's like you said—they seem always lookin' for somethin' that ain't there. Anyway, he's quiet, an' he minds his own business. At it looks like he aims to stay on Halfaday. He's pickin' up all the savvy he can about prospectin'. An' he's choppin' wood to burn in with next winter."

"Yeah—but them quiet ones is the ones you got to watch. That there third wife of mine—she was kinda quiet, too—fer a woman. But if I hadn't skipped out on her jest when I did, by God, I'd be dead!"

III

THE MAN HAD subjected Olson's old shack to a thorough cleaning, had repaired the roof, and replaced numerous broken and sagging puncheons in the floor. He had fashioned curtains for the windows out of squaw cloth he bought at Cush's, and had even transplanted a number of young trees and landscaped the dooryard, after removing the litter of tin cans and discarded trash that had been heaved out the door by the previous occupants.

Clumsy at first in the use of an axe, he soon got the hang of it and put in his time cutting and piling the wood to be used in thawing the gravel to be shoveled from his shaft during the coming winter.

Quiet and unassuming, he was generally liked by the men of Halfaday Creek, who willingly explained the functions of flumes, sluices, grizzles, and riffles and numerous other bits of useful information. He visited Cush's frequently, drank moderately, and learned to play stud and enjoy it. He hunted moose, generally with Black John, who was a frequent visitor at Olson's old shack. Frankly, the big man was puzzled. Here was a man probably in his middle fifties, a man of culture and refinement who, even in the course of long conversations had never dropped a word that could throw the slightest hint as to his identity, or his previous mode of life—a man whose past was a book closed and sealed.

He had deposited no gold nor any sum of money in Cush's safe, nor had he made use of the cache used by so many of the previous occupants of the cabin. In vain Black John racked his brain for a crime that would fit the man's temperament and personality—and always he gave it up.

One evening, after a session of stud, One Armed John stood at the bar with several others, and glanced toward the doorway through which Custer had just disappeared. "That there Jube, he's a damn good guy. Never gits drunk an' raises hell. I never even heard him cuss. I wonder what the hell he done that put him on the run? He don't look like no one that would rob no one."

"Might of knocked someone off in a scrap," ventured Short John.

"He ain't the scrappin' kind," One Arm replied. "It musta be'n somethin' damn important, er a guy like him wouldn't never of skipped out. He's a damn liar, though—claimin' he can't rec'lect his name. Cripes, no one could fergit their name!"

Pot Gutted John grinned. "The hell they couldn't! Every man's name on Halfaday has be'n fergot—yourn inclooded."

"Oh, shore. But hell, Pot Gut, everyone knows we're damn liars. Jube—he don't look like none. Fer all he's ever said, you'd think he don't even know that most of us on the crick is outlawed!"

Old Cush mopped at the bar with a rag. "No matter what he done before he come to Halfaday, it ain't none of our business.

"All I got to say—if everyone that come here wouldn't raise no more hell than he does, we wouldn't never have no more hangin's."

A FEW days later Corporal Downey stepped into the saloon to find Black John and Cush at the bar, two glasses, a bottle, and the inevitable dice box between them.

The big man greeted the officer heartily. "Belly up, Downey! Yes just in time. Cush is buyin' one."

"I'll buy one all right, after we've got this here one drunk," Cush said, sliding a glass toward the officer. "But this un's on John. I jest stuck him a round."

"What's on yer mind?" Black John asked, as Downey poured his drink. "Has someone broke a law?"

"Jest a sort of routine patrol. Had to go up to Father Cassatt's village to get the figures on that Siwash census they want down to Ottawa. The father was askin' me if a certain party ever got to Dawson. He said he found this man wandering in the mountains a while back. The man claimed he couldn't remember his name, nor where he came from, nor where he was goin'. In fact, he couldn't remember nothin' except findin himself on the sea coast where there was a lot of dead men. The father says he gave a couple of Siwashes the money the fellow had in his pocket to take him to Dawson, but that the Siwashes came back in a few days an' claimed they saw you at the mouth of Halfaday, so they beached the canoe on the other side of the White, an' hit for home. They claimed you'd threatened to shoot 'em on sight if they ever showed up around here. Know anything about it?"

"You've got the facts straight. Them Siwashes was the two Shirttail boys. They robbed Old Man Hizer an' Solomon Albert a while back, an' we called a miner's meetin' an' voted a hangin' onto 'em, but I let 'em off with a warnin' that if they ever showed up around here agin they'd be shot on sight."

"An' what became of the white man? Did he go on down the river?"

"No, he couldn't never have made it. Never handled a canoe. He moved into Olson's old shack."

"Oh, so he's the one, eh? I stopped there an' talked with him fer a few minutes comin' up the crick. He's shore fixed the place up. Cleanest I ever saw it."

"Yeah, Jube's got it fixed up nice down there."

"Jube?"

"Yeah, he draw'd the name out of the can—Jubal Custer. It's as good a name as any—seein' he can't rec'lect his right one."

Downey grinned. "There ain't but damn few men hit Holladay that can recollect their names, is there?"

"Not many. Their recollections run mainly to John Smith, till me an' Cush invented the name can."

"This Jube, as you call him—how you got him pegged, John?"

The big man downed his drink and refilled his glass. "I ain't. He's quiet. Minds his own business. Apparently he's got a good education. Takes a drink, now an' then. Learned to play stud, an' seems to enjoy it. That's about all we know about him."

Downey's brow puckered. "Seems like we've got a pickup on him—I sort of remember a description that fits him. But I can't rec'lect who wants him, nor what for. I'll look it up when I get back. He must figger on stickin' around. I see he's got quite a bit of wood chopped."

"Yeah, he'll prob'ly stick around," Black John agreed.

"Does he seem to be well heeled?"

"Well, first time he showed up here fer supplies he shoved me a thousan' dollar bill," Cush said. "I busted it fer him. He'd ort to have most of that left. How many more of 'em he's got, I couldn't say."

"Thousan' dollar bill, eh? Did he ever mention any place he's be'n—any place in the States, fer instance?"

"Nope. Claims he can't rec'lect his name, nor where he come from, nor what he ever done before he found himself there on the coast amongst a lot of dead men. He did ask me if I ever heard of some place called Mariposa. But I never heard of no sech place. Did you?"

Downey shook his head. "No *place* named Mariposa. There was a steamer wrecked somewheres along the coast by that name a while back. Hell of a lot of people went down with her, from all reports. There's a piece about it in this newspaper I fetched along." Tossing the paper onto the bar, he turned toward the door. "Well, I'll be trottin' along. I'll look up that dodger, an' if the description fits this Jube, I'll be back."

When the officer had gone Cush glanced across the bar at Black John, who was reading the story of the wreck of the *Mariposa*. "See there—what did I tell you?"

The big man pocketed the paper and glanced across the bar. "You've told me so damn many things, most of which wasn't worth hearin', that I can't answer yer question."

"Yeah, well by God, I told you this here Jube must be some kind of a crook, er else he wouldn't be on Halfaday. An' you claimed he might be an honest citizen. Now Downey comes along an proves I was right."

"Downey ain't proved nothin', yet. All he says—he thinks he remembers a police dodger describin' some bird that might look like Jube."

"Where would a quiet guy like Jube, which his hands showed he hadn't never done no work when he come here, git a thousan' dollar bill, if he didn't steal it off'n someone?"

Black John grinned. "Hell, Cush, he might of got it a hundred an one way—might of found a bunch of 'em blowin' down a street, somewheres, an' stopped to pick 'em up. Cripes, most anyone would stop to pick up a thousan' dollar bill."

"Huh," Cash grunted, in disgust "Sometimes, John, you talk like a damn fool!"

Later, in his cabin, Black John reread the newspaper account of the shipwreck, clipped the story and placed the clipping in his wallet.

IV

ONE DAY, SOME five weeks after his departure from Halfaday Creek, Corporal Downey reappeared. As Black John was about to enter the saloon, he paused and glanced toward the landing to see the officer ascending the steep trail from the creek. "Back again, eh? You fellas shore get around, don't you? Cripes, if you got paid by the mile you'd have a better proposition than any claim on Bonanza!"

The officer joined him and the two stepped into the saloon and crossed to the bar. The big man eyed Cush, "Bein' as we're a couple of newcomers, the first drink is on the house, ain't it?"

Cush frowned. "It ain't." Methodically he set a bottle, three glasses, and the dice box onto the bar. "You fellas might be newcomers somewheres you'd go to—but not here. There's the box. The drinks is on the one that loses 'em."

"Sech penuriousness is reprehensible, not to say downright niggardly," remarked Black John, picking up the dice box.

"Yeah? Well, four sixes shook outa that box would be worth more to you than all the big words you kin think up in a week. So go ahead an' roll out them dice—an' keep yer thumb off'n the front end of the box whilst yer doin' it. An' as fer bein' niggerly, you're a damn sight more niggerly lookin' than I be, what with them black whiskers of yourn."

"Okay," grinned the big man, raffling the dice in the box. "One shake all around, an' the loser pays."

"We'll shake jest like we allus do," Cush replied, "an' the one that gits two horses on him first buys the drinks. One shake ain't no dice game, no more than one shot is a pool game, er one move is a game of checkers. If some guy could stand around an' make up the rules, he'd allus win."

Black John shook a pair of treys the first shake, and the other three treys in the two following shakes. Downey shook three fives, and added another five in the next two shakes. Cush threw three aces the first shake, and failed to better them. He lost the next horse also, and Black John grinned across the bar. "You see, Cush, if you'd followed my suggestion, you'd have stuck me for the drinks on that first throw. You must remember, my good man, that I always have your best interest at heart. Let that be a lesson to you."

"Huh," Cush grunted, with a glance at Downey. "They can't nothin' happen that John don't wangle it around to make it look like he's right an' the other fella's wrong. An the hell of it is, what with the luck he's got, he gen'ly is. What fetched you back so quick? Seems like you ain't had no more'n time to git down to Dawson an' back—onlest you went like hell. Er mebbe you didn't go down to Dawson?"

"Yes, I went to Dawson, all right. Things are kind of quiet along the river so I hunted through the files till I found that dodger I was tellin' you about, describin' that fella down in Olson's old shack. I figgered I'd better come up an' get him before he took a notion to pull out. I caught the *Sarah* goin' down, at the mouth of the White, an' come back up there on the *Hannah,* so I saved a hell of a lot of paddlin'. I stopped at Olson's shack as I come by, but he wasn't there. I figgered mebbe he was up here."

"He ain't showed up this mornin'," Black John said. "But he ain't far away. Prob'ly out in the hills somewheres huntin' a moose. He told me yesterday he was plumb out of meat. So you figger he's the fella they want back there in the States, eh?"

For answer Downey drew the printed dodger from his pocket and spread it on the bar. "Here's the description," he said. "It fits him to a T—name, Joseph Bracken. Five-foot eleven. Hundred an' seventy pounds. Age, about fifty-five. Hair brown. Eyes blue. Smooth talker. Well educated. Gentlemanly appearance. Gambler by profession. Mild, even temper, except when aroused, then flies into a killin' rage."

The big man's eyes followed the lines as Downey read them. "Too bad they ain't got his picture on there," he said "an' his fingerprints, too. I thought most of them pick-up dodgers had 'em."

"Only when the man had been in serious trouble before—like he'd done time, or broke out of some prison, so the police would have a photo, an his prints on file. But you can see for yourself, John, not many men would fit that description."

THE BIG man grinned. "Oh, I don't know, Downey. There must be a hell of a lot of men in the world that's five-foot eleven. An' a lot of 'em prob'ly weighs around a hundred an' seventy. An' if they keep on livin', they're bound to be fifty-five sometime. An' as for brown hair an' blue eyes—they're too common to mention. Also there's a hell of a lot of gamblers—an' a lot of 'em would be smooth talkers, an' even tempered, an' gentlemanly appearin'. What's this here Bracken wanted for?"

"Murder an robbery. Shot another gambler named Buck Whiting over a card game in the Oriental Club, in Seattle. Then turned the gun on the house, reached through the pay-off wicket, an' grabbed off a packet containing five one thousan' dollar bills, an' some smaller stuff, an' disappeared."

BEHIND THE bar Cush nodded emphatically "By God, he's him all right! That there thousan' dollar bill part proves it! When he first hit here, the same time he draw'd the name outa the can, he bought him a bunch of supplies, an' give me a thousan' dollar bill, an' I give him back his change." He turned to Black John. "An' what's more, Jube *is* a gambler—jest like I claimed! No one but a gambler would have long supple fingers like he's got—an' no calluses on his hands! I spotted him fer a gambler, first time I seen him. But John, he figgered he worn't. Gamblers ain't got no calluses, 'cause they don't never work—an' if a man won't work, how in hell would he have a thousan' dollar bill, onlest he win if off'n someone? Besides, gamblers like thousan' dollar bills."

"Well, who the hell don't?" grinned the big man.

"I mean, if a man's got thousan' dollar bills, he kin pack around a hell of a lot of money in a common wallet. Like the handbill claims, there, Jube was gentlemanly appearin'. Most of them city gamblers is. But like if they packed their wad around in fives an' tens an twenties their pockets would bung out like a couple of saddlebags an' they'd look like hell."

"He must be a hell of a gambler—the way he plays stud," Black John retorted. "Claimed he'd never played the game—an' I believe him. He's be'n at it fer a couple of months, an' he don't play even a middlin' good game yet."

"Huh," Cush grunted. "If I would tell someone I never played no stud, an' then started in an played as good as I know'd how, everyone would figger I was a damn liar!"

The big man grinned, and winked at Downey. "Oh, I don't know, Cush. I guess they'd believe you, all right—the way you play."

"Is that so? Well, I take notice I win about as often as you do! An' they can't no one claim you don't know the game!"

A shadow darkened the doorway, and a man stepped into the room. Stepping to a card table, be removed the cartridges from the rifle he was carrying, pocketed them, laid the gun on the table, and joined the two at the bar. "Hello, Jube!" Black John greeted, stepping aside to allow space for the man between himself and the officer. "Meet Corporal Downey, of the North-west Mounted Police. An' Downey, this is Jube Custer, accordin' to the name can."

The officer smiled thinly, his eyes on the other's face. "I'm more interested in what your name was back where you come from."

The man's brow puckered into a slight frown, and he passed his fingers lightly across it. "Back where I came from?" he repeated, slowly. "Yes—certainly—I must have had a name. The priest asked me the same question—back there in the mountains. But for the life of me, I couldn't remember it. It is all very annoying."

"Joe Bracken," Downey pronounced the name distinctly. "Does that name mean anything to you?"

"Joe Bracken," the man repeated the name slowly, and slowly he shook his head. "No, I don't think I ever heard the name before."

"Where did you come from?"

"From the seashore. There were many dead men. Some bodies had been tossed ashore by the waves, some were lodged among the rocks, and other bodies were floating in the water, battering against the rocks. One man was alive. He had built a small fire. I tried to talk to him, but he could only mutter the name Mariposa. I fell asleep, and in the morning when I awoke, the man was dead."

"The *Mariposa* was a ship that was wrecked somewhere down along the coast, a while back," Downey said. "Was you on the *Mariposa?*"

The man shook his head. "No—on the shore. It was a rocky shore, with the waves pounding incessantly. I wake up in the night even yet, and hear the thunderous roar, and the suck and gurgle of the waves among the rocks. I started to walk, following the coastline until I came to a turbulent river that I could not cross, so I followed it back away from the sea. For many days I followed its course farther and farther into the mountains—glad to get away from the sea—from that damned sound—the pounding of waves against rocks. Then I came upon the priest. This Father Cassatt, after asking me many questions, sent me on to Dawson City, in company of two Indians, who, when the canoe rounded a bend of the river, and they saw Black John standing there at the mouth of Halfaday, beached the canoe on the opposite side of the river and fled into the woods. Black John kindly allowed me to occupy Olson's old shack, and I have been here ever since. And," the man concluded with a smile, "that is about all I can tell you."

Downey frowned. "An' it ain't enough—by a damn sight Do you mean to stand there an' tell me you don't remember your own name, nor where you come from?"

THE MAN nodded. "I remember nothing. It is as if that morning there on the seashore was the beginning of things—the first morning of my life. I know, of course, that this cannot be so. I am a grown man. I must have been a youngster, and many years must have passed since that time, because, as you can see, I am not a young man. I must have had a mother and a father. Maybe brothers, sisters—friends. Maybe even a wife and children. My God, man," he cried suddenly, "the thought is torturing! Maddening! Or—am I mad? For hours on end, in the daytime, and at night, I strive to concentrate—to force my mind to penetrate the blank wall that separates me from my past. But it is no use. Always my recollection carries me back to the seacoast and the dead men, and the thunderous pounding of the waves—and no farther."

The frown on Downey's face deepened. "Chicago!" he exclaimed suddenly. "Ever be'n in Chicago?"

"C-h-i-c-a-go," the man's lips formed the word slowly—deliberately, and again he passed his long fingers across his brow.

"Y-e-s. Dr. Senn—Dr. Oxner. The Augustana Hospital. There were many others."

"You was in a hospital, there? Was you sick?"

"Sick? No. That is—I don't remember of being sick."

"What business did you follow?"

"Business?"

"Yeah. How'd you make a livin'? Was you a store-keeper, er a doctor, er a lawyer. Er, mebbe you was a gambler?"

The man was silent for several moments then shook his head. "It is no use trying. I can't remember."

"Ever be'n to Seattle?"

"S-e-a-t-t-l-e. Yes, the name seems vaguely familiar. I may have been there."

"Ever play cards there?"

"No, not that I remember."

"Look here, Bracken," Downey said impatiently, "yer pretty good at this 'don't remember' stuff: But it won't get you anything. Why did you shoot Buck Whiting?"

"Who—me? You are calling me 'Bracken'? I certainly don't remember shooting anyone. Who is Buck Whiting?"

"He's a corpse now. Before you shot him that night in the Oriental Club, in Seattle, he was another gambler. You shot him over a card game, then swung yet gun on the house, scooped up all the loose change, an' skipped out. Does that help yet memory any."

THE OTHER smiled. "Sort of a Wild West play, eh? If you are really in earnest, officer, you have the wrong man. I know nothing of any Oriental Club. And I am certain I never shot anyone during a card game—nor at any other time."

"You got any thousan' dollar bills?" Downey asked, abruptly.

"Yes. I seem to be well supplied with money. I tendered one to Cush, here, for some supplies, when I first came, and I have four others in my bolt." He loosened a money belt and handed it to Downey, who slipped it into his pocket.

"Where'd you get them bills?" he asked sharply.

"Get them? Why, I—I don't remember where I got them. They are evidently mine. What difference does it make where I got them?"

"It makes a hell of a lot of difference," Downey replied grimly. "These four bills, an' the one you give Cush, was snatched through the payoff wicket at the Oriental Club the night you shot Buck Whiting—an you done the snatchin'. Come on, Bracken. The jig's up. We'll be goin' down to Dawson where you'll be held fer the American authorities. We can stop in an' pick up yer pack on the way down."

Black John turned to the officer. "Guess I'll go along, Downey," he said. "Wait till I throw some stuff in my pack. We'll take my canoe. It's bigger. You know, Jube here is a friend of mine. This is a mighty interestin' case—an' somehow I can't help but feel that it ain't comin' out jest the way you think. Tell you what I'll do—I'll bet you the drinks you've got the wrong man."

"You're on," grinned the officer, "an' if I was a bettin' man I'd lay a month's salary on top of it. But I ain't."

V

AS THE CANOE bearing the three men felt the pull of the fast water at the head of the Fish Rapids on the White River, Black John, who was paddling the stern, leaned heavily on his paddle to swerve the craft toward the bank at the head of the portage trail. At the same instant Downey, in the bow, shifted his paddle and with a mighty back stroke designed to break the increasing speed, threw the canoe broadside to the current. The next moment it was swept against a rock that protruded above the surface and overturned.

As Black John came to the surface he managed to grab hold of the gunwale at the stern of the canoe and an instant later was whirling down through the turbulent whitewater. The weight of his body, serving as a drag, kept the canoe in front of him, and he held on with a grip of iron as the light craft, tossing on the crests, raced down through the canyon, ricocheting from rock to rock, serving as a buffer which kept him from any contact with the obstructions.

Almost before he realized it he shot out onto the surface of the placid, slowly revolving eddy at the foot of the rapid to see Downey, flat on his belly at the edge of the gravel bar, reach out and grasp the unconscious form of Jube Custer as it floated slowly past him. A moment later the big man hauled the damaged canoe ashore, and turned his attention to the two at the edge of the gravel. Custer he pulled clear of the water and turned to speak to Downey, to find that the officer had passed completely out and lay with his face in the gravel, his legs still in the water.

Realizing that inasmuch as Downey had been conscious only a moment before, in all probability he had little or no water in his lungs, he turned to the other whose only visible injury was a slowly swelling lump high on the forehead. Grasping him by the ankles, he threw the man's knees over his shoulders so the body hung against his back in an inverted position. Then he trotted up and down the gravel for a few moments so that the rough jolting would empty the man's lungs of any water he might have inhaled.

As no water gushed from the open mouth, he laid the man on the ground and, with his hands under Downey's armpits dragged him clear of the water. As he did so he noticed that the officer's left foot dangled loosely, lying sidewise on the gravel, while the toe of the right foot pointed straight up.

Dropping to his knees, he removed the boot and sock and with his belt knife slit the trousers to the knee. Drawing the cloth back, the big man emitted a low whistle as he stared at the badly shattered leg. Blood oozed from a wound at the shin through which nearly an inch of splintered bone protruded. Two other irregularities between the knee and ankle showed that other misplaced bone fragments were on the verge of breaking through the skin. Black John's brow furrowed into a frown as he gazed down at the injured member. "Don't believe he'll ever walk on that leg again," he muttered. "Might's well cut the damn thing off an throw it in the river for all the good it'll ever do him." Raising his eyes he glanced helplessly about. Then, leaping to his feet, be dashed waist deep into the water, and retrieved a pack sack that was floating on the surface of the slowly revolving eddy. It was his own pack, and carrying it ashore, he opened it, and removed a shirt. "Guess I'll jest tie his leg up in this an' see if I can patch up the canoe."

SPREADING THE shirt on me gravel, he squatted beside the injured man, and as he was about to slip the shirt underneath the leg, a slight sound attracted his attention, and he glanced over his shoulder to see that the prisoner had risen to his knees and was staring wide-eyed at the shattered leg. "So you come to, eh? By God, you're lucky to get out of it with a crack on the head. Downey, here, his leg must of got jammed between two rocks, an' the current done the rest—an by the looks of things it was plenty. Give me a hand, here, an' we'll wrap it up in this shirt an' get to work on the canoe." As he spoke, he was about to fold the shirt over the wound when a sharp exclamation stayed him.

"No! No! For God's sake, man, don't touch that wound with that poisonous rag!"

"Pizenous rag—hell! This here's my other shirt. An' it's clean. I worshed it myself! Just took it out of my pack sack." >

"Just the same it's a poisonous rag as far as that wound is concerned. In all probability it would start an infection that might well cost the man his leg. Don't let anything touch that protruding bone!"

The big man frowned. "It's twenty mile from here to the Yukon, an' eighty mile from the mouth of the White to Dawson. Besides that, we the canoe to patch. What the hell we goin' to do—leave his leg lay open like that for the flies to blow? Or mebbe we could bang it over the side, an' drag it down to Dawson through the water."

The man was squatting beside him, now, gazing down at the injured member. He reached down and gently ran his long supple fingers over the skin, feeling the lumps, but carefully avoiding any contact with the protruding bone. "Multiple and compound fracture of the tibia. Fractured fibula, too. Mighty interesting case in a hospital—doubly so here."

"Yeah," grinned Black John. "Ain't it? 'Specially to Downey."

"There's no time to be lost. We must hurry," the other replied.

"Hurry! Hurry—an' what?"

"Why—hurry and get to work on this leg! If possible before he regains consciousness—at least before those muscles begin to contract." He glanced swiftly about him, and the big man noted that the peculiar baffled look was gone from the keen blue eyes as they flitted from the open pack sack, to the damaged canoe, and swept the barren gravel bar. "If we had a rope we might work it," he muttered.

"I've got a length of babiche line in my pack. Always carry it, jest in case." Producing the stout line, he glanced at the other. "Here's yer rope—now what do we do with it—hang him an' put him out of his misery?"

The man smiled and pointed to two spruce trees that stood some ten feet apart at the edge of the gravel. "We must move him over between those trees. Then, with our belts and the straps from that pack, we can anchor him to one of them, and then, with the line made fast to his ankle and passed around the other tree, we'll be able to get power enough to draw that bone back into place."

Together the two carried the injured man across the narrow reach of gravel and placing him in a sitting position against one of the tree trunks, made him fast to it by strapping his body tight to the trunk by means of the belts and straps passed about his chest and under his arms. Slipping the boot onto the foot and lacing it to prevent laceration, they made one end of the line fast to the ankle, and passed it around the trunk of the other tree.

Black John then grasped the line firmly. "Want me to pull on it, eh, an' stretch the leg out?"

The other shook his head doubtfully. "Manipulating those bones into place is going to take quite some time. I don't believe you could maintain a steady pull until I finished," he said. "Let's try it this way." Bringing the line back, he tightened it, and took two half hitches around the ankle, thus doubling it between the ankle and the tree. "Now cut a short stout stick, thrust it in between the two lines, and twist them together. In that way we get all the power the need."

As the big man twisted the stick round and round, the leg was pulled taut, and kneeling beside it, the other worked deftly with his fingers, kneading at the flesh, working the shattered bone fragments into place.

Presently Black John paused in the twisting and stared in fascination at the manipulating fingers. "That ort to be tight enough," he said.

The other shook his head, and pointed to the wound through which the bone fragment still protruded for a quarter of an inch. "A little tighter. A little more stretching. We've got to pull that bone back out of the wound." He glanced apprehensively at the taut twisted line. "I only hope the line holds," he said.

Black John twisted on the stick. "The line'll hold," he replied grimly, "I only hope Downey does. It would be a damn sight easier to whittle that leg off than pull it out by the roots."

After a few more twists the man spoke. "That will do," he said. "If we could keep that line from untwisting and slacking off, you might be working on the canoe."

"Hold this stick a minute an' I'll make it fast," Black John said, and as the other took the stick, he cut a sapling, and with a piece cut from the end of the babiche line, he spliced the two sticks together, the longer piece braced firmly against the ground, preventing the rope from untwisting.

EXAMINATION OF the canoe showed a few cracked ribs, but only one hole in her near the bow. Gathering pitch, the big man heated a stone, and with it ironed a small square of canvas cut from his pack sack neatly over the hole.

The task completed, he returned to the wounded man who was mercifully still unconscious, as the other finished fashioning a number of splints from a length of cedar. "Have you any soap?" he asked. Black John handed him a cake of soap from his pack, and the man proceeded to make a thick, heavy lather, with which he smeared the wound and a greater part of the injured leg. "Nearest thing we've got to an antiseptic," he said, "And probably not so bad, at that. Anyway, it's the best we can do till we can get him to a hospital. How is the canoe?"

"All set," the big man replied. "An' the quicker we got goin' the better. I grabbed my pack out of the river—but the grub pack must of gone on down."

"You can help me with these splints. We'll have to use that shirt, now, and whatever else we can find to wrap his leg in. It must be held rigid just as it is. Any slight movement between the knee and the ankle, and all our work might go for nothing."

When the splints and the shirt were bound into place, and the line slacked off, Black John's eyes rested for a moment upon a white birch tree, some eight inches in diameter. "By God!" he cried. "I believe we can fix that leg so it can't move if you'd jump on it!" Stepping to the tree, he worked for several minutes with his belt knife, and came back with a section of heavy bark, round and stiff as a length of stovepipe. Spreading this section of bark, they slipped it on over the bandage, and punching holes along the edges, laced it tight. As he finished the job, the big man looked around for approval. Jube Custer lay sprawled on the gravel beside the still unconscious officer. "Well—I'll be damned!" be muttered. "Passed plumb out! It's a good thing he held out as long as he did. If Downey keeps two legs under him he's shore got Jube to thank—not me. Gambler—hell!" he grinned and drawing the account of the *Mariposa* wreck he had clipped from the newspaper he glanced at it and returned it to his pocket. "When Downey reads this he's goin' to sort of revise his guess about who Jube is. At that, I ain't goin' to show it to him till I get good an damn ready."

VI

SLIPPING THE PATCHED canoe into the water, Black John turned his attention to the two men to find that Corporal Downey had regained consciousness and sat with his back against the tree to which he had been strapped, seriously contemplating his bark-wrapped leg.

"Busted, eh?" the officer asked. "I figgered it was when I dragged myself out on the gravel. Then Bracken come floatin' by an' I made a grab for him an felt a hell of a pain go shootin' through my leg—an' that's the last I remember."

"I'll say it's busted," the big man replied. "Damn near pulverized, if you ask me. You're goin' to be in the hospital quite a while when we get down to Dawson."

Downey glanced at the unconscious form sprawled on the gravel. "Ain't Bracken come to, yet? Mebbe he's dead."

"No, he ain't dead. He come to for a while, but he passed out again. Got a hell of a rap on the head comin' down through the rapids. You set there till I get him loaded in the canoe, an' then I'll help you in. We've got to get to hell out of here. The grub pack's gone on down the river. The three of us are lucky to be alive, an' if our luck holds, we might connect up with a steamboat when we hit the big river."

Their luck did hold. A couple of miles below the mouth of the White the light craft was overtaken by the steamer, *Delta*, and the two wounded men were placed in bunks. Several times during the downriver run Jube Custer regained consciousness, but each time, after a few minutes of staring about him in a dazed, puzzled manner, he relapsed again into unconsciousness.

On arrival at Dawson, both were removed on stretchers to the hospital where Corporal Downey was placed immediately on the operating table.

Black John, who had helped lift him onto the table, turned to white-clad Dr. Sutherland with a grin. "Cripes, Doc, you look like a cross between Father Judge in full dress, an the Grand Beagle of a Ku Klux outfit!"

The doctor returned the grin, and eyed the bark-wrapped leg. "Not a bad idea—that birch bark wrapping. I'll remember that. It may come in handy, sometime."

"Oh, shore. It ain't so bad—fer a rough job. A man's got to do the best he can with what he's got to work with."

When the bark casing and the shirt that wrapped the leg were removed, the doctor eyed the perfectly shaped cedar splints that encased the leg between ankle and knee. "That's a mighty good job of splint work, John," he commended. Then bent closer to examine the wound in the shin, "Didn't the bone protrude through the skin, there?" he asked.

"Yeah, about an inch er so."

"But—how did you retract it?"

"Pounded it back with a rock," the big man replied, with a perfectly straight face. "A hammer would have be'n better. But I didn't have none along. Didn't have no antiseptic along, neither, but I softened up a bar of soap an' give it a good thick swashin' of that."

As the big man talked the doctor's fingers were exploring the leg, moving back and forth along the tibia. A few moments later, he glanced up. "John," he said, "you're a damn liar! Who set that leg?"

Black John grinned. "Fella from up on Halfaday. He's a prospector. We call him Jube Custer, on account of him drawin' that name out of the can. But, Downey, here, he claims he's a gambler from down in the States."

"Prospector, gambler, hell! The man who handled this case could only be a trained surgeon—and a mighty fine one, too! Three fractures of the tibia—one of them compound—and at least one of the fibula—tell me, now, how he did it? How did he retract that sliver of bone? And don't tell me you don't know! You were there. You must have helped."

"Well—first we strapped Downey to a tree, an' then we made a len'th of babiche line fast to his ankle, an' passed it around another tree, an' that back to the ankle agin. Then I stuck a stick between the two lines an twisted, an' kep' twistin' till we damn near pulled Downey in two. Then the bone went back by itself. It was Jube's idea. Like I told you, if I'd had it to do alone, I'd have pounded it back with a rock. How he done the rest of it—fittin' them broken bones together I don't know. After we'd got Downey stretched out between them two trees like a clothes-line, I went to work patchin' the canoe, an' left the leg-patchin' job to Jube."

"Where is this Jube, now?"

"He's here in the hospital somewheres, I reckon. At least we brought him here. Couple of other fellas was handlin' him while I helped with Downey."

WITH A few words of instruction to a younger doctor and a white-clad nurse, Dr. Sutherland stepped from the room, followed by Black John. After an inquiry at the desk the doctor led the way down a hall, pushed open the door of a room, and the two stepped inside. The man's clothing had been removed, and he lay there in bed. As the two stood looking down at him, his eyes opened, and he glanced about him with the same bewildered expression that Black John had noticed during his brief intervals of consciousness on the *Delta*. His glance swept the room, and focused upon the white clad figure of Dr. Sutherland, standing at the foot of the bed. Then, suddenly, the form beneath the covers seemed to stiffen, the eyes again swept the room, and again they came to rest upon the doctor. The bewildered look was still there—but Black John noted that there was a difference. It was not the hopelessly bewildered look he had seen in those eyes before—rather the frankly puzzled expression of a man finding himself placed suddenly amid half familiar surroundings. As the man's glance shifted to his own face, Black John smiled. "Hi, Jube!" he said, "How you feelin'?"

The man stared at him for a moment, then shifted his glance to the other. "I realize that I am in a hospital, doctor—as a patient. But why? And where? Who is this man? And why did he address me as 'Jube'?"

Dr. Sutherland smiled. "You were brought here to be treated for an injury received when the canoe in which Corporal Downey and Black John, here, and you were coming down the White River, overturned in a rapid. You are in Dawson. And this man is Black John Smith of Halfaday Creek."

"A canoe—the White River—Black John Smith—Halfaday Creek." The man repeated the words slowly, as he drew his fingers across his brow. "It's all Greek to me," he said, rising to a sitting posture. "I have never heard of the White River, nor of Black John Smith, nor of Halfaday Creek. And why should I have been in a canoe?"

Dr. Sutherland smiled reassuringly. "Let's just take it easy, and we'll get this thing straightened out. Just what is the last thing you do remember clearly?"

"Why—the storm. And the broken rudder. And the ship tossing on the waves—drifting inevitably toward the rocks. And the frantic passengers rushing back and forth from one rail to the other, with the ship's officers and crew vainly trying to control them, and to launch the boats. Then—the shock as the ship struck. The terrible grinding crash, then the deck rising, and men and women sliding into the sea. I held to the rail for some time—then—then—" He paused, and for several moments sat there with furrowed brow, evidently striving to remember.

Finally he shook his head. "That's all," he said. "That's the last thing I remember."

"You spoke of the ship. What ship was it?"

"The *Mariposa*, I had been working rather hard for a long time and felt the need of a rest—a change of some kind so I went to Seattle and took passage on the *Mariprosa*, for a trip up the coast. Then, the storm—the broken rudder—and ship-wreck."

DR. SUTHERLAND nodded. "A terrible disaster," he said. "There were mighty few survivors.

"I remember it particularly because the medial profession suffered a severe loss in the death of—"

His words were cut short by the voice of Corporal Downey, who ordered the attendants who were wheeling him past the open door of the room to halt. The officer raised himself on an elbow. "So, you come to, eh, Bracken? I'm havin' a constable sent up from detachment to lock you up jest as soon as they get you fixed up, here."

The man on the bed glanced at the officer. "Bracken? Were you speaking to me?"

"You know damn well who I'm speakin' to," Downey replied.

"But—why the constable? Why lock me up?"

Downey, grinned. "It's a kind of a quaint custom we've got in these parts—lockin' a murderer up. We find we can keep track of 'em better, that way."

The man on the bed shook his head in resignation. "First it's 'Jube'—then 'Bracken'. I was in a canoe on a river I never even heard of. Now I'm a murderer. I must confess, it's all rather confusing, to say the least."

Black John grinned broadly. "It won't take long to straighten it out, Doc—yeah, we're forgettin' the 'Jube', and the 'Bracken' aliases. It's my guess that you're Dr. Howard B. Macleod, of Philadelphia—right?"

The other nodded. "Certainly. Now we seem to be getting someplace."

Fumbling in his pocket, Black John drew out the account of the sinking of the *Mariposa* he had clipped from the newspaper, back in his cabin. He handed it to the man on the bed. "Here you are, Doc. It might interest you to read of yer demise—an' what a hell of a loss you was to the medical profession."

The man read the story, wide eyed, and then glanced at the others. "But—Dawson City—that's inland, isn't it? On the Yukon River?"

Dr. Sutherland nodded, "Yes, and I'm mighty proud to meet you, Doctor—and to know," he added, with a smile, "that the account of your death has been greatly exaggerated."

The other returned the smile and glanced at the clipping in his hand. "As has also this highly flattering estimate of my value to the medical profession. But—how did I get here? And how much time has elapsed since the wreck."

"A little better'n three months," Black John said. "You lived in Olson's old shack, on Halfaday, better'n two months, after them Siwashes run off an' left you there on the White."

"Three months! Oh—my poor wife! Is there a telegraph office here? I must wire her immediately!"

"Oh, shore. Just write out the message, an' I'll see that it gets sent."

THE MAN'S brow furrowed. "Three months," he repeated. "And I haven't the slightest recollection of anything that transpired, from the time I was clinging to that ship's rail until a few minutes ago, when I awoke in this room."

"Well," Black John grinned, "quite a bit transpired in the interim, at that. After we get that message to your wife on the wire, I'll give you the low-down."

"But—what is this about a murder? And my being locked up?"

"Oh, that's jest a mistake of Downey's. Some gambler name of Bracken shot a guy down in Seattle over a card game an' Downey figgered you was him, on account of the description fittin' you fairly well."

Dr. Sutherland smiled, and glanced at the officer, who had been an interested listener. "It's a mighty good thing for you, Downey, that Doctor Macleod isn't a gambler.

"He is the one who set your broken leg—and believe me, under the circumstances, it is one for the book—a remarkable accomplishment, indeed. If you'd been left to the tender mercies of Black John, you'd have had to hobble around the rest of your life on a wooden leg."

Dr. Sutherland stepped from the room and returned a few moments later with a newspaper in his hand. The man on the bed glanced up at him. "There is no reason for my remaining here in bed, is there, doctor?" he asked.

The other smiled. "None that I know of. You look fit as a fiddle." Stepping into a closet, he returned with an outfit of clothing which he placed on a chair beside the bed, setting a pair of heavy laced packs beside it. The man on the bed eyed the clothing dubiously. "Those—er—garments? Are you sure they're mine? There must be some mistake."

Black John, grinned. "Nope. They're yours, all right, Doc. You bought 'em up to Cush's. Them store clothes you was wearin' when them Siwashes run out on you there on the river, that day, was only hangin' on you by the grace of God, after two, three hundred miles of scramblin' through the mountains in 'em."

LIFTING THE heavy twill trousers, the man explored the pockets. He also felt in the pockets of the heavy wool shirt. Then he glanced up at Dr. Sutherland. "It isn't only that I fail to recognize these garments as my own, but I seem to be totally without funds. If you are satisfied as to my identity, doctor, will you advance me the money to defray my expenses to Philadel-phia?"

In the hall Corporal Downey spoke to an attendant who reached into a pocket of the uniform trousers he held in his arm, and withdrew a money belt. Downey motioned for him to hand it to the man on the bed. "Guess you won't need to borrow no money, doctor," he said. "There's your own belt. It's got four thousan' dollar bills in it. I was holdin''em for evidence."

"Evidence?"

"Yeah. You see, this gambler Bracken, grabbed off five one thousan' dollar bills the night he shot the gambler. You had passed a thousan' dollar bill on Cush, an' had these four on you when I arrested you. Them bills, together with the description I had of Bracken, made a pretty strong case against you."

Black John chuckled. "That's the trouble with the law, Downey. It goes too much on circumstantial evidence. Hell, take a miner's meetin' now—an' if we figgered Doc, there was a murderer we'd had him hung long ago. An' here the law's got to turn him loose!"

Dr. Sutherland joined in the laughter and handed the man on the bed the week-old Seattle newspaper he held in his hand, indicating a certain headline.

HOSPITAL TO BE ERECTED IN PHILADELPHIA IN MEMORY OF EMINENT SURGEON WHO WENT DOWN WITH THE "MARIPOSA". COMMIT-TEE APPOINTED TO DRAW UP PLAN FOR THE HOWARD D. MACLEOD MEMORIAL HOSPITAL.

"If you make good connections, doctor, you may get to Philadelphia in time to help that committee out with their plan."

As the man read the article, Corporal Downey spoke. "Funny how things works out sometimes, ain't it? If it hadn't be'n fer me figurin' the doctor, there, was this Bracken, he might have gone on bein' Jube Custer, an' livin' up there on Halfaday fer

God knows how long. An if it hadn't be'n for his comin' to long enough to work on my leg, I'd prob'ly lost it. An' if it hadn't be'n fer Black John, we wouldn't neither one of us be'n here. Looks like everyone but Black John got somethin' out of it. An," he added with a broad grin, "if you all knew Black John like I do—that's one hell of a good joke!"

"Don't worry, Downey," the big man replied, "I'll get mine. Remember I win that drink! I knew damn well Jube wasn't no gambler!"

SKIN GAME

BLACK JOHN SMITH stepped into the barroom of Cushing's Fort, the combined trading post and saloon that served the little community of outlawed men that had sprung up on Halfaday Creek, close against the Yukon-Alaska border, crossed the floor, elevated a foot to the battered brass rail, and eyed the lugubrious proprietor with a frown. "What the hell's ailin' you?" he demanded. "Spit out that chaw of tobacco, an' set out the dice box. I'm dry."

Without a word Cush set out a bottle and two glasses. Filling one of the glasses to the brim, he shoved the other and the bottle across the bar. Then, raising the glass, he downed its contents at a gulp, rasped the dregs from his throat, and eyed the big man.

"I ain't got no thaw of terbacker. My jaw's swole. I got a back tooth that's achin' the hell outa me. I wouldn't git no kick outa shakin' dice—even if I win, I wouldn't."

"Toothache, eh? Well, don't let that worry you none. I'll get a hammer an' a spike an' knock it out. You remember last year I got a toothache, an' you offered to operate on me that way— claimed you saw a Hudson's Bay Company factor fix up a Siwash like that one time."

"Yeah—but it was me seen him do it, not you. You wouldn't know how to go at it."

"Cripes, I can try, can't I?"

"Nor on me, you can't. This damn tooth's hurtin' enough the way it is, without you whammin' away at it with no hammer."

"But hell, Cush, you could sort of give me instructions as I went along, correct any mistakes I might make—like knockin' out the wrong tooth, or spearin' a tonsil."

"Nothin' doin'. I'm hittin' fer Dawson, an' you're goin' along."

"Me! Cripes, I jest got back from Dawson!"

"I don't give a damn if you jest got back, et didn't jest git back. Listen—when Downey come up here an' arrested Jube Custer you went back with 'em, claimin' Jube was a friend of yourn, an' you didn't figger he was no gambler an' murderer, like Downey claimed he was. Well, I'm a friend of yourn, too—ain't I?"

"Oh, shore."

"Well then, yer goin' down with me, too. I ain't no great hand with a canoe, an' if you an' Downey tipped over in a rapids, what the hell would I do in one? An' on top of that, the safe's gittin' full. We kin take the dust down with us an' bank it. I sent the klooch up to git One Armed John to run the saloon till we git back. They'll be showin' up pretty quick, so you better throw yer stuff in yer pack sack whilst I git the dust outa the safe. I'll throw in half a dozen quarts, too. And if this here tooth gits to hurtin' any worst than what it does now, I wouldn't give a damn if I tipped over in a rapids, er not!"

The big man grinned. "If you get half a dozen quarts in you, you won't give a damn whether you tip over or not, either. But, go ahead—get out the dust, an' I'll throw my stuff together. Be back anon, as a poet would say."

"Who gives a damn what a poet would say?" Cush growled. "That's one kind of a guy that ain't never showed up on Halfaday, anyhow."

"Ah, my friend, the loss is ours, I assure you. Take it on a beautiful morning like this, what could be more inspirin' than—"

"Listen," Cush interrupted, "if a man's got a toothache he don't give a damn if a mornin's beautiful, nor neither he wouldn't take no pleasure in hearin' no pome spoke. He'd want to git to a dentist, an' not no damn poet. Here's One Arm now—so you git to hell outa here!"

II

THE CANOE TRIP downriver was made without incident, and late in the afternoon, ten days later, they beached the canoe at the Dawson landing. Cush hit straight for the dentist, while Black John visited the Tivoli Saloon where Cush found him an hour later in desultory conversation with the bartender. "Don't look like no hell of a lot goin' on here," he grunted, glancing about the nearly deserted barroom.

"It's too early in the day," the bartender said. "The boys'll begin driftin' in after supper."

"We might start out by shakin' a game of dice for the drinks," Black John suggested, "an' later we can prob'ly get up a stud game."

Cush frowned. "The hell with shakin' dice fer the drinks, an' playin' stud! We kin do that on Halfaday. If a man's got a toothache fer a couple weeks solid, an' then gits it yanked out so it don't ache no more, he feels like doin' somethin' lively."

"Like what, for instance?" Black John asked.

"Well, like goin' down to the Klondike Palace an' doin' some dancin'. We kin stop in to the *ho*tel an' git supper, an' then go on over to the Palace."

The two proceeded to the hotel, and as they finished their meal, the big man glanced across the table at Cush. "Do you still feel like frivolin' the evenin' away at the Palace? Tellin' you about me, I don't like Cuter Malone."

"I don't like Cuter no better'n what you do," Cush replied. "But I wasn't aimin' to dance with Cuter. They's a lot of girls there to dance with."

"A man of your age should be more serious minded," Black John replied. "As we come past Al Scougale's store I saw a notice in the window where some missionary jest back from China, is goin' to lecture tonight in the Methodist Church on the evil effect of Buddhism, Confucianism, Shintoism, and Zoroasterism on the Chinese nation. If we hurry, I figger we might be able to get a couple of tickets."

Cush scowled. "Listen—I wouldn't give a damn if some Chinee had all them things, an' rheumatism on top of 'em. Chances is, if they got all them thing's ailin' 'em they ain't a-goin to git well nohow—so what's the use lecturin' about it. Besides, I went to a lecture onct, when I was tendin' bar back in Cincinnati. A guy give me a ticket."

"What was the topic of the lecture?"

"The which?"

"What was the lecture about?"

"Oh. Damn if I know. I went to sleep. Come on, let's be gittin' over to the Palace. I don't git down here very often. I figger we might's well make a night of it, an' pull out fer Halfaday in the mornin'."

ALONG TOWARD midnight, Cush led his scantily clad dancing partner to the bar, bought her a drink, and scowled as he watched Black John whirling about the floor with a big blonde in his arms.

When the dance was finished, the big man led his partner to the bar, ordered a couple of drinks, and was about to return to the dance floor when he caught Cush's eye. He turned to the blonde. "Friend of mine, there, wants to speak to me. I'll skip this next one."

The woman's eyes met his, she smiled and patted his arm. "All right, honey. Just this one, though. You're one baby I sure love to dance with."

Cush scowled as the big man joined him at the bar. "Honey! Baby!" he snorted. "If some woman's good lookin' an' yaller headed, she kin do any damn thing she wants to with you!"

Black John grinned. "I haven't noticed you passin' many of 'em up."

"Shore you ain't. An' that's jest it—I be'n dancin' with all of 'em. But I take notice you ain't danced with no one but that big taffy-head all evenin'.'"

"She's a good dancer."

"So's all the rest of 'em a good dancer," Cush replied. "Hell, they'd ort to be—they do enough of it. It's jest like I allus claim—any good lookin' woman that comes along could take you—an' take you fer plenty. Some day one of 'em will!"

The big blonde made her way toward them across the floor. "Come on, big boy," she said. "Time for the next dance!"

As the two left the bar, a man who had been standing beside Cush drinking alone, turned to him with a grin. "Drink up," he invited, "an' have one on me. So yer friend falls for the dames, eh?"

"I'll say he does," Cush replied, filling his glass from the bottle the other shoved toward him. "An' like I was tellin' him, one of 'em's goin' to take him fer plenty. Any good lookin' woman, special' if she's yaller headed kin git anything she wants off'n John."

"He don't look like no millionaire, at that," the other observed. "If she took him for all he's got, she prob'ly wouldn't be gettin' much."

Cush slanted him a glance. "No? Well, I'm tellin' you, brother, there ain't but damn few men in the country got more'n him."

"Prospector?"

"Yeah, he's a prospector, all right—an' a damn good one."

"Made a strike, eh?"

"Yeah, he's made a lot of strikes. He's smart, John is—except around some good lookin' woman. Then he's a damn fool."

The man laughed and sauntered toward the rear of the room as four men entered and approached the bar. Old Bettles, dean of the sourdoughs, greeted Cush vociferously. "Hi, Cush! Where the hell's Black John? We heard he was in town."

"Figgered on gittin' up a stud game," supplemented Moose-hide Charlie.

For answer, Cush nodded toward the dance floor. "You won't git him in no stud game tonight," he replied glumly. "Not if that there big yaller-head's got anything to say, you won't. He's be'n dancin' with her ever sence supper—an' they're still at it."

Camillo Bill eyed the dancers. "Cripes, that's Bovey's wife! Er at least they claim she is. They're a couple of crooks. Smooth, too. Took Jack Hammond fer ten thousan' on some kind of a fake deal."

"Yeah, an' the talk is that they took the manager of the Consolidated for a damn sight more'n that," Moosehide Charlie added.

"You better tip John off, Cush," Burr McShane said.

Cush scowled. Then a sudden gleam in his eye, he glanced into the faces of the sourdoughs. "Not by a damn sight I won't tip him off! An' I don't want none of you boys should, neither. I've warned John a hundred times agin foolin' around with wimmin'—but it don't do no good. Let some good lookin' woman come along, an' John allus falls fer her. I've told him sometime one of 'em would take him—an' I shore hope this un does. It would learn him a lesson—an' serve him right, to boot! The way I figger it, John's took plenty others—it won't hurt him none to git took hisself."

Bettles laughed. "It would be a hell of a good joke, at that!"

"It shore would," Camillo Bill agreed.

"Let's shet up an' see what happens," Moosehide said. "Hell, John's got plenty. What she takes him fer won't bust him."

"If she does take him," Burr MacShane said, "we'll never let him hear the last of it!"

A COUPLE of hours later, Cush accosted Black John as he stepped to the bar with the big blonde. "Hey, John," he said, "I've had about enough. Let's be gittin' over to the *ho*tel an' git to bed. We want to git a good early start in the mornin'."

The big man stepped closer and eyed him with a grin. "You do look a little the worse for wear, Cush. A man of your age hadn't ort to keep sech late hours."

"Is that so! Well, I'm a-tellin' you that I could keep right on dancin' from now till mornin', except these here damn pacs of mine is too tight, er somethin', an' my feet's hurtin' me. An' besides that, this here damn licker of Cuter's ain't settin' none too good on my stummick, neither. An' on top of that, it's like I said—we'd ort to git an early start in the mornin'."

As they talked, the big blonde stood waiting, her drink on the bar before her. Unnoticed by either of the two, the man who had bought Cush the drink just before the entry of the sourdoughs, slipped to her side and whispered in her ear, "Hook him if you can, Sadie. The little guy there claimed he's got plenty—an' I checks with Cuter. I asks him if the big guy's worth makin' a play fer, an' he laughs, an' says if we can take him we're in luck, 'cause he's got more loose dough than any guy in the Yukon. So it's up to you—go after him." The woman nodded, and the man faded into the crowd that rimmed the faro layout.

Black John's grin widened. "I don't see no call to hustle back to Halfaday," he argued. "Hell, Cush, we're havin' a good time right here. Remember, it was you that got me over here. I wanted to play stud, but you was hell-bent on dancin'—an' now you want to run out on me! Cripes, we don't get down here very often. We'd ort to make a week of it! You can trust One Arm to run the saloon."

"Yeah—an' the longer he runs it the more money I lose. I kin trust him jest twict as much as I kin trust any of the others—'cause he ain't only got one hand to git in the till. But at that, I'm losin' money every day I'm gone."

"But hell, Cush—it's worth it. Look at the fun we're havin'."

"Fun! Where's the fun in bein' sick to yer stummick, an' havin' yer feet hurt? Cripes, I'll bet I could have more fun in hell than here!"

"Well," grinned the big man, glancing about the room, "the two places is ondoubtless sim'lar. Anyway, you're headed in the right direction to find out. An' when I get there, I'll bet you a damn good snort of brimstone, we'll both wish we was back in Dawson!"

Cush scowled. "Listen—be you comin', er ain't you?"

"I ain't. Here I'm jest beginnin' to get acquainted with Sadie, an' you butt in an' try to ruin a beautiful friendship."

"Beautiful friendship!" Cush snorted in disgust. "You give me a pain in the pants! Of all the damn fools I ever seen, you're the damnedest! Me, I'm hittin' fer the *hotel* an' git me some sleep. An' in the mornin' I'm hirin' a Siwash to paddle me back to Halfaday. You kin stay here a week—er a month. But when yer beautiful friendship peters out on you, an' the big taffy-top takes you fer a roll, don't come to me fer no sympathy! Yer askin' fer it—an' fer once I hope you git it!"

As Cush made his way toward the door the big blonde nudged at Black John's elbow. "Come on, big boy—here's your drink. What's the matter—your friend run out on you?"

"Yeah, says he's had dancin' enough. Claims his feet hurt."

"His and mine both," the woman said. "You know, honey, we've been doin' quite some dancing ourselves. You know what I'd like to do—I'd like to go over in one of those booths, just you and me together, and sit out three or four dances over a good bottle of wine. How does that strike you?"

"Let's go. I'll tell the barkeep to fetch a bottle an' a couple of glasses."

THE WOMAN led the way to a booth and drew the curtains. Settling into a chair, she kicked off her slippers, hoisted a pair of shapely legs onto the table, drew a flat case from her stocking top, lighted a cigarette, and settled back with a sigh of contentment. The barkeeper appeared, set a tray on the table, and withdrew. Black John drew the cork, filled the two glasses, handed one to the lady, and sat down.

"This is what I call solid comfort," she said, wriggling her toes as she sipped the wine.

Black John smiled, his eyes on the shapely legs. "It ain't so hard to take, at that."

She eyed him through half-closed lids. "You don't live here in Dawson, do you?" she asked. "We've been here a week, and I never saw you before."

"Who's we?"

"Why, me an' my husband."

"Oh, you've got a husband, eh?"

"Sure I have. Listen, big boy—don't get me wrong. This isn't my regular grift. Living costs money in this man's town, and I'm working here to help pay expenses, while we try to raise the rest of the money."

"The rest of what money?"

"The rest of the money we've got to have to buy and outfit the ship we need."

"You needin' a ship?"

"You bet we do—and a good one. Amos, he's my husband, he knows the very ship we want—and the price is right, too. The trouble is, we've only got half enough to finance the deal."

"How much do you figger on raisin'?"

"We ought to have fifty thousand more. We might skimp through with forty thousand. They want sixty thousand in cash for the ship—and she's a bargain, at that price. We sold everything we had, and hustled around among our friends and borrowed all we could, but the most we could raise was forty thousand. So, seeing there was no chance to raise any more in Vancouver, we came up here, hoping to find someone—some miner, maybe, that had struck it lucky, and would be glad of the chance to invest forty thousand in a proposition that will pay him right around two hundred and thirty-five thousand in sixty days."

"H-u-m, not a bad investment, at that," Black John said, a gleam of interest in his eye. "This here forty thousan' you said you was able to raise—you've got it in cash?"

"That's right—forty one-thousand dollar bills—just about half of what we need. You don't know of anyone who'd be willing to match the roll for a fifty-fifty split on a half-million-dollar proposition, do you?"

"W-e-e-l-l, I wouldn't mind gettin' in on a proposition of that kind myself."

"Have you got forty thousand in cash?"

"Oh, shore. That is, I ain't got that much loose change on me right this minute. But I've got it in Cush's safe."

"Who's Cush? And where is his safe?"

"Cush? Oh, he's the fella I was talkin' to back there at the bar—the one who claimed his feet was hurtin' him. His safe is up in his saloon. He runs a little tradin' post an' saloon on a crick up the White River a piece."

"How long would it take you to go up there and get the money?"

"You mean, go up an' get it, an' fetch it down here?"

"Sure. We've got to have the spot cash to buy that ship with."

"Is the ship here in Dawson?"

"No, of course not! You don't suppose we'd fool around with one of these river scows, do you? The ship we're going to buy is a sea-going vessel."

"Going to make a trip on the ocean, eh?"

"That's right."

Black John pondered the statement for a few moments. "It looks like this here ship would have to be middlin' spry to make a trip acrost the ocean an' back in time enough for us to cash in on our investment in sixty days," he said. "An' it looks like we'd have to charge a hell of a freight rate to pick up half a million dollars on the round trip. 'Cause, if the ship costs us sixty thousan', we'd only have twenty thousan' left fer wages fer the crew, an' supplies—it's a cinch we couldn't be buyin' no cargo of our own to show a profit on."

The woman smiled. "You've got a good head on you, big boy. And that's what I like. You're not dumb. You're smart enough to figure things out. You'd be dead right—if we had to make a round trip across the ocean. But we don't. And the cargo we bring back will be ours, all right. It's worth half a million dollars—and all it's costing us is the difference between what we pay for the ship and what we can sell her for when we're through, plus the wages for the crew and the supplies—and the price of one first-class passage for one Jap, from Vancouver to his home in Japan."

"Offhand, the proposition sounds a mite involved, if not downright abstruse."

"You mean you can't figure it out?"

"Well, there seems to be a pint, here an' there, that ain't quite clear."

"Don't worry about that—when it's explained to you you'll see that it's as simple as A B C. When we see the color of your money we'll tell you all about it."

"Where is this ship you figger on buyin'?"

"It's in the harbor at Vancouver."

"An' you want I should go get the cash an' turn it over to you an' Amos, an' you'd take it on down to Vancouver an' buy this ship?"

"That's right."

BLACK JOHN shook his head. "I wouldn't hardly like to do that. You see, ma'am, in spite of our friendly attitude toward one another, you ain't hardly more than a chance acquaintance."

"You don't think I'd beat you out of forty thousand dollars, do you?"

"No, I don't believe you will. But at that, when you come to think it over, handin' forty thousan' in cash over to a chance acquaintance couldn't be called a good conservative business procedure—now, could it?"

"Well—maybe you're right. But if that's the way you feel about it, I don't see how we're going to get together on the proposition."

"How about me goin' on down to Vancouver with you?"

"Are you acquainted in Vancouver? Got any friends there?"

"No. But I could stay at some hotel till we got the ship ready. Then we could all make the trip together. I'm good an' husky. It would save hirin' a hand, if someone was there on the ship to tell me what to do."

"That's a fine idea!" the woman exclaimed enthusiastically. "You go ahead and get the money so we can start right out. The quicker we get down there, the quicker we can cash in on our our investment!"

"I was thinkin' that same thing," Black John said. "An' I can see how we can save a good month gettin' to Vancouver. You see, it would take me two weeks to go up to Cush's, an' a good ten days to come back. Then we'd have to start from here an' go on out by way of Skagway. But if you an' Amos was to come on along with me, we could stop in to Cush's an' get the money, an' then keep right on goin' outside by way of the Dalton Trail. It would save better'n a month. Prob'ly right around six weeks."

"Well—I don't know," the woman replied doubtfully. "I—I'd have to talk to Amos first."

"Where's Amos at?"

"Oh, he's around here somewheres. Prob'ly out in the barroom. He sort of sticks around—just to see that no one gets fresh with me."

"Kind of a dotin' husband, eh?" the big man grinned. "Well, takin' you by an' large, as the Good Book says, I don't know as I blame him none. Why not fetch Amos in here an' we can kind of thrash this proposition out in all its aspects? Tell him to fetch along another bottle, an' I'll pay for it."

The woman swung her legs from the table, put on her slippers, and disappeared. A few minutes later she returned in company with a rather shifty-eyed individual. "Meet my husband, Amos Doolittle," she smiled. "Amos, this is Mr.—Mr.—why—I don't believe you told me your name!"

"Guess you're right at that. It's Smith—jest plain John Smith, not even a middle initial to sort of relieve the monotony."

"You see, Amos," the woman explained, "I was telling Mr. Smith that we had a mighty good investment for someone with forty or fifty thousand in ready cash, and he's interested. He has the money, but it's in a safe in a trading post back where he lives, on some crick up the White River. He figures that if we'd all go up there, we could stop at this trading post, he could pick up the money, and we could all go on out to Vancouver on the Dalton Trail, and save a good six weeks' time."

The man nodded. "Well, I guess that would be all right. I've heard about the Dalton Trail. Goes on up the White River a ways, don't it, an' then swings over an' comes out at Haines?"

"That's right," Black John agreed.

"You see, Amos," the woman said, "I suggested that Mr. Smith go up and get the money and bring it down here and turn it over to us. But he said it wasn't good business to hand over that much to mere chance acquaintances. He'd rather go on down to Vancouver with us—and make the trip on the ship, too."

"I don't blame him none fer not wantin' to hand over that much cash—not knowin' us no better'n what he does," the man said. "He's got the right idee—to go along with us, all the way. Then he can see there ain't no shenanigan about the deal. When can we start?"

"We could start in the mornin'," Black John said. "But I figger it would be better if you folks sort of give me the lowdown on this proposition before we start. You see, if you waited till we got clean to Cush's before explainin' it—an' then if, for any reason, it didn't look good to me—why, you folks would have made quite a trip for nothin'."

"That's right," Amos agreed. "I claim everything ort to be open an' aboveboard before we start."

"There's just one thing you must bear in mind," Black John said. "I wouldn't care to engage in no illegal venture. So, if this enterprise is in any ways shady, you might as well save yer breath, an' count me out before you start."

"Oh, it's legal, all right—legal as hell!" Amos exclaimed. "I s'pose Sadie told you about the skins?"

"Skins? No, she didn't mention no skins."

"I thought you could tell him about them better than I could," the woman said. "You have been there and seen 'em, and I haven't."

"Yeah—sure. It's like this: I'm a fur trader. Had a little schooner an' run up and down the coast buyin' fur here an' there, wherever I could pick it up. Couple months ago I was runnin' around amongst them little islands east of Chignik Bay. Mostly them islands ain't nothin' but a rock without no one livin' on 'em, but there's a few trappers on the bigger ones, an' a man can pick up some fur along there—fox mostly. Well, I was runnin' along clost in the lee of one of them islands, an' on a kind of a rock point I seen somethin' white waving back an' forth like a flag. So I run in clost, an' damn if it wasn't a Jap! The pore devil was damn near all in, so I took him aboard. He could talk some English, an' he told me he'd be'n there ten days livin' on what he could scavenge. There wasn't a livin' thing on the island, an' he'd be'n eatin' dead fish that blow'd agin the rocks, an' a couple of gulls he killed with rocks. He was all there was left of the crew of one of them damn Jap seal poachin' ships that prowls around in American waters. He said they had a full cargo of sealskins, an' was headin' fer home with 'em, when the revenue cutter *Bear* sighted 'em an' give chase. It was rougher'n hell an' night comin' on, an' they give the *Bear* the slip amongst the islands, an' run into a harbor, an' spent the next day onloadin' an' cachin' the skins—better'n half a million dollars' worth. Then the next night they pulled out, figgerin' on cruisin' around a while till the *Bear* went on, er else lettin' her overhaul 'em an' find 'em empty.

"The storm had lulled down, but onct they got out of the harbor she picked up somethin' fierce, an' along towards mornin' the ship hit the rocks off'n that island where I picked him up. She went down before they could launch a boat, an' this Jap was the only one that made the island. He claimed all he wanted was to git back to Japan, an' offered to show me where the skins was cached if I'd give him his passage money to Japan, an' take him to Vancouver where he could ship out.

"Well, I give him the money, seein' how there was three of us on the schooner, an' only one of him, so if he couldn't show no skins, we could take it away from him.

"Well, sir, we cruised around amongst them islands fer three days, an' I was beginnin' to think the Jap was lyin', an' there wasn't no sealskin cache, when along about noon he gives a yell an' pints to a narrow slot betwixt two high rocks. We run in through a kind of a passage, an' come into the snuggest harbor I ever seen. We went ashore, an' there in a kind of rock cave, an' protected from the weather by tarps was the damndest biggest bunch of sealskins I ever seen, er heard tell of.

"So we hit back to Vancouver, an' the Jap he shipped fer home."

"Why didn't you take the skins along?" Black John asked.

The man laughed. "Hell, man—there was four, five times as many as that damn little tub of mine would hold!"

"Looks like you could of made four, five trips, then," the big man said. "If them skins is worth as much as you claim, it looks like it would have paid to."

"There's two, three reasons why I couldn't do that. In the first place the schooner was old, an' I wouldn't trust no valuable cargo on her—that is, no full load. Then agin she was slow. We got to have a ship that is as fast, er a little faster than the *Bear*. Then, agin, it's a damn sight less risk to run one cargo in than four or five of 'em."

"Why would you have to outrun the *Bear?*" Black John asked. "You ain't no Jap poacher. An' you claimed this venture was legal."

The man smiled and winked. "When I said legal, I meant it ain't like we was hijackin' the cargo, er piratin' it. Them skins is abandoned by the owner, an' is legal salvage fer anyone that gits 'em. But there is a couple of small laws a man's got to kind of wink at. Like the one that claims possession of any seal skins is illegal, an' the other one about smugglin' 'em into the country. I wouldn't do nothin' criminal, you onderstand. But every place has got a bunch of small laws that no one pays any attention to—like spittin' on the sidewalk, an' cuttin' corners acrost vacant lots. Down along the coast we regard the smugglin' law, an' the illegal possession of fur, like city folks regards them other little laws. Take you, now—you wouldn't hold it agin a man if he spit on a sidewalk, would you?"

"W-e-e-l-l, I wouldn't consider a man to be steeped in original sin, nor regard him as utterly depraved if he spit on one—provided he didn't persist in the habit. It seems that yer desire to acquire a bigger an' faster ship for this enterprise is commendable. Yes sir, Amos, it shows that yer a right-thinkin' man—to be willin' to spend good money to get a ship that would allow this venture to be consumated in one small violation, instead of four or five. It proves you have no intention of becomin' a habitual violator, of even them small laws. On the whole, I believe I can wink at the slight irregularity, an' go along with you on this proposition. Your wife tells me you've managed to scrape up some forty thousan' in cash."

"That's right. I sold the schooner, an' borrowed here an' there amongst my friends—but they ain't none of 'em rich, an' I got all they could spare. Then I made arrangements for handlin' the stuff when we get it in. You bet, I know a dozen furriers that'll fall all over theirselves to get their hands on them skins at a damn good fancy price. So, seein' yer satisfied, we'll be pullin' out in the mornin', eh?"

"Okay. You come over to the hotel in the mornin' an' we'll pick up Cush, an' pull out in a couple of canoes, quick as we've et breakfast."

BLACK JOHN slept late the following morning and it was nearly noon when he descended the stairs to find the two waiting for him in the hotel lobby. Inquiry at the desk revealed the fact that Cush had checked out early in the morning and left the hotel in company of an Indian. He eyed the two a bit dubiously. "Ever handle a canoe, Amos?" he asked.

"Yeah, quite a bit. Us free-traders, we got to git out in the back country an' ketch the Injuns on their trappin' grounds before they git a chanct to take their fur to some reg'lar tradin' post. But looks like, what with me an' you an' her, an' a tent, an' blankets, an' what grub we'll be needin' we've got a damn sight more 'n a canoe load—'specially when it's all upstream paddlin'!"

"We'll make it, all right," Black John said. "I know where I can get holt of a Strickland freight canoe." He turned to the desk clerk. "Any boat pullin' out for Whitehorse today?"

The clerk nodded. "The *Herman's* due to leave at two o'clock."

"That'll work out fine," the big man said. "We'll hustle around an' git the outfit together, an save a good eighty miles of upriver paddlin'. The *Herman'll* set us ashore at the mouth of the White. From there on it won't be so bad. There's only a few portages on the White, an' where she's a little fast for good paddlin' we can trackline."

III

ONE MORNING, SOME two weeks later Black John stepped into Cushing's saloon, crossed to the bar, and elevated a foot to the brass rail. Deliberately, Cush set out a bottle, two glasses, and the leather dice box. The big man picked up the box and cast the dice. "I feel lucky, this mornin' he said. "I'll leave them three fives in one."

Cush failed to beat the fives, and lost the next horse also. "You prob'ly need all the luck you felt like you've got," he said. "How much did she take you fer?"

Black John smiled. "Why—what do you mean, Cush? How much did who take me for?"

"You know damn well who I mean! That there yaller-head you was froze to in the Klondike Palace. How much did she cost you—outside of the drinks an' the dancin'? By God, I've told you right along that some good-lookin' woman would take you one of these times! An' I give you fair warnin' that night. Even before I know'd she was a crook, I told you you was makin a damn fool of yerself!"

"What do you mean—before you knew she was a crook? Who told you she was a crook?"

"Bettles, an' Camillo Bill, an' Moosehide Charlie, an' Burr McShane—that's who. She's married to a guy name of Bovey, an' they took Jack Hammond fer better'n ten thousan' on some kind of a crooked deal, an' the manager of the Consolidated fer a damn sight more'n that."

The big man smiled broadly. "That just goes to show, Cush, how easy it is to be mistaken. They got her all wrong. In the first place, her husband's name ain't Bovey. It's Doolittle—Amos Doolittle. An' instead of bein' a crook, he's a fur trader down along the coast."

"Huh! That's what you think! Listen—if you had a brain in yer head, you'd know damn well them old sourdoughs ain't wrong. Who told you their name is Doolittle?"

"Why, Sadie told me herself. An' not only that, she introduced me to Amos. Cripes, Cush, it stands to reason they'd know their own name better'n them old sourdoughs would! Amos, he seems to be a nice sort of a chap. An' as for Sadie, why she's one of the most friendly an' engagin' women I know."

"Yeah," Cush sneered, "the kind of wimmin' you know, she could be all them things, an' still ort to git hung fer what she'd do to a man, onct she got the chanct. But you ain't told me yet how much they took you fer—her an' this here Amos."

Black John downed his drink and shook his head in resignation. "It's sad to contemplate, Cush—but I don't know as I blame you, at that—the experience you've had with those first three wives of yours has made you suspicious of all women."

"I ain't no sech a damn thing," Cush contradicted. "Only them big taffy-heads that hangs around dance halls waitin' fer a chanct to hook some sucker—even if they was little an' black-headed I'd suspicion 'em!"

"Very fortunately in this instance I am in a position to disabuse your mind of your preconceived, and wholly onfounded suspicion. Far from any desire to swindle me, these two friends have offered me the chance to engage in a venture with them that will net me a profit of five or six hundred percent within sixty days."

"Oh, yeah? An' how much cash have you got to shove into this here venture?"

"Exactly the same amount that they are investing—a mere forty thousand."

"So they figger you're four times as big a damn fool as Jack Hammond, eh? They only took him fer ten thousan'. Well—I guess they're right, at that."

"You forget that, according to the sourdoughs, the couple who took Hammond were named Bovey. These folks are named Doolittle—like I told you before."

"I s'pose you handed over yer forty thousan' to 'em down there in the Palace, an' come on up here to wait fer yer profits to come rollin' in. I'll bet Cuter Malone an' his gang is gittin' a hell of a kick out of that deal—an' believe me, when them sourdoughs hears how easy you was, it'll cost you another forty thousan' buyin' 'em drinks!"

BLACK JOHN grinned. "Why, Cush—you shorely wouldn't think I'd be fool enough to hand over forty thousan' in cash, an' then come on up here without no security whatever?"

"What kind of security you got—their note for forty thousan'."

"I've got the Doolittles."

Cush's eyes widened. "You've got the which?"

"The two Doolittles, in person. They're down in Olson's old shack, right now. They were a bit fagged out when we reached there last evening, so I advised 'em to hole up there an' rest up fer a while. I come on last night. I told 'em how to get here. They'll be along this afternoon."

"By Cripes, John! Ain't there enough damn crooks on Halfaday already, without you fetchin' them two up here? An' what kind of a skin game be they gittin' you into?"

The big man chuckled. "Skin game is right, Cush—yup, litterly it's a skin game—sealskins. Half a million dollars' worth, cached on an island down off the coast. You see, Amos was cruisin' around in his little schooner, pickin' up what fur he could here an' there from the trappers, when he found a Jap on a rock."

"Did he kick him off—I hope?"

"No, he took him off, an' the Jap told him about this sealskin cache. It seems he was the sole survivor of the crew of a Jap seal poacher loaded with skins. The *Bear* took after 'em, an' they run into a harbor an' cached the skins, then pulled out in the night, an' a storm come up an' wrecked 'em, an' this Jap was the only one to reach the rock—the others went down with the ship. The Jap said all he wanted was to get back home, an' he offered to show Amos where the cache was if Amos would take him to Vancouver an' pay his passage to Japan. He done so, an' Amos took him down an' shipped him off fer home. Then Amos sold his home an' his schooner, which it was too slow an' too little to handle them skins, an' borrowed what he could off his friends, an' raised forty thousan' in cash. But the ship we need will cost sixty thousan', an' the outfittin', crew wages, an' so forth will cost another twenty thousan'. So they come to Dawson in hope that someone who had struck it lucky would match their forty thousan' an' go in partnership on the venture. After hearing the details, an' thinkin' it over, I decided that the proposition was a sound investment—so I agreed to go in. This afternoon, right here at this bar, I'll match their forty thousan', an' then the three of us will hit out for Vancouver over the Dalton Trail an' buy that ship. You see, Cush, I'm not takin' any chances—I'm goin' right along with 'em, till he gets those skins into the hands of the buyers, an' I'll be right there to pocket my share of the profits."

Cush scowled. "Listen, John—if you pull outa here on the Dalton Trail with them two damn cusses, you won't never git nowheres. They'll knock you on the head some night when yer asleep, an' roll you into some gulch somewheres, an' they'll go on outside with them forty thousan' dollars of yourn, an in the spring we'll be huntin' along the trail to find yer body to give it a decent funeral. But chances is, the wolves won't leave enough of it so's we kin tell if it's you, er someone else we're buryin'."

Black John grinned. "You're takin' a pessimistic view of the venture, Cush. Cripes, you've got to remember I've be'n a hell of a lot of places with a damn sight worse folks than the Doo-littles, an' I ain't be'n knocked on the head yet. An' by the way—open up the safe an' sort out forty one-thousan'-dollar bills. Lay 'em to one side where you can get 'em handy tomorrow mornin'. They've got their money in thousan'-dollar bills—it packs handier that way."

"The older some folks gits, the damner fools they git to be—'specially if there's a woman in it if it worn't fer that big taffy-head snuggerin' up to you there in the Palace like she done, this here Amos couldn't of got within rifle shot of you with no damn-fool proposition like a bunch of sealskins cached in some rocks! Look at it sensible—why would he have to pay sixty thousan' dollars fer a ship to git them skins? Cripes, there's plenty of ships in any port he could charter fer the trip. Might cost a couple thousan'—er even five. But that ain't no sixty thousan', by a damn sight."

"I asked Amos about that one night when we was campin' there by the river comin' up. An' he explained that on a venture of this kind it was inadvisible. You see, there's a p'int er two of law involved in the enterprise. While the seizure of the skins is perfectly legal, amountin' merely to the salvage of abandoned property, the landin' and disposal of the skins, runs foul of a couple of minor statutes, like the smugglin' act, an' another one regardin' the illegal possession of sealskins. As Amos p'inted out, if we was to charter a vessel for the venture, as soon as the cargo got loaded, the captain would have us dead to rights. He could declare himself in for a one-third cut, or even a half, an' if we didn't come acrost, all he'd have to do is contact the *Bear*, or else steam right into port, an' report the cargo to the customs officials. He'd collect his twenty-five percent of the appraised value of the cargo for informin' on us—an' we'd not only lose the whole cargo, but be in a hell of a fix besides. Amos, he's smart all right. He don't overlook no bets. He wants his own ship, an' his own crew—men he can trust to do as he orders 'em to do, an' keep their mouths shut."

"Yeah, an' even if they let you git to Vancouver, an' bought this ship, an' you went out on her with 'em—what he'd order 'em to do would be to heave you over the rail some night—an' we wouldn't even find some wolf-gnawed bones to bury."

"Such skepticism is woeful to contemplate," the big man said, with a sigh of resignation. "All I've got to say is that when you know the Doolittles better, you'll trust 'em the same as I do. I shore wish you could have be'n along on that trip up the White. I'll never forget 'em—those nights—settin' there by the little campfire, with the low hum of mosquitoes in the air, an' Sadie settin' close beside me, an' the moon shinin', an' now an' then a wolf would howl in the distance, an' Sadie would crowd even closer, an' sort of shiver like—right up against me. Amos, not being broke in good to the hard paddlin', would roll up in his blanket right after supper, an' his snorin' was the only jarrin' note in them idyllic evenin's, as a poet would say. It's nights like them, Cush, that a man never forgets."

"Huh," Cush snorted in disgust. "A month from now you'll be wishin' you could fergit them idiotic evenin's. If yer alive— which the chances is, you won't be! Experience is the best teacher, like the Good Book says, an' I s'pose forty thousan' is cheap enough to pay fer the lesson—but when yer rememberin' them forty thousan', don't fergit to remember you could of got the same lesson fer nothin' if you'd listened to me."

"You wouldn't, perchance, care to go into this proposition with me—on a fifty-fifty basis, would you, Cush?" Black John asked. "A man don't get a chance like this every day."

"No, I wouldn't! An' I wouldn't want no damn big yaller-headed wench crowdin' into me by no campfire 'cause a wolf howled, neither!"

"There is much of suspicion, and little of romance in your make-up, I fear. However, be that as it may—remember I offered you a cut.

"Since you have turned it down I will go on about my business. There are certain things to be done." Stepping into the storeroom, he procured two squares of heavy wrapping paper. One of these, he placed in his pocket, the other he carried into the saloon, folded, and told Cush to place it on top of the safe. "Leave it there so it'll be handy to do up them bills in, this afternoon," he said. "You see, when the Doolittles come, I'm goin' to take their forty thousan'-dollar bills, an' put mine on top of 'em, an' do 'em up in a neat package. I've got some sealin' wax over to my cabin which I'll fetch over. You throw it in the drawer there in the back bar, an' when I ask you if you've got any, you fish around an' find it. Now I ort to have somethin' I could use fer a seal—somethin' distinctive to press into the hot wax, so the package could be readily identified. Once sealed, the package can't be tampered with till we get to Vancouver without my knowin' it. Let's see—what could we use for a seal?"

"How about pressin' the bottom of a whiskey glass down on it?"

"Not distinctive enough. By gosh, I've got it! You remember that time I ripped my pants, an' went in your bedroom to sew 'em up? Well, I remember seein' a large cameo broach lyin' there in the sewin' basket. That'll be just the thing!"

"You mean that there big bres'pin my fourth wife had with George Worshin'ton's face on it, er St. Peter's, er someone?"

"That's the one. It will make a swell seal. Can I use it?"

"Oh, shore. It's be'n kickin' around fer years an' I ain't never found no use fer it yet. I'll go git it."

CUSH HANDED the bauble across the counter and Black John pocketed it. "Okay," he said. "I'm gain' over to my cabin now, an' make up my trail pack. Be back after a while."

Proceeding directly to his cabin he took a pair of shears from a shelf, and proceeded to cut eighty pieces of paper the exact size of paper currency. These he wrapped tightly in the square of heavy paper, tied the package securely with stout twine, produced his sealing wax, and sealed each side of the package at the crossing of the twine, pressing the cameo into the warm wax to make a very effective seal. Placing the package in a fold of his mackinaw, he proceeded to the cabin of Pot-Gutted John, a short distance down the creek and gave him some very definite instructions.

Returning to his cabin, he procured his pack sack, and picking up the folded mackinaw, proceeded to the saloon. Carefully depositing the mackinaw on the bar, he tossed Cush the brooch. "Put that in the drawer along with this sealin' wax, an' fish 'em out when the time comes. An' here—put this piece of twine somewhere on the back bar where it'll be handy to find when I call for it. I'll step out an' loaf around by the landin'. The Doolittles ort to be showin' up pretty quick. An' by the way— don't touch that there mackinaw of mine, leave it jest as it lays."

IV

A SHORT TIME later the canoe beached at the landing and the Doolittles ascended the steep trail to the little plateau where Black John awaited them.

"Quite a place here," Amos said, eyeing the long low log building.

"Yeah, Cush, he's got about everything a man wants in the way of liquor an' supplies. He's got a damn good stout safe to keep our dust an' bills in, too."

The woman's eyes rested on the little rows of wooden slabs toward the edge of the clearing. "Must be awful unhealthy up here if those are graves," she said. "Looks like there's a lot more dead folks than live ones."

The big man smiled. "No, ma'am. It's just that the live ones are scattered out along the crick, while the dead ones are what you might say concentrated. The crick's healthy enough—if a man minds his own business—that is, if his business is prospectin'."

"How do you mean by that?" Amos asked.

"Come on over here an' I'll show you," Black John replied, leading the way to the little cemetery. "You'll notice that every one of the slabs has got a check letter on it followin' the corpse's alias, an' the date of his demise."

"What do you mean—alias?" Amos asked.

"Meanin' the name he went by here on Halfaday. You see, quite a few of our citizens are outlawed, one place or another. They settle here because, layin' close to the line, like we do, it's handy for 'em to step across into Alaska if the police shows up. Such bein' the case, it's a safe bet that whatever name a man goes by is an alias."

"But those check letters?" the woman asked, "What do they mean? They're all either M's or H's. Oh, yes—there's a few D's, too."

"Yes, ma'am," the big man agreed, "but not many. That's what I meant by the crick bein' healthy. D on a slab means that its owner died natural. M means he got murdered. An' H signifies he got hung."

"Hung?" Amos exclaimed. "What do you mean—hung?"

"It's an expression we use to indicate that a rope was slipped around his neck an' the other end throw'd over a rafter, or a tree limb as circumstances permitted, an' he was hauled up an' left to dangle till Cush pronounced him dead. Cush, he's the coroner—and a man ain't officially dead till Cush claims he is."

"But," Amos said, eyeing the slabs, "it don't make sense. Accordin' to that, there hadn't ort to be no more H's than there is M's—even if you caught every damn one of them murderers."

"You're in error. You see, Amos, bein' as you might say, an isolated community, we not only enforce the laws of the Territory as herein made an' provided, but we've got a special law of our own that we invoke as circumstances indicate. It's known locally as the Skullduggery Law, any infringement of which earns a man a prompt an' thoroughgoin hangin'."

"What the hell is skullduggery?"

"Skullduggery is any offense which I deem detrimental to the welfare of the crick, or any citizen thereof. Take that first slab, there—Olson's. He was the original owner of the cabin you're located in. His offense was palmin' out a king in a stud game an' slippin' it into his hand a deal or two later to the detriment of One-Eyed John. That's One-Eye's slab over there. We hung him later, for stealin' a shirt out of Cush's storeroom. The next slab, there—Big Pete, it says there; we found out later his real name was George Magoofus, not that it made any difference we hung him for lyin'."

"Lyin'! Good God—you can't hang a man fer lyin'!"

"The hell we can't! We did. Pete, he claimed he saw three moose over on a feeder to the White, an' Pot-Gutted John went over there the next day to get one, him bein' out of meat, an' not only he didn't find no moose—but there wasn't even a track where Pete said he saw 'em. An' it hadn't snowed, either. Pot-Gut was damn near bushed when he got back—so we hung Pete for lyin'. You see, Amos, any infringement of rectitude, with or without malice aforethought, if it in any way injures another, is hangable under the Skullduggery Law. I personally preside at the miners' meetin's that mete out the jestice an' the boys, relyin' on my judgment, always vote as I indicate. In that way we manage to keep the crick moral as hell. But come on, let's go over to the saloon. I'll buy a drink. Then we'll put up our money, an' be on our way to Vancouver. Cripes, I can't hardly wait till we get holt of them sealskins!"

LEADING THE way to the bar, Black John called for a round of drinks, and as Cush set out bottle and glasses he introduced the pair. "Cush, these folks are Amos Doolittle, an' his wife, Sadie. They're the ones I was tellin' you about this mornin', that I'm goin' in pardnership with on that there sealskin proposition."

Cush acknowledged the introduction with an uncivil grunt.

"Yes sir, an hour from now we'll be on our way," the big man continued and pointed to a well-filled pack sack on the floor near the doorway. "There's my pack all ready to swing into the canoe. First off, though, we ort to get the financial arrangements made to the satisfaction of all parties concerned. I claim we each ort to count out our money right here on the bar, an' then bunch it an' tie it up in a neat package an' seal it up tight, so it can't be tampered with till we get to Vancouver. What do you say, Amos? Ain't that fair, an' reasonable?"

"Why—yeah. Looks like it's all right. But—who carries the package?"

"We-e-e-l-l," Black John said. "I could carry it. So could you. But bein' as we're what you might say, the parties in interest, I'd say that Sadie, bein' a third party, an' not in on the transaction, except by marriage, would be the logical custodian of the funds durin' the trip. That is, providin' she'll accept the responsibility."

"Suits me," Amos approved.

"I'll handle the money, if you boys want me to," the woman said.

"Okay, then we'll make up the package," the big man replied. "Hey, Cush, open up the safe an' count me out forty one-thousan'-dollar bills an' charge 'em to my account." He turned to the others. "I believe Sadie claimed that your money was in thousan'-dollar bills, too, didn't she?"

Amos nodded. "That's right. It don't take up so much room that way." Producing a packet of bills from beneath his coat the man laid it on the bar. With the eyes of both on his every movement, Black John cut the string, and counted out the money. "Right, to the last thousan'," he approved with a smile. "Now, Amos, you count mine." He indicated the currency Cush had counted out on the bar.

The man complied, and nodded. "It's right," he said.

Black John gathered the two stacks of bills, and bunched them. "Hey, Cush," he called. "There's a piece of wrappin' paper there on the safe. Hand it over, an' some stout string, too." Shoving his folded mackinaw slightly aside, he spread the paper before him on the bar, placed the packet of bills on it, folded the paper tightly around the packet and securely tied it with several turns of the stout cord. He regarded the packet with approval. "Eighty thousan' dollars," he said. "Don't take up a hell of a lot of room, when it's tied up good an' tight, does it? Now, Cush, hunt around there somewheres an' dig up that hunk of sealin' wax we found in Jake Krug's stuff after we hung him, that time. Seems like you tossed it in one of them drawers under the back bar there." He glanced at the two Doolittles. "We never throw nothin' away, up here—never can tell when it might come in handy." Cush tossed the sealing wax onto the bar, and Black John's brow furrowed. "Cripes, I can't melt this stuff good with matches. Have to keep lightin''em all the time—shove me out one of them candles, Cush. An'—hey—hold on—what's that there thing in there with a face or somethin' on it? Shove that out, too. That'll make a damn good seal!"

Picking up the brooch, he showed it to the others. "Look, we'll press this into the hot wax, an' it'll leave an impression of this face there. That way, nobody can monkey with the seals without us knowin' about it. Someone might bust the seals, an' have some wax along to fix 'em up with, but they shore as hell wouldn't have a trinket like that to seal it with."

He set to work and five minutes later, the three gazed at the result with approval. Behind the bar, Cush looked on in scowling silence.

HIS EYES on the packet before him, Black John lifted the hat from his head and ran his fingers through his hair, as Amos ordered a round of drinks. Suddenly, from the clearing outside came a loud-shouted command. "Stop! Damn you stop, er I'll shoot!" The command was followed by two quick rifle shots, close outside the door.

The Doolittles whirled about and glanced fearfully toward the doorway through which a huge man catapulted into the room. Amos suddenly faced the bar again, his eyes seeking the packet which still reposed on the bar in front of Black John.

"What the hell's ailin' you, Pot-Gut?" the big man asked, regarding the intruder with a frown.

"It's that damn Bill Haley!" Pot-Gut panted. "He stoled my poke off'n my shelft with a good five ounces of dust in it! I seen him do it—stud right there at the edge of my clearin' an' seen the damn skunk stop by the door an' look all around then slip in the cabin, an' lift the poke off'n the shelft an' slip it in his pocket, an' slip outa the cabin. I yelled at him to stop, but he started to run, an' I tuk out after him. I couldn't ketch up to him, an' I couldn't git no good shot at him neither, the way he kep' dodgin' amongst the trees. By God, John—stealin' pokes is skullduggery, ain't it? We'd ort to git him an' hang him!"

The big man nodded gravely. "It certainly is skullduggery, Pot-Gut. An' if he's guilty we'll shore hang him. But Bill Haley lives a good forty miles back on that feeder. It'll take nigh three days to get him, an' another three to fetch him back here."

"Looks like a hell of a trip to make fer five ounces of dust," Amos opined.

Black John regarded him with a frown. "It ain't the amount that was stole—it's the principle of the thing. Here on Halfaday, we'd go a damn sight further than that to recover five ounces of stolen dust—an' other amounts in proportion."

"You mean yer goin' to put in six days of hard work jest to bring that dude down here an' hang him?"

"That's right," Black John replied. "It shore raises hell with our plans, Amos—but duty is duty. We can't afford to get lax on Halfaday." Picking up the packet, he handed it to the woman. "Here you are, Sadie. Take good care of the stuff, an' don't let nothin' happen to it. You two go back down to Olson's an' hole up till I get there. This here job ortn't to take over a week. Then we'll pull out over the Dalton Trail an' hit for Vancouver—an' a damn good profit." Lifting his folded mackinaw from the bar, he turned to Pot-Gutted John. "Come on, Pot-Gut, let's get goin'!" Pausing at the doorway he retrieved his pack sack, and the two stepped from the room, and disappeared up the creek.

"Where the hell we goin'?" Pot-Gut asked, a mile further on. "Cripes—they ain't no Bill Haley, no more'n what I lost no five ounces!"

Black John grinned. "I'm low on meat," Black John replied. "I expect you could use some, too—an' I know Cush could. Me an' you'll hole up fer a week in Whiskey Bill's old shack an' do a little huntin'."

V

AS THE DOOLITTLES stepped from their canoe at the Olson cabin the woman glanced at Amos, a flicker of fear in her eyes. "My God, this place gives me the creeps—all those graves, and hanging anyone, no matter what they do! They're screwy, I tell you! And that big John Smith is the screwiest one of the bunch. Let's get out of here while the getting's good!"

"You tellin' me! That big pot-gutted guy bustin' in the way he done sure was a break fer us! We'll have a good week's start on Smith. We kin be to the Yukon by that time, an' believe me, we'll flag a steamboat an' hit for the outside. To hell with this country! We done all right—but I don't want no more of it."

"There's still good pickings around Dawson," the woman said.

"The hell with Dawson! You heard what he said—he'd go further than Bill Haley's place to git a man an' hang him fer snitchin' five ounces—*an' other amounts in proportion!* By God, I want to be a damn sight further from here than Dawson when he finds his forty thousan' is gone! Tellin' you about me—I ain't even goin' to stop in Vancouver!"

"I guess you're right, at that," the woman agreed. "What'll we do with this haul? It's a cinch I'm not going to carry it in the front of my shirt clear through to Vancouver. Let's take it out and divide it up, right now."

"Not by a damn sight! We'll shove it down in the bottom of the pack sack, an' leave it there till we get on the boat out of Skagway. I've got enough loose money on me to pay our way to Vancouver. There's plenty of grub here in the cabin—we'll throw what we want in the canoe, an' be on our way. Every mile—an' every minute we kin put between us an' that damn Smith, is so much to the good. Hangin' a man fer lyin' about seein' a moose!"

VI

A WEEK LATER Black John stepped into Cush's saloon, crossed the floor, and laid his folded mackinaw on the bar. Cush set out bottles and glasses. "Drink up," he said. "I'll buy this un."

The big man smiled. "Why, thanks, Cush. Here's lookin' at you." He tossed off the drink, and motioned toward the bottle. "Fill up, an' have one on me. Then I'll be hittin' out."

"Fer where?"

"Why, for Vancouver, of course. I'll pick up Sadie an' Amos at Olson's an' we'll hit the trail."

"Where you be'n fer the last week?"

"Who—me?"

"Yeah, you—an' Pot-Gut, too. You know damn well they ain't no Bill Haley on no feeder nor forty mile back nowheres! An' Pot-Gut never shot at him, neither."

"That's right," the big man grinned. "I found that out. We couldn't locate no Bill Haley nowheres, so me an' Pot-Gut holed up in Whiskey Bill's old shack an' hunted moose. Got a dandy, too. Fetched a quarter down fer you. I figgered there wasn't no hell of a hurry about gettin' down to Vancouver. Them sealskins'll be there when we want 'em."

Cush snorted in disgust. "Sealskins—my foot! An' if you're hittin' out fer Vancouver, yer hittin' out alone."

"What do you mean—alone? Cripes, Sadie an' Amos are goin' along. Hell, Cush—we're pardners!"

"Yeah? Well, yer pardners has flew the coop on you! Yup—jest like I told you when you fell fer that damn yaller-head! She took you—her an' Amos, er Bovey, er whatever his name is—took you fer forty thousan'! An' I'm damn glad of it! Mebbe now you'll listen to folks like me an' Bettles, an' the rest of the sourdoughs an' not go nuts over the first good-lookin' woman that comes along!"

"You mean that Sadie an' Amos have gone—have departed from Halfaday, without waiting for me? When did they go?"

"They went when they left here. One-Arm was fishin' down by Olson's shack that evenin', an' he seen 'em land the canoe there. They stud an' talked fer a few minutes, then they went in the cabin an' fetched out a bunch of grub, an' throwed it in the canoe, an' hit hell-bent downstream. An' they ain't be'n back sence. One-Arm's be'n down there every day."

"Tch, tch, tch," Black John's head moved slowly from side to side. "I guess I've got to admit that this time you an' them sourdoughs was right when you figgered Sadie was a crook. Don't it beat hell, what some folks will stoop to!" Casually, he reached under the fold of his mackinaw and tossed a packet onto the bar. Cush's eyes widened as he regarded the seal.

"What—where the hell did you git that?" he gasped. "By God, that there Sadie had it on her when she went out of this room. I seen her shove it down her shirt!"

Black John grinned. "Not this packet, Cush! Another one, maybe—but not this one. I've had it in my mackinaw all along."

Picking up the packet, he cut the string and broke the seals, carefully he undid the wrapping and shoved the thick packet of thousand-dollar bills toward the other. "Jest stick 'em in the safe, Cush, an' credit my account with eighty thousan'. I'll earmark ten thousan' of it fer Jack Hammond. He shore can't afford to lose no sech amount."

"An' I s'pose you'll give the rest of it back to the manager of the Consolidated," Cush said. "They claim he lost a damn sight more'n Jack did."

Black John shook his head. "No. You see, Cush, he has on-doubtless reimbursed himself from the coffers of the Company for any loss he may have sustained—an' charged it off as op-eratin' expense. An' by the way, you might reflect that I offered to let you in fifty-fifty on this venture. Too bad you turned it down. You could have made a rather neat profit—not no six-hundred percent, like the Doolittles offered me, but a nice little profit, jest the same. It shore saddens me to think about the morals of them damn crooks. Seems like they never can learn that honesty is the best policy."

MINER'S MEETIN'

CORPORAL DOWNEY, ACE officer of the Northwest Mounted Police force in Dawson, looked up from his desk as Black John Smith stepped info the little office at detachment headquarters and greeted him with a grin. "Hello, John, draw up a chair an' fill your pipe. What brings you back so soon? Lookin' for anyone in particular?"

The big man seated himself, tilted the chair back against the wall, elevated his heels to a corner of the desk, and drew pipe and tobacco from his pocket. "No—no one in particular. Just thought I might round up enough of the sourdoughs to get up a stud game. Who'd you think I'd be lookin' for?"

"Well, from a few little remarks the sourdoughs dropped the other day in the Tivoli bar, I thought mebbe you'd be lookin' for a certain big blonde. But if you are, you're out of luck. Her an' that damn husband of hers, Bovey, have pulled out. No one's seen 'em around here for a month."

"Oh, I guess you mean Sadie. Boy, there's a gal for you!"

Downey's grin widened. "Not for me! An' I don't mind tellin' you I'm glad she's out of the country. That is, if she is out, I hope to hell she stays out."

"You're just like them damn sourdoughs, Downey—you've got Sadie wrong. Bettles, an' Moosehide Charlie, an' a couple of the others tipped Cush off, the last time we was down, that she an' her husband was crooks. But hell, Downey—that's all they know about it! Cripes, the sourdoughs ain't even got their

name right—claimin' it's Bovey, when it's Doolittle. Sadie told me herself, an' she introduced me to Amos—Amos Doolittle—that's her husband. An' they ain't no more crooks than I am!"

"Oh," Corporal Downey chuckled. "Them sourdoughs shore must have be'n misinformed!"

"Shore they was. Sadie's got all them other good time gals that hangs out around the Palace beat a mile fer looks—an' she can dance rings around any of 'em. Holds her licker well, too. I'm tellin' you, Downey, for right down takin' ways, I never saw her beat."

"Guess you're right," the officer agreed dryly. "Come clean, jest between friends, John—how much did she take you for? The sourdoughs are makin' plenty of guesses."

Black John shook his head in resignation. "You've shore got a suspicious mind, Downey. It's owin', I s'pose, to your occupation. But them sourdoughs ort to know better. Just to show you how wrong you are, I'll you that Sadie an' Amos let me in on a business venture that netted me a forty thousan' dollar profit. You can take it from me, Downey—an' honester couple never robbed a bank!"

"I'll think that one over," the officer grinned. "But they shore took poor Jack Hammond for ten thousand—every damn cent he had. An' they did it so slick we haven't got a thing on 'em. An' the talk is that Sadie took the Honorable Algernon Bentley for plenty, too."

"Algernon Bentley!" Black John exclaimed. "You mean old mutton-chops, himself? The manager of the Consolidated—the guy that master-minded the Consolidated into losin' that hundred thousan' dollar gold shipment by disregardin' the tip I give him to substitute lead for gold in them boxes?"

"He's the one. Of course, he never made any complaint—so there's nothin' we could do about it. But there's plenty of talk around the bars. An' where there's that much smoke, there's bound to be some fire."

"Pore old Al!" Black John said in mock sympathy. "My heart shore bleeds for him. He gets it comin' an' goin', don't he? But this Jack Hammond deal—that's different." Drawing a wallet from his pocket, he counted out ten one thousand-dollar bills, which he shoved toward the officer. "Just slip this money to Jack, next time you see him," he said. "He shore can't afford to lose it. Sadie wanted I should return it to him. That little deal her an' Amos entered into with Jack proved onprofitable, an' ruther than have Jack think there was anything onderhanded about it, she an' Amos decided to return his investment, an' shoulder the loss themselves."

Corporal Downey picked up the money, placed it in an envelope, sealed it, scribbled Jack Hammond's name on it, and slipped it into a drawer of the desk. He slanted the big man a glance. "They didn't perchance, entrust you to return an even larger amount to the Honorable Algernon Bentley, did they?" he asked.

Black John shook his head. "No. I never heard either one of 'em even mention Al's name. Fact is, Downey, if I was you I'd disregard rumor. Now that you've got good proof that Sadie an' Amos are honest, you can see that there's ondoubtless nothin' to this Bentley squawk."

"Where are they now—Sadie an' Amos?" Downey asked.

"How the hell would I know? Havin' brought our business venture to a successful conclusion, as a business man would say, they headed for the outside. I believe they did mention Vancouver as their ultimate destination—but I ain't sure."

"What was the nature of this profitable venture?" Downey asked.

"Oh, it was jest a little flyer we took in sealskins."

"Sealskins! Where the hell would you get any sealskins in this country?"

BLACK JOHN grinned broadly, "You know, I was wonderin' about that, too. But shucks, Downey—as long as the deal was successful, I didn't bother my head with the details. I let Sadie an' Amos worry about the sealskins. I just took my profit an' retired."

The officer returned the grin. "There's a lot of them details I'd shore like to hear about. But I don't s'pose I ever will."

"Most likely not, Downey—onlest sometime you'd run onto Sadie or Amos! Even if you did, the chances are they wouldn't care to talk. I've noticed that these business folks don't do much talkin'—afraid of givin' away trade secrets, I guess. Well, I'll he driftin' over to the Tivoli. You don't seem to be overly busy. Must be a kind of a lull in the activities of the sinful."

"Yeah, things are a bit quiet along the river, right now. The boys down to Forty Mile have got a murder on their hands—an' a damn dirty one, too, accordin' to the report. They've asked us to pick up a tall, dark guy with narrow brown eyes an' black hair, an' some tattooin' on his forearms—a full rigged ship on one, an' a naked woman on the other. He worked for Bill Oatley for a few days on Coal Crick, an' then quit, claimin' he was goin' to try his luck downriver. A day er so after he'd gone, Bill went down to Forty Mile fer supplies. When he got back, four days later, he found his wife layin' dead on the floor of the cabin. She'd be'n beat up an' choked to death, prob'ly to try an' make her tell where Bill's cache was. But apparently she didn't tell, because the cache was okay. They know it was this guy, because they found his belt knife on the floor under the edge of the bunk. It had evidently dropped out of the sheath durin' the rookus, an' he never noticed it was gone till he got away from there, an' then was afraid to go back after it.

"Of course, him claimin' he was goin' downriver, it's a cinch he come upriver, an' we're keepin' an eye out for him. I told all the storekeepers to let me know if any tall, dark guy come in to buy a belt knife, an' Al Scougale told me I was too late. He said this bird was in an' bought a Double-X knife in a yellow leather stamped sheath only a couple of days before. So if he should show up on Halfaday, sort of keep your eye on him till I get up there."

"I shore will, Downey. You bet your life I shore will! I ain't forgot the time Bill Oatley's wife nursed me through a spell of pneumonia a few years ago on Birch Crick."

The officer noted a certain gleam in the steel-blue eyes. "I want you to promise me, John, to let the law deal with this man. I'll be up there before long an' you can turn him over to me."

"Okay. I promise to turn him over to you—if you want him. When I get through with him, how the law deals with him won't make no difference, nohow."

"Our main headache, right now, here in Dawson is a robbery. It's the Consolidated again. They've got a dredge on a crick way up the Klondike, an' someone tapped the night watchman on the head a couple of weeks ago, an' robbed the strong box of twenty thousan' in dust. Bentley has be'n raisin' hell about it ever sence. But we haven't made any arrests yet."

"Did he kill the nightwatch?"

"No—but he damn well would have if the fellow hadn't be'n smart enough to rig up a contraption for the inside of his cap. The robber lammed him over the head from behind with a pick handle, an' the watchman dropped, an' played possum. Got a damn good look at the guy, an' give us an accurate description. Chances are we'll pick him up when he shows up along the river. Didn't meet anyone on the White while you were comin' down, did you? He might hit for Halfaday."

BLACK JOHN shook his head, "No—but that don't mean nothin'. I didn't come down the White. Swung off over toward Sixtyimile, to look over a crick a Siwash told me about."

"Siwashes are always tippin' someone off about some good crick," Downey observed, "but I never yet heard of anyone makin' a strike on one of 'em—have you?"

"Well, one tipped me off not so long ago to a damn good proposition way up the Stewart. You've got to remember, Downey, there's a hell of a lot of Siwashes—an' a hell of a lot of cricks. Most Siwashes are liars—an' most cricks are barren. But some cricks are rich—an' some Siwashes tell the truth. An' sometimes the law of averages brings a truthful Siwash to a rich crick. You rec'lect how no one believed Carmack when he made the original strike on Bonanza. Of course, Carmack wasn't a Siwash—but he was married to one, which amounts to the same thing.

"What fer lookin' guy was this robber. I'll be hittin' back to Halfaday in a couple of days, an' if he's there I'd like to spot him. We shore don't want no club-whammin', dust-stealin' son of a gun on the crick, even with the mitigatin' circumstance of robbin' a dredge company in his favor. If I know what he looks like I could, mebbe, take steps to get rid of him."

Downey consulted a notebook. "According to the nightwatch, he's about five-foot-seven, light haired, wears a reddish mustache, about twenty-five or thirty, heavy built."

"Okay, I'll keep an eye out for him."

"An' let me know if he shows up?" Downey asked.

"That would be as circumstances dictates," the big man replied. "You know that on Halfaday we don't neither help nor hinder the police. In case the guy refrains from committin' murder, robbery, or some other form of skulduggery while a resident of the crick, you might be able to locate him there. If he does not, we'll p'int out his slab in the graveyard, when you show up at Cush's. So long."

II

ONE MORNING, SOME two weeks later, Black John stepped into the barroom of Cushing's Fort, the combined trading post and saloon that served the little community of outlawed men that had sprung up on Halfaday Creek, close against the Yukon-Alaska border, crossed the floor and elevated a foot to the brass rail.

Old Cush laid aside the month-old newspaper he had been reading, shoved the steel-rimmed spectacles from nose to forehead, and reaching onto the back bar, set out two glasses, a bottle, and the leather dice box. He won the round in straight horses, made the proper entry in the day book, and as the glasses were filled, glanced toward the newspaper. "I be'n readin' a piece in the paper where the English has got their army down some-wheres in Afriky fightin' some Boers they claim is down there. Why the hell would they do that, John?"

"Why, to lick 'em, I s'pose. Same as we've got our army over in the Philippines."

"But Cripes, John—them Philippinos is folks! They're some kind of niggers like—but they're folks. Why would England send their army clean to Afriky to lick some pigs?"

"Pigs!"

"Shore, boars is pigs. I seen pichers of 'em in a magazine, one time. They got long tushes curvin' up outa the side of their mouth, an' there was a piece in the magazine which claimed them German Kisers go out in the woods an' hunt 'em with spears but it didn't say nothin' about 'em bein' down in Afriky."

Black John grinned. "You seem to have overlooked a little matter of orthography."

Cush scowled. "I went to school when I was a kid an' I might not know everything there is about georg'fy—but by God, I know if some German Kisers go out in the woods to kill some pigs with a spear, they do it in Germany, an' not down in Afriky!"

"Your geographical comprehension, in this instance, seems onimpeachable, but I was referrin' to a matter of spellin' rather than of *locus operandus.*"

"If them big words mean anything, you have wasted every damn one of 'em, except spellin'. An' what I claim, them English is damn fools to send their army clean down to Afriky to kill some pigs, no matter how they're spelt."

"What I was gettin' at," the big man explained, "is that the word used in designating the wild pig, is spelled b-o-a-r. If you will refer to the newspaper, you will see that word under discussion is spelled B-o-e-r, and also that it starts with a capital B, indicating a proper name. I might also add that the word is pronounced boor, not boar. By the way, has anyone showed up on Halfaday sence I've be'n gone?"

"Yeah, one guy has. He claimed his name was John Smith till I p'inted out that the name was outlawed on the crick, so he draw'd the name of William Henry Van Buren outs the can."

"Where is he domiciled?"

"He ain't got no scars on him that I could see. Only some tattooin' on his arms. I seen it when he rolled up his sleeves one night in a stud game."

"I was askin' where he's livin'."

"Why the hell didn't you say so, then? He moved into One Eyed John's shack."

"Does he appear to be—er—well heeled?"

"Yeah, fairly well heeled. When he swung off his pack sack there in front of the bar it hit the floor with a twelve, thirteen-hundred-ounce tunk."

"H-u-u-m," Black John calculated, "right around twenty thousan' dollars in dust, eh?"

"Somewheres around there."

"I'm wonderin' if, perchanct, he'll find that inconspicuous piece of string that protrudes from the wall—the one that removes the section of log and discloses the secret cache?"

"Shore he found it. Couple of nights ago, whilst he was in a stud game here, I snuck over an' peeked in the cache. The dust's there, all right—an' by God, I'll have you to know that when the time comes to divide it up, I git my share!"

"Why, Cush—how you talk! As though here on Halfaday, anyone would rob a cache!"

"I ain't talkin' about robbin' no cache—an' you know it. But when you know this guy, you'll see he ain't pin' to be around here long before we hang him. He's about as ornery a coot as ever showed up."

"Sort of light-haired guy with a reddish mustache, twenty-five or thirty years old, about five foot seven, ain't he?"

"He ain't. He's better'n six foot, black-headed, no whiskers, an' he's forty er more, if he's a day."

"H-u-u-m, that's interestin'—extremely interestin'."

"Why is it interestin' if some guy is black-headed an' forty, an' ain't got no whiskers? Hell, lots of folks is like that! If someone didn't know you was smart, they'd think you was a damn fool."

BOTH TURNED to look as a man stepped into the room and advanced to the bar. He was a small man with mild blue eyes and a stubble of blond beard liberally besprinkled with gray.

"This here's Cushing's Fort, ain't it?" he asked.

Reaching for a glass, Cush slid it across the bar. "Yup," he replied. "Fill up. This un's on the house."

The man filled the glass. "Thanks," he said. "A drink of licker goes good when a man's tired. Quite a ways up here, ain't it?"

"That," smiled Black John, "is accordin' to where a man started from."

"I come clean from Detroit," the man replied, his right cheek twitching nervously. "But right now I come from Dawson. Fella name of Bettles told me about Halfaday Crick. He told me to hunt up a fella name of Black John Smith that hung out at Cushing's Fort. So I come up here. An' you might be him, accordin' to what Bettles claimed you looked like."

The big man nodded. "I'm Black John," he said. "Was there somethin' you wanted to see me about in particular?"

"Yeah. My name's Joe Smiley. Bettles, he claimed you might help me out."

"Out of what?"

"He claimed about all the outlaws in the country hit fer Halfaday Crick, an' you kind of run things, up here."

"You an outlaw?"

"Cripes no! I'm huntin' one. I was night watchman on the Consolidated Minin' Company's dredge on a crick up the Klondike River, an' one night a damn cuss whammed me over the head with a club an' robbed the strong box of twenty thousan' dollars worth of gold. I told Mr. Bentley—he's the big boss down to Dawson—I told him when I hired out to him that he better give me a revolver to carry, but he claimed there worn't no danger of no robbery way up there, that all I had to do was keep the night fire gain' under the b'iler, an' see that the pump didn't freeze, an' stuff like that. The crew sleeps in a cabin on the bank an' he claimed if there was any trouble all I'd have to do is yell an' wake the boys up. Mr. Bentley, he ort to listened to me.

Black John grinned. "Old Muttonchops Bentley, he won't listen to anyone. He knows it all. He wouldn't listen to me one time—an' it cost the Consolidated a hundred thousan' in gold."

"Nightwatchin's my business. I was nightwatchman in a factory down in Detroit, an' I know dang well that wherever there's somethin' that can be stole handy, like money er gold, er stuff like that, there's allus someone lookin' fer the chant to steal it, no matter if it's in Detroit, er the Klondike River, er wherever it's at. So I got to figgerin' on how I'd go at it to rob that strong box if I was a robber, an' I figgered that I'd sneak up an' wham the nightwatchman on the head with a club because that way it wouldn't make no noise to wake up the crew. So I hunted around an' found an old iron kettle an' knocked the bottom out of it, an' padded it good with moss, an' I wore that in my cap— an' it's a dang good thing I did, 'cause one night this here robber snuck up on me an' whammed me on the head so hard it dang near drove me through the deck. It knocked one down, an' I laid there like I was dead, but I got a dang good look at the robber, an' you bet I never yelled, like Mr. Bentley told me to, er he'd of clubbed me to death, fer shore.

"Mr. Bentley, he fired me fer not yellin'—but I'd ruther be fired than dead. A policeman name of Corporal Downey asked me a lot of questions. An' then one night in the Tivoli Saloon I was tellin' a nice old fella name of Bettles about it, an' he told me if I'd come up here you might help me out. He claimed the robber prob'ly hit fer here."

"What do you want of the robber? Are you aimin' to take him back to Dawson?"

"No. But I want to get that gold back. You see, when Mr. Bentley fired me I ask him if he'd give me back my job in case I got his gold back, an' he promised he would. But he said it like he didn't figger I could get it back."

"Now that you're here, how do you figger on gettin' it back, in case you'd locate this robber?"

"Why, I'd keep an eye on him every dang minute. He's got that gold hid somewheres, an' if he robs someone else he'll stick that gold in along with it. Or if he's spendin' it, like here in the saloon, he'll have to go an' git more, now an' then, an' either way, I can find out where it's hid, an' sneak in an' swipe it off'n him an' take it back to Mr. Bentley an' get my job back."

"Why are you so hell-bent on gettin' that job back? Was he payin' you good money?"

"Well, not the way prices is. He paid me ten dollars a night."

"Ten dollars! Hell, man, an ounce a day is goin' wages! An' that's sixteen dollars."

"Yes, I know. But there's a lot of men in the country an' dang few jobs. An' I'm gettin' kind of old. That's all he'd pay me. He told me to take it, er leave it. So I took it."

"He throws in your grub, I s'pose?"

"No, I have to pay fer my grub. But I don't eat much. An' daytimes, the boys let me sleep in the cabin, so my lodgin' don't cost me nothin' You see, I've got to save up enough to buy me an outfit so I can go out on some crick an' dig me some gold of my own. It's on account of my boy."

"Your boy?"

"Yeah. He's in the army—over there in the Philippines. I got a letter from him a while back, an' he's goin' to be discharged come fall, an' he wants to go to college an' learn how to be a doctor. His ma died last spring, an' I was alone there in Detroit, so when I got that letter I started figgerin'. I run up to Ann Arbor where the University is, an' I talks to quite a few folks, some perfessors, an' some of the boys that was goin' to the college, an' I found out it would take more to send him to college than I could make workin' at my job. So I quit, an' come up here to Dawson to dig out some of the gold the newspapers is printin' about. When I got to Dawson I was broke, an' so I had to hunt me a job to earn enough money to buy me a prospectin' outfit."

"He's a mighty good boy, Sammy is—allas good to his ma an' me. Altus sent home part of his pay. I kep' puttin' it in the bank so he'd have it when he got out of the army, but when his ma got sick, there was doctor's bills to pay, an' medicine, an' then the horspital—an' at last the funeral. So I had to use up all we'd saved, an' the money Sammy sent home too. I'd do anything fer my boy. I never had no education to speak of. But I want he should have one. Do you think that there robber is up here on Halfaday Crick?"

BLACK JOHN shook his head. "No, I don't believe he is. You see, I was down to Dawson—just got back, an' while I was there Corporal Downey told me about that robbery, an' he gave me the description of the robber that you gave him. The only newcomer on the crick is an altogether different lookin' man."

"He might be him, then," the little man replied. "You see, I lied to Downey about what fer lookin' guy this robber was."

"You lied to him! Why?"

"Well, you see I want to get my job back so I can buy an' outfit, so I can dig some gold, so my boy can go to college. If the police found the robber an' arrested him it wouldn't do me no good. I've got to get the dust back myself, an' give it to Mr. Bentley."

"Well, I'll be damned!" Black John grinned. "How much money do you figger it'll take to send your boy through college?"

"It'll take a sight of money—mebbe five, six thousan' dollars. It's accordin' to whether Sammy can get some kind of a job an' go to the college too. But I'd ruther he didn't have to git a job, so he could put in more time studyin'!"

"What'll you do, if you get enough to finance the boy's education—go back to your job?"

"Oh, I'd find some kind of a job. It don't make no difference about me. My wife, she's gone. I'm all alone, now. I'll git along. I never did amount to no hell of a lot, nohow. But if I could dig enough gold between now an' fall to send Sammy through college—then he would amount to somethin.' He'd make a fine man. An' if I could live long enough to see that, I'd sort of feel that mebbe I had amounted to somethin', after all."

The big man nodded slowly. "Yeah—I guess that's right, Joe. When a man sets out to do somethin', an' has got the guts to carry it through, he's a damn good man, anyway you look at him. Come on with me. You can throw your stuff in my cabin. You are liable to be around here fer a few days till we sort of figger things out—an' you don't want to let this guy get a look at you till you're ready."

"I'm shore obliged to you, Mr. Smith," the little man said as he picked up his light pack and followed Black John out the door. "But I don't hardly think that robber would know me if he seen me now, 'cause I've let my whiskers grow sence the robbery—an' I don't look like me, no more."

III

WHEN THEY REACHED the cabin Black John indicated one of the two bunks. "That one's yours as long as you're here," he said. "Just slip your pack under it, an' I'll light the fire. It's time to eat an' I'm hungrier'n hell."

"You go ahead an' make the fire, Mr. Smith," the little man said. "But I'll do the cookin'. I can cook good. Learn't how off'n my wife. She was a good cook, an' when she got sick she showed me how, an' I done the cookin' fer the two of us, till she died. An' sence then I've be'n batchin' it. You're shore good to me—takin' me in, this way—an' it's little enough I can do to pay you back. I'll do the cookin' an' sort of red up the place a little, like sweepin' out, an' the like of that. I like to keep things middlin' neat. My wife, she was a good woman, but she was too dang neat—allus scrubbin' the floor, an' dustin', an' wipin', an' sweepin', worshin', an' puttin' fresh paper on shelves. Take a woman like that, there ain't no halfways about 'em, if a thing don't shine like a nigger's heel, it's filthy—an' off they go to fetch the scrub pail. I don't figger a man's got to be that neat—do you, Mr. Smith?"

"Well, no. I can't see the sense in a man's runnin' hog-wild with his neatness. It's about like anything else—a middle course is generally the sensible one. You go ahead an' take over, if you want to. Cookin's a chore I never did like. You'll find the tea an' canned stuff there on the shelves. If you need anything else you can get it at Cush's an' charge it to me. I'll go out an' cut some more firewood."

At supper that evening, Black John eyed the little man with approval. "You're all right, Joe," he approved. "This chunk of meat is roasted to a turn. I like roast moose meat. I like it good an' rare in the middle. But I damn seldom get any because it's quicker to fry it when I'm cookin' my own, an' if you order it in a restaurant it's always so damn well done there ain't no flavor to it. An' this macaroni's good, too, fixed up with cheese the way you've got it. You must have just naturally took to cookin'."

"Well, I dunno's it was so dang nache'l. If I didn't do it right, my wife she'd make me throw it out, an' do it over. I had to learn to do it right, er I'd of gone broke buyin' stuff to throw out.

"I hope if that feller that stole that dust in here on Halfaday Crick, he don't live very far from here, 'cause I want to watch him every dang minute I can—an' yet I want to be around here to do yer cookin' fer you, too."

"I've never seen this newcomer, myself," Black John said. "Cush told me about him this mornin' when I got back from Dawson. Claimed he's a tall, black-haired man, around forty, or so, with tattooed arms."

"I wouldn't know if his arms is tattooed, er if they ain't. But I'll bet he's the feller, all right. Do you know where he's livin'?"

"Yeah, Cush said he moved into One Eyed John's shack. It's only a little piece down the crick—first cabin you come to on the left-hand side, goin' down. Cush claims he hangs around the saloon most of the time—said he draw'd the name of William Henry Van Buren out of the can."

"Out of the can?"

"Yeah, the name can. Livin' up here clost to the line, like we do, a lot of men that's tryin' to evade the police, for one reason or another drifts in on us, an' damn near every one of 'em claims his name is John Smith. It wasn't so bad as long as the physical characteristics held out—like long, an' short, an' red, an' black, an' one-eyed, an' one-armed, an' pot gutted, an' slim—but after that we run into more or less confusion. So Cush an' I copied the names out of a history book, an' mixed 'em up a bit, an' wrote 'em on slips of paper an' put 'em in a molasses can we keep on the end of the bar, an' now when someone comes along an' claims his name is John Smith, we call his attention to the lie, an' make him draw one out of the can. This name becomes his property until such time as he gets murdered or hung, or leaves the crick."

"But—how would they get hung, up here?"

"The feat is accomplished by slippin' a rope around their neck an' jerkin' 'em up to a rafter or tree limb—whichever's handiest."

"But, I mean—there ain't any court, or judge here, is there?"

"Well, not in the generally accepted use of the term. We call a miner's meetin', an' try 'em. If they're guilty of murder, or larceny, or any other form of skullduggery, we hang 'em. If they ain't, we turn 'em loose. We have found the method to be both convenient an' effective."

"After we worsh up the dishes I'm a-goin' over to the saloon an' hang around there till that feller shows up. I'd know him quick as I seen him, if he's him. An' if he is, I'm a-goin' to hang around in the brush an' watch him every dang minute till he goes to where he's got the gold hid. An' when I find out where it's at, I'll wait till he goes over to the saloon, and I'll sneak up an' grab it an' take it back to Mr. Bentley an' get my job back."

"The plan has its merits," opined Black John, "but you better be damn careful he don't see you prowlin' around, or he might knock you off. Of course, if he did, we'd hang him—but from your angle it wouldn't be so good."

When the two arrived at the saloon, several of the men of Halfaday were already there. Joe Smiley settled inconspicuously into a chair. Cush spoke a few words to a tall, dark-haired man who moved along and ranged himself beside Black John as Cush slid a glass across the bar.

"Drink up, pardner," the man invited. "I'm buyin' this one." When the glass was filled, he regarded the bearded face through a pair of swinish eyes. "So you're this here Black John Smith I've be'n hearin' all about, eh? I'm William Henry Van Buren, accordin' to the name I draw'd outa the can yonder. Jest call me Bill fer short. I be'n waitin' till you got back. I figger me an' you kin do business. Guy down to Dawson name of Cuter Malone put me wise to you boys up here bein' outlaws—claimed you're king of the bunch. You know Cuter—he runs the Klondike Palace."

"Oh, shore. I've known Cuter for quite a while. What's the nature of the business you figger you an' me might transact?"

"I'm an outlaw, too. I figgered on j'inin' up with yer gang."

BLACK JOHN regarded the man with an appraising glance that didn't fail to take in the new belt knife in its sheath of yellow stamped leather. "Quite a lot of chechakos drifts in on us, claimin' to be outlaws," he said. "But hell—not one in a dozen of 'em ever done more'n steal a washin' off some woman's clothesline. An' to tell the truth, Bill, you don't look no better'n any of the rest of 'em."

The vicious dark eyes narrowed slightly. "Is that so! Well, jest between you an' me, I've got twenty thousan' in dust, barrin' the few ounces I spent gittin' up here—an' I never dug a damn ounce of it—see?"

"You mean you got away with a twenty thousan'-dollar job—here in the Yukon?"

"That's right. I took the strong box on a Consolidated dredge way to hell an' gone up the Klondike River one night. Slipped up an' clouted the nightwatchman over the head with a pick handle an' the rest was easy."

"Kill him?"

"I don't know if I did, er didn't. He laid like a log, whilst I pried the strong box open, an' he was still layin' there when I come away. What difference does it make? I got the dust. How about it? Do I rate in with you boys?"

Black John nodded slowly, his eyes on the little row of beads that rimmed the liquor in his glass. "Yeah, you stick around a few days, Bill. We'll find a place for you all right—a place that'll fit you to a T."

"Okay. I figgered you could use a guy like me. I'm hard—see? A guy's gotta be hard to git along. Jest slip me the word when you want me. I'm livin' in the first cabin down the crick—One Eyed John's place, they call it. One of the boys was sayin' you hung him a while back. What did you hang him fer?"

"Oh, damn if I rec'lect. Most likely for something he done."

"That's why I like it up here. You boys is hard, too. What I claim—if someone makes a wrong move, hang him an' be done with it."

"I'm glad you feel that way about it, Bill. I was afraid we might be pullin' off a hangin' one of these days that you wouldn't approve of."

"Oh, hell—fergit it! Any time you boys pulls off a hangin', jest count me in."

"We'll do that, Bill. Yeah, we'll shore do just that." The big man paused and glanced toward a card table where some of the men of Halfaday were seating themselves.

"Looks like they're startin' a stud game," he said. "We might as well set in."

IV

WHEN THE GAME broke up shortly after midnight, Black John returned to his cabin to find Joe Smiley snoring in his bunk. In the morning he awoke and lay for a few minutes breathing in the aroma of frying steak and listening to the cheerful sizzle of grease in the pan.

Joe Smiley greeted him with a smile as he tossed off his blanket and swung his feet to the floor. "Good mornin', Mr. Smith. Have a good sleep? Breakfast's about ready. That's him, all right—that's the dang cuss that snuck up an' whammed me over the head, an' stole the gold that night. Cripes, I know'd him the minute I seen him! I was kinda tired, so while you an' him was talkin', I slipped over here an' went to bed. I'm a-goin' to start watchin' him, an' you bet when I find out where he's hid that gold, I'm a-goin to git it."

"Okay, Joe," the big man replied. "Just don't let him catch you at it—that's all." During the next five days the little man appeared at the cabin only long enough to cook and eat. In the evenings he would hang around the saloon watching the stud game, hoping, as he explained to Black John, that the robber would go broke in the game, and be forced to visit his cache for more dust. But the man's luck was running. He won steadily.

At breakfast on the morning of the sixth day, the little man regarded Black John with puckered brow. "You know, Mr. Smith, I believe that dang cuss has got that dust hid right there in his cabin. I be'n watchin' him every day, an' he don't go no place except to rustle some firewood, an' go over to the saloon. I figgered on slippin' in his cabin whilst he's over there—but I don't dast to in the daytime, 'cause, you can't never tell when he'll come back. Sometimes he stays away quite a while, but most times he comes slippin' back every little while, an' stands there at the edge of the clearin' lookin' around, jest like he figgers someone might try to find his gold.

"I've follered him back there nights after the stud game broke up, to see if he would not sneak out an' stick his winnin's in with his gold—but he don't—so he must have it hid in the cabin. But that won't do him no good. The only time he stays away very long is at night when he's playin' stud—an' tonight I'm goin' to slip over there an' hunt all over that cabin till I find the gold."

The big man nodded approval. "Yeah, I believe you've got somethin' there, Joe," he said. "I wouldn't be surprised if that's where he's got that dust cached. Tonight ort to be a good time to sort of look the place over. It's Saturday night an' a lot of the boys'll be in to Cush's. There'll probably be two, three games goin'—an' the bets'll run high. Van Buren plays a good game of stud. He'll have his mind on the game—figger on makin' a killin'."

That evening, as Black John had predicted, some twenty-five or thirty of the men of Halfaday congregated in the saloon. Numerous drinks were had, and before long three stud games were in progress.

For several nights the big man had noticed that Van Buren's glance strayed frequently to Joe Smiley who stood idly at the bar, or hovered about the table watching the game. As they sat down to play, Black John seated himself directly across the table from Van Buren. The game proceeded for an hour or more, when he saw Smiley slip unobtrusively from the room. Out of the tail of his eye he noted that Van Buren also saw the little man disappear. Van Buren stayed on the next deal, then cashed in his chips, and strolled from the room. As the door closed behind him, Black John also cashed in, and making his way through the storeroom, slipped out the back door. Keeping well back, he followed Van Buren, whose figure was distinctly visible in the bright starlight. At the edge of the little clearing that surrounded One Eyed John's cabin, the man paused and eyed the square of dim light that showed at the window. Drawing a pistol from his pocket, he cocked it, and crossing the clearing, stood for several minutes peering in through the window. Close behind him Black John peered around the corner of the outhouse, his forty-five Colt cocked and ready.

Presently Van Buren walked to the door and threw it open. Stepping into the room with the cocked gun in his hand, he eyed Smiley. "What the hell you doin' here?" he demanded.

The little man turned startled eyes on him—eyes that strayed from the intruder's face to the gun. "Why—I—I—"

"Come on—you might's well spit it out! You ain't got more'n a minute to live, nohow. You might's well come clean. I know who you be. Yer the nightwatch up there on the Consolidated's dredge. I thought I'd croaked you with that pick handle—but this time I'll make a job of it."

SMILEY GULPED, and swallowed, his cheek twitching spasmodically. "How—how'd you know me—with these whiskers—an' you only seen me from behind—at night, too?"

"Oh, I seen you before that night. I cased the damn job fer two days before I pulled it. Laid there in the brush an' took it all in. I know'd you by the way you squinch your cheek every few minutes. I stumbled on that dredge job by accident. I was hittin' acrost country from Coal Crick—didn't dast to go by the big river, on account of the police might want to ask me about somethin' that happened in a cabin back there. But to hell with that! You ain't told me what yer doin' here in my cabin this time of night."

"I—I was huntin' fer that gold you stole that night. I—I want to give it to Mr. Bentley so he'd give me my job back. It's—it's on account of my boy."

"To hell with yer boy! You mean if you'd located that swag you'd of give it back?"

"Sure I would. It ain't mine—an' it ain't yourn, neither. It belongs to the Consolidated—an' you stole it."

"Of all the damn fools I ever heard of, you take the cake! Well, you won't make no more fool plays, anyhow. Here's where you git yourn!"

"Please don't shoot me! I didn't find the gold. Let me go—please!"

"Let you go—so you kin slip down an' give my description, an' where I'm at to the cops, eh? To hell with that! Git ready, bud—'cause this is it."

As he raised the gun a voice sounded at his elbow. "Just drop the gun, Bill—an' drop it quick."

THE MAN whirled at the sound and stared straight into the steel-blue eyes behind the black beard—stared, also squarely into the muzzle of a cocked forty-five. "What? What the hell?" he gasped, as his pistol hit the floor with a thud. "What you doin' here? You was settin' in that stud game a minute ago!"

"So was you."

"But I come over here 'cause I seen that damn little sneak thief slip out the door, an' I figgered where he was goin'."

"An' I come because I saw you slip out the door—an' I figgered where *you* were goin', too."

"A man's got a right to shoot a damn thief that's prowlin' around his house at night," Van Buren growled.

"That's true," Black John admitted. "The evidence will be presented at the proper time. We'll adjourn now, to the saloon, an' I'll call a miner's meetin'."

"What the hell's a miner's meetin'?"

"It's a sort of quasi-legal institution we've got up here for adjudicatin' such crimes as murder, larceny, an' general skulduggery. You'll ondoubtless get the gist of it before the evenin's over."

"You mean we're goin' to take this damn little thief over an try him—like in a court?"

"That's right."

"Cripes, you kin see for yourself he's guilty as hell! What'll he git when he's convicted?"

"If he's convicted, he'll get hung. We've only got two verdicts. If a man's guilty, we hang him. If not, we turn him loose."

"Come on then—let's git goin'!" The man grinned and winked at Black John. "First time I ever enjoyed going into court."

"You're shore welcome to all the enjoyment you can get out of it," replied the big man dryly. Reaching down, he picked up the cocked revolver from the floor, slipped it into his pocket, and turned to Smiley. "Come on, Joe. We're goin' back to Cush's."

ENTERING THE saloon accompanied by the two, Black John strode to the bar and, with the butt of his revolver, knocked loudly to attract attention. "All stud games is temporarily adjourned. I'm callin' a miner's meetin' to try one Joe Smiley for night prowlin' in One Eyed John's cabin, at present occupied by, to wit, alias William Henry Van Buren. Five minutes will be allowed for the cashin' of chips."

When the time was up the big man rapped on the bar for order and glanced into the faces of the men who had crowded up and stood in a close-packed semi-circle. "For the first witness call the aforementioned alias William Henry Van Buren. Step out here, Bill, where everyone can hear you. Do you swear to tell the truth, the whole truth, or any part of it, s'l'pe God?"

"Sure."

"Okay. Now tell the boys what come off."

"I was playin' stud in here a little bit ago, an' I seen this here guy slip out the door, so I cashed in, an' follered him, figgering he aimed to prowl around my cabin, an' when I got to the clearin' I seen a light in the winder, which I'd blowed out the lamp before I come over here. I looked in an' seen this guy huntin' around in under my bunk, so I draw'd my gun, an' opened the door, an' ask him what the hell he's doin' in there." The man paused, and Black John frowned.

"Go on," the big man urged. "That ain't all you said, is it?"

"Well—I dunno. I prob'ly said more, but I disremember what it was. It don't make no difference, nohow. The main thing is this guy was prowlin' around my cabin in the nighttime, an' I ketched him redhanded."

"There's one little thing you're overlookin', Bill—the fact that I'm the one to judge whether what you said makes a differ-ence—not you. In this instance I deem it does make a difference, an' bein' as I was right behind you an' overheard every word, I'm in a position to sort of jog your memory a bit. When Smiley didn't answer you, did you, or did you not tell him he might as well come clean, because he didn't have more'n a minute to live?"

"Well—I might of said that."

"Did you, or did you not tell the defendant that you knew he was the nightwatch on the Consolidated's dredge that's located somewheres up the Klondike?"

"Sure, I told him that"

"Did you, or did you not tell him you thought you'd croaked him with a pick handle—and also tell him that, this time, you'd make a job of it?"

"I guess I told him that."

"Okay. Now, Bill, would you mind telling the boys why you tried to croak him with the pick handle?"

The man glanced into the expectant faces of the men of Halfaday. "Sure. I'll tell 'em. Why not? We're all outlaws up here together. I knocked him out so I could go ahead an' rob the strong box—same as any of you would of done."

"An' did you, or did you not, rob the strong box?"

"Sure I robbed it. Got twelve hundred an' fifty ounces of dust."

"Did you, or did you not tell Smiley that you stumbled on that job by accident—that you were hittin' acrost from Coal Crick the back way because you didn't dare to go up the river for fear the police might question you about somethin' that happened in a cabin, back there?"

THE MAN hesitated, the glance of the narrowed dark eyes shifting swiftly from one face to another. He frowned. "Sure I said that! What if I did?"

"Did the defendant tell you why he was there in your cabin?"

"Yeah—the damn fool claimed he was tryin' to locate them twelve hundred an' fifty ounces so he could give 'em back to the boss of the Consolidated, so he could git his job back."

"An' then did you, or did you not tell him he wouldn't make any more fool plays—that here's where he gets his? And ain't it a fact that you, then an' there, raised your cocked gun with intent to shoot the defendant?"

"Sure I'd of shot him, if you hadn't pulled yer gun on me an' made me drop mine. Hell, a man's got a right to shoot a thief in his house, ain't he?"

"Have you got them twelve hundred an' fifty ounces cached there in the cabin where he might have found it?"

The man hesitated only an instant. "No," he answered, "I've got 'em buried way out in the bresh where no one could find 'em."

"That'll do," Black John said. "Witness is excused."

He allowed his eyes to travel over the faces of the assembled men. "You've heard the evidence against the defendant. As most of you know, Joe, there, has be'n stayin' with me ever since he came to Halfaday. It would be a waste of time to have him testify in his own defense, because Cush can verify the fact that he told us about that robbery when he first got here, an' he told us that he had come in hope that the robber had hit for here, an' that by watchin' his chance, he could locate his cache, remove the stolen dust, and return it to its rightful owner.

"While the ethics of returnin' dust to an outfit like the Consolidated is open to question, it is clear to any right thinkin' man that his motive in searchin' Van Buren's cabin was not robbery or larceny in any form. In fact, from his angle, it was a laudible motive. Therefore it's clear that the defendant is in no wise guilty of a criminal act. We'll take a vote, now—all them in favor of conviction signify by sayin' 'Aye.'" The silence was broken by a single vote—the voice of Van Buren.

"Contrary, 'No.'"

A loud chorus of 'No's filled the room.

"Meetin's adjourned," Black John said, and as a buzz of conversation rose, he again banged on the bar for order. "Meetin' reconvened to try one, alias William Henry Van Buren for general skullduggery an' attempted murder."

Van Buren's swinish eyes suddenly widened. "What—what the hell do you mean?" he cried.

"Have patience," Black John replied. "Like I told you before, you'll get the gist of it before long." He turned to the others. "You all heard this defendant admit under oath that he threatened to shoot Joe Smiley there in One-Eyed John's cabin, and that he would in fact, have shot him if I hadn't interfered. The shooting of Smiley under these conditions would have be'n a cold-blooded murder, because you also heard the defendant swear that the dust he stole from the Consolidated is not cached in the cabin but is buried somewheres out in the brush. There-fore—"

"Hold on!" Van Buren interrupted. "I lied! The dust is—"

"Shut up!" Black John roared. "You've spoke your piece!"

"As I was goin' on to say, such bein' the case, the defendant here knew damn well that the said Joe Smiley couldn't have located that dust no matter how long he hunted for it.

"Not wishin' in anyway to prejudice the defendant's case, I'll digress here to relate that the other day, in Dawson, Corporal Downey told me of a particularly dirty murder that was re-cently pulled off in a cabin on Coal Crick. Some of you boys might know Bill Oatley, some of you might even know his wife, as fine a woman as ever hit the Yukon. She nursed me through a spell of pneumonia on Birch Crick. Doc Sutherland told me afterward that if it hadn't be'n for her I'd never have pulled through. She didn't have to do it, an God knows she had enough to do without botherin' to walk them two miles from her cabin to mine every day—an' plenty of them days the strong cold was on.

"Accordin' to Downey, Bill Oatley hired a hand to help him with his sluicin'. This man was a tall, dark guy with brown eyes an' black hair an' had a ship tattooed on one forearm, an' a naked woman on the other one. He worked a few days an' quit, claiming he was goin' downriver. Bill went to Forty Mile for supplies a few days after he'd gone, an' when he got back three or four days later he found his wife layin' dead on the cabin floor—she'd be'n beaten an' choked to death. But she hadn't told where Bill's cache was. Whoever murdered her dropped his belt knife on the floor, an' Al Scougale told Downey that only a couple of days after the Consolidated robbery, a tall dark guy bought a Double-X belt knife in a yellow stamped sheath from him.

"Now you all heard the defendant admit that he told Smiley that he was cuttin' acrost from Coal Crick when——"

"I lied!" The defendant's voice rose hysterically shrill, and there was a look of terror in his shifting eyes. "I never seen Coal Crick! I—tell you, I lied!"

"Lyin'," replied Black John dryly, "is a bad habit. It's liable to get you in trouble." He turned to the others. "Now, we can all see that this here defendant comes up to the physical specifications Downey mentioned. I never saw his arms—they may, or may not be tattooed."

"Yer damn right they be!" Pot-Gutted John interrupted. "He rolls up his sleeves sometimes playin' stud, an' plenty of us has saw them there pichers—the ship an' the naked woman!"

Black John nodded. "The matter can be easily verified—an' that leads us to the matter of the knife that a tall dark guy bought off'n Al Scougale recently. I notice that this defendant has a new belt knife strapped to him—an' that the sheath is of yellow stamped leather. So if it's a Double-X, we can safely assume it is the identical knife that Al sold.

"Now I want you boys to bear in mind that we ain't tryin' this defendant for anything except his attempted murder of Joe Smiley, right here on Halfaday. If you're so minded, you can disregard the similarity of the defendant an' the damn cuss that murdered Bill Oatley's wife, an' also his attempted murder of Smiley when he conked him with that pick handle up the Klondike. At best, they're only straws that shows which way the wind blows, as the Good Book says—an' in the present case, are irreverent an' immaterial. So it's up to you boys to decide whether or not the defendant is guilty or not guilty as charged. If you boys want a woman-chokin', head-whammin' son of a gun livin' amongst us, it is your duty to vote for acquittal. If not, you should vote for conviction. Al! them in favor of acquittal, signify by hollerin' 'Aye.' Contrary 'No.'"

When the boisterous chorus of 'No's died down Black John turned to the defendant. "You was askin' me, back there in One-Eyed's cabin what a miner's meetin' was. I trust you've found out. But the information came a little late to do you any good. I rec'lect that you told me that anytime we felt like pullin' off a hangin' to count you in. Well—you're counted in, all right. I might add, however, that you'll have time to h'ist a couple of drinks whilst Pot-Gut is tyin' the knot."

V

WHEN THE SENTENCE had been duly carried out, the body was cut down and carried into the storeroom, it being deemed too dark to dig a grave. The stud games were resumed, and after looking on for a while, Joe Smiley slipped over and went to bed.

Later, when the men of Holladay had returned to their cabins, Black John and Cush slipped over to One-Eyed John's cabin, retrieved the dust from the secret cache, carried it back to the saloon and divided it equally between them. "She weighs up thirteen hundred an' ten ounces," Cush said. "Van Buren played a little ahead on his stud. That makes ten thousan' four hundred an' eighty dollars apiece. An' jest think, John—if Joe Smiley had happened to find that cache, the damn fool would of give all that dust back to the Consolidated! I kinda like the little cuss, too. He thinks a heap of that boy of his'n. I'd shore like fer him to make a strike so's he could send him to that there college. But Joe, he won't never make no strike—he ain't got a chanct in a thousan'."

"Oh, I don't know, Cush—sometimes those long shots pay out."

Joe Smiley accompanied Black John to Cush's after breakfast the following morning, and after a round of drinks, the big man turned to Cush. "Jest count out ten thousan' in big bills, an' charge 'em up to me," he said. "I'll pay Joe that there reward money, an' collect it later from Downey. If Joe had to hang around to collect it, he might be here till it was too late fer his boy to start in college, this fall. There's too damn much red tape to these here police matters."

Without a word, Cush counted the money onto the bar, and picking up the bills, Black John handed them to the astonished Smiley.

"Reward money!" the little man gasped, the hand that clutched the bills trembling slightly. "What reward money? Reward money for what?"

"Why, for furnishin' us the information whereby we was able to hang Van Buren, of course. Hadn't be'n for you identifyin' him for us, he might have gone scot-free. I plumb forgot to mention it, but down there in Dawson Downey said there was a ten thousan' dollar reward posted for Van Buren, dead or alive, on account of that Coal Crick murder. The reward belongs to you. You earn't it, fair an' square."

The little man blinked rapidly, and furtively wiped an eye with the back of his hand. "But—ten thousan' dollars!" he uttered, in a voice that was not quite steady. "Why—why—now Sammy can go to college!"

"That's right—so he can," the big man smiled. "An' you won't have to worry about makin' no strike." He paused abruptly, and glanced through the open doorway toward the landing, where a uniformed figure had just reached the top of the bank. "Look—there's Downey now!" he cried. "Hey, Joe, you slip back through the storeroom an' get over to my cabin as quick as you can make it! Don't let Downey see you, under no circumstances! Cripes, he's liable to take you back to Dawson an' stick you in jail from now on fer lyin' to him about what that Consolidated robber looked like. Git, now—he'll be in here in a minute!"

A few minutes later as the officer stepped into the room, Black John greeted him heartily. "Well, damned if it ain't Downey, himself! Come on up an' wet your whistle. Cush is about to buy one. We were just talkin' about you—wonderin' if you ever located that Consolidated robber you were tellin' me about."

The officer shook his head, as he filled the glass Cush slid toward him. "Nope. Just swung around this way to see if he was here."

The big man shook his head. "He ain't here. No one of that description has showed up. We've be'n on the lookout for him. But we ain't had any luck."

"An' that other damn cuss—the one I told you about that murdered Bill Oatley's wife—I s'pose he ain't showed up either."

"Such supposition ain't founded on fact."

"What do you mean?" Downey asked. "I'd sure like to get my hands on that bird! I'd a damn sight rather get him than the other one. Bill Oatley's wife was a fine woman. An' what with his description—them tattooed arms, an' all, we could convict him sure, especially if he was carryin' a new belt knife. You don't mean to tell me he's be'n here, on Halfaday?"

BLACK JOHN nodded. "Yeah, he was here, all right."

"What do you mean—he *was* here? Has he gone?"

"Well—yes—an' no."

"What do you mean—yes an' no?"

"His material entity is still with us. His soul, if any, is on-doubtless disportin' itself somewhere in hell—or else the theologians arc way off on their guess."

"You mean—he's dead?"

"Cush so pronounced him. An' he's the coroner. We called a miner's meetin' an' convicted him, an' give him a suspended sentence."

"Suspended sentence! Then what did he die of?"

"Of the sentence! We suspended him by a rope from that rafter over your head."

"You mean, you tried him for that Coal Crick murder? That's carryin' things too damn far, John! Away from the law, like you are, up here, miner's meetin's are legal enough to be winked at, when a crime has be'n committed right here. But that murder was entirely out of your jurisdiction, and should have be'n dealt with by the proper authorities."

"By Cripes, Downey—you shore jump at conclusions. That damn scoundral was tried for a crime he committed right here in this room. That Coal Crick murder was disregarded entirely."

"What crime did he commit here?"

"He spit on the floor. Yes, sir—just beyond where you're standin'. He deliberately spit on the floor! An' he done it with premeditation an' malice aforethought, an' before numerous witnesses. I told the boys about Bill Oatley's wife walkin' a couple of miles through the strong cold every day there on Birch Crick to nurse me through that case of pneumonia—an' I told 'em that the defendant had choked her an' beat her to death on Coal Crick. But I expressly told 'em to disregard those facts, an' consider only the crime he was bein' tried for. They done so—an' we hung him."

Corporal Downey nodded, slowly. "I see," he said. "An' now, if you buried him, we'll have to dig him up, so I can verify the identification. Anyway, he got what was cumin' to him—the dirty crook."

"We laid him aside to bury this afternoon," Black John said. "He's there in the storeroom. You can look him over, an' then write him off the book."

"Okay. Glad I didn't make the trip up here for nothin'. Sorry that other one ain't here—you remember his description, don't you—twenty-five or thirty, five-foot-seven, light-haired, reddish mustache, heavy built?"

"Oh, shore. I'll keep my eye peeled for him."

"An' will you let me know if he shows up?"

"You bet I will, Downey! By God, you can depend on us, up here, on Halfaday, to work hand in glove with the police!"

Downey grinned. "Yeah, I know. Much obliged, John. I shore hope I can get that dust back. Bentley's squawkin' his head off about it."

"Well—it don't cost nothin' to hope, Downey. You might get it. But I doubt it. Them damn crooks is cagey as hell."

After Downey had departed, some time later, Cush reached for his account book on the back bar, opened it, and made a notation. "That there ten thousan' reward money you give Joe Smiley," he said. "Only five thousan' of it is charged agin you."

"No, no, Cush! Charge me with the whole thing."

"Like hell I will! You can't play the hull hog all the time! Not whilst I'm around, you can't."

PERMANENT RESIDENT
ON HALFADAY

ONE MORNING EARLY in September Black John stepped through the doorway and crossed to the bar of Cushing's Fort, the combined trading post and saloon that served the little community of outlawed men that had sprung up on Halfaday Creek, close against the Yukon-Alaska border, as Old Cush, the proprietor, shoved aside the month-old newspaper he had been reading and set out a bottle, two glasses, and the leather dice box. Black John won in straight horses, and when the glasses were filled Cush folded the newspaper and laid it on the back bar. "I seen a piece in the paper there, where some preacher name of Billy Sunday built him a tuberkle an' converted three thousan', six hundred an' seventy-three folks in three weeks in Chicago. By God, what I claim, that's good convertin', even fer a town like Chicago!"

Black John nodded. "Yeah, I read that piece. It give the attendance figgers, the cost of the tabernacle, an' also the amount of the collection. I got out my pencil an' done a little figurin' an' found out that Billy made a net profit of three dollars an' sixty-two cents per soul. Which, when you come to think about it, ain't bad for three weeks of gymnastical devil-baitin'. Well—every man to his own racket." He paused and glanced at some penciled sheets that lay just beyond the newspaper. "Looks like you be'n doin' a little figurin' yourself."

Cush shook his head. "No, I wouldn't give a damn what souls is worth in Chicago. Them figgers is what I need to winter through on. I be'n goin' through my stock the last couple of days an' on top of four bar'ls of licker, I gotta have a lot of pants, an' shirts, an' blankets, an' underwear, an' a hell of a lot of groceries. An' I've got to git 'em up here before the freeze-up. Boat-freightin' is a damn sighter cheaper than dog-freightin'. I'm tellin' you, runnin' a tradin' post way out here, a man's got his troubles.

"Take it like them places where I tended bar in Cincinnati an' Seattle—Cripes, there wasn't hardly a day but what some licker er beer salesman didn't come in, settin' up free drinks fer the house, an' houndin' you fer an order. An' when you give 'em an order an' the stuff come, it was delivered an' tuk right down cellar where you wanted it.

"But, up here, they ain't no travelin' men to take yer order, an' no railroad to haul the stuff in, so I gotta go clean down to Dawson an' buy what I need an' then dicker with a bunch of damn pirates to git it delivered, an' some of it's allus gittin' dropped in the river an' lost er spoilt."

THE BIG man grinned. "Standin' around belly-achin' about it don't do no good. Hell if I felt the way you do about it, I'd take a trip outside an' get in touch with the right parties, an' promote' a railroad connectin' Halfaday Crick with Chicago an' all way p'ints. An' I'd stop in an' arrange with the wholesalers to have their travellin' men drop in on us occasionally. Cripes, the boys would appreciate a free drink now an' then, when one of them licker salesmen hit the crick."

"Huh," Cush grunted, "the kind of travellin' men that shows up on Halfaday could keep right on travellin' fer all of me. But gittin' back to this here stuff I need—me an' you's got to take a trip to Dawson, an' do it damn quick. The freeze-up'll hit us next month."

"Why rope me in on it? You know the way to Dawson as well as I do."

"Yeah, I know the way all right. But you know damn well I ain't no good in a canoe alone. I can't run them rapids, an' I ain't stout enough to pack the canoe around 'em. Besides that, we gotta take a bunch of dust down to the bank. The safe's gittin' clogged up with it. An' besides that, you'd ort to set in the stud game nights down to the Tivoli an' git back them three thousan' dollars them sourdoughs tuk you fer the last time you was down. An' besides that—"

"Hold on, Cush!" the big man interrupted. "The cogent reasonin' an' logical presentation of yer case percludes the necessity of further enumeration—"

"Yeah, an' further 'numeration of a lot of big words ain't gittin' you nothin', neither. So you slip over to yer cabin an' throw yer other shirt in yer pack whilst I send the *klooch* to fetch One Armed John to run the place whilst we're gone. All I'm hopin' is you don't run onto some good-lookin' woman down there that'll take you fer all you've got."

Black John smiled. "The contacts I've had with good-lookin' women haven't hurt me any, so far. In fact, on several occasions they've proved financially very profitable."

"Yeah, but you be'n lucky. An' you know damn well luck like that can't hold. One of 'em's goin' to take you one of these times—an' don't you fergit it! Tellin' you about me, I'm through with all of 'em. Them first three wives of mine run me ragged. I'm damn lucky to be alive, even—what with one of 'em wearin' a stiletto strapped to her leg, an' another one soakin' flypaper in under the bed! Time a man's had four wives, like I've had, an' only one of 'em worth a damn, he's learnt that when it comes to wimmin, the odds ain't right! I'm givin' you fair warnin', John—an' I'm givin' it to you free. But if yer goin' to be pig-headed about it, an' fall fer every good-lookin' woman you see—why then you'll learn about 'em the hard way—like I done."

II

THE TRIP TO Dawson was made without incident. After securing a couple of rooms at the hotel, Cush attended to his business with the big commercial companies, while Black John loafed about town fraternizing with the sourdoughs. He dropped into police detachment for a chat with Corporal Downey, to find Constable Rollo Buck, a rookie whose inflated ego was a source of constant amusement to the sourdoughs, seated behind Corporal Downey's flat-topped desk. "Why, hello, Rollo!" he greeted, eyeing the officer with an amused grin.

"What do you want?" the younger man snapped.

"Nothin'. Just stopped in to thaw the fat with Downey."

"Well, Corporal Downey's not here. He and Constable Peters are up the McQuesten investigating a reported murder. I'm in command of detachment until Downey's return."

"H-u-u-m. When you headin' for Halfaday?"

"What?"

"Well, I rec'lect that time I found you camped on that p'int upriver a piece, gnawin' on a chunk of loon that you thought was duck, after missin' a couple of shots at a moose, an' then goin' off half-cocked an' arrestin' the wrong Siwash on that trap stealin' complaint—I rec'lect you claimed that as quick as you got in command of the detachment here, the first thing you'd do you'd hit out for Halfaday Crick an' clean up Black John Smith an' that bunch of outlaws that's reported to hang out up there. I was just wonderin' when you figgered on startin' in on us."

The rookie's face flushed and his eyes narrowed. "My time will come—don't forget that. Just because Corporal Downey sees fit to leave you unmolested, is no sign I will. At present, I'm only in temporary command here. My orders are to stay right here until Corporal Downey returns."

Black John's grin widened, as he eyed the other appraisingly. "Yer uniform's all spick an' span, an' yer shoes are shined nice, Rollo," he approved. "An' I s'pose Downey figgers as long as you stay in the office you can't make many mistakes. But at that, you look quite a bit narrow acrost the hips to fill Downey's chair right—quite a bit narrow between the ears, too. Well, so long, sonny—good luck to you. An' whenever you get ready to invade Halfaday, come on up an' I'll buy you a drink." Turning on his heel he stepped from the room with Constable Buck's angry retort ringing in his ears.

At suppertime, as they waited to be served in the hotel dining room, Cush eyed Black John whose glance kept straying to a young woman and a little boy seated at a nearby table. "There you go," he said in an undertone, "jest like I said—if they's a good-lookin' woman shows up somewheres you don't look at nothin' else."

The big man smiled. "Well, Cripes, Cush—look around you. That old-timer over there in the corner ain't much to look at, what with needin' a clean shirt, an' a shave, an' a haircut. An' the sprinklin' of *chechakos* scattered around at the other tables shore ain't no hell of a sight. Besides, there's an air of tragedy about that young woman that rather intrigues me."

"She'll do a damn sight wors't than that, onct she gits her hooks into you," Cush growled. "I s'pose now, you won't be settin' in no stud game, tonight."

Black John ignored the jibe. "Yes, sir—if I ever saw sadness an' misery in a woman's eyes it's in hers."

Cush gave a contemptuous snort. "The sadder an' more miserable they look the more they kin take you fer. That there first wife of mine—she was the saddest lookin' woman I ever seen. She looked so damn miserable I up an' married her—an' after that, up to the time I got shet of her, by God it was me that was miserable—not her!"

A waitress brought in the food and the meal proceeded in silence. At its conclusion Cush glanced across the table. "Be you goin' to play stud, tonight—er ain't you?"

"Why shore I am."

"Let's be gittin' over to the Tivoli, then. I'm goin' to cash in around midnight. I got a hard week ahead of me, what with pickin' out all that stuff I need, an' then findin' a crew to freight it up to the fort."

Shortly after midnight the two quit the game and, returning to the hotel, sought their rooms. For a half-hour or more before he fell asleep, Black John lay in bed and listened to the sound of muffled sobbing that reached his ears through the thin partition between his room and the next. "It's that young woman," he muttered to himself. "She's in some kind of trouble, all right. It's too damn bad—what with that little kid, an' all."

IN THE morning he awoke and glanced at his watch. "Seven o'clock," he muttered. "What the hell does anyone do in Dawson at seven o'clock in the mornin'? I was a damn fool to quit the game early, last night, just because Cush did. If I'd have played on till four or five o'clock, I'd have slept till noon."

Swinging his feet to the floor, he dressed, washed, and descended the stairs to find the young woman and the little boy the sole occupants of the dining-room. Hesitating only a moment, he stepped into the room, crossed to her table, and smiled down into her upraised eyes. "Good mornin', ma'am," he said. "I noticed you an' the little fella in here last evenin', an' I couldn't help but feel that you're in trouble of some kind. Then, when I went to my room soon after midnight, I could hear someone cryin' in the next room—an' I can see by your eyes this mornin' that it must have be'n you. Of course, it's none of my business, ma'm—an' if I'm talkin' out of turn, just tell me so. But the fact is, I sort of know my way around in this country, an' if I could help you out in any way, I'd shore be proud to do it."

For a long moment the woman's gaze centered upon the kindly gray eyes that smiled down at her from above the heavy black beard. Then, suddenly, she spoke. "Oh, I am in trouble," she said, "terrible trouble. But I—there isn't anything anyone can do about it, but the police—and—somehow the policeman there at the post doesn't inspire me with much confidence."

White teeth flashed behind the black beard as the big man smiled. "No, ma'm, Rollo ain't no inspirin' sight, anyways you look at him. If Corporal Downey was here, or Constable Peters, it would be different. But they're both off on a long patrol. At that, ma'am, it's be'n my experience that things generally look worse than they really are. An' when they get so bad they can't get no worse, there's always a change for the better. S'pose I just set down here an' while we're eatin' our breakfast, you can tell me about it. Police, er no police, I think I can promise to be more help to you than Rollo."

Hardly had he seated himself, than Cush stepped into the room, paused abruptly in the doorway, scowled as he eyed the three, advanced into the room and without a word, seated himself at the next table and buried his face in a newspaper.

A waitress appeared from the kitchen and paused beside the table. Black John glanced up at her. "Couple of big thick steaks, couple dozen pancakes, plenty of butter an' syrup an' coffee." He glanced across at the woman. "What does the little fella like?" he asked.

"Oh, he just takes cereal of some kind, and milk, if they have it."

"Okay, sister," he said to the waitress, "fetch in a big dish of cereal, an' a quart er so of milk—an' real cow's milk, what I mean—nothin' out of a can. An' tell the cook to fry my steak damn near raw, an' find out how the lady likes hers."

As the girl turned away, the woman cleared her throat, nervously. "We lived in Colorado—my husband, and little Freddie, and I. He was a mining engineer, and he became involved in a venture that failed to pay out. He had sunk every cent we had in it and when the vein faulted out, we were busted flat. The men with whom my husband was associated realized that it was through no fault of his that the venture failed. They had every confidence in his honesty and his ability, and when he told them of another proposition he knew of that could be developed, they agreed to go in on it, provided my husband would put twenty thousand dollars of his own in. As I said, we were broke, so my husband told them he would try to raise the money within a year. He scraped together every cent he could get hold of and we came to Dawson, arriving here early this spring. My husband realized that trying to locate a good placer claim was a long shot—but it seemed the only way possible to get so much money.

"When we reached here, he bought a good tent, and the things necessary for me to keep house in it. We pitched it on the edge of town, then he got a prospecting outfit, gave me all the money he had left, and hit off up the Klondike.

"Two months later he came back. He had located a promising claim on a small feeder, and had sold it for twenty-five thousand dollars to a man named George Ingram, who was working a proposition on a nearby creek. Ingram said he could spare only fifteen thousand dollars at the time, but would pay the balance in September. Inquiry among some sourdoughs up the Klondike developed that George Ingram's word was as good as his bond, so my husband took his check for fifteen thousand.

When he presented it here at the bank, it was honored without question, and the bank officials also vouched for Ingram's integrity."

Black John nodded. "That's right, ma'm. I know George Ingram well. If he promises a thing, he'll do it, come hell or high water."

"So my husband stayed here in Dawson, waiting for September. About three weeks ago, he came home and picked up his prospecting outfit. He said he had run across a fellow who, hearing he was a mining engineer, wanted his opinion on a hard-rock proposition he had run onto somewhere back in the mountains." The woman paused, her voice faltered, and her eyes filled with tears. "Ten days later some men brought the body of my husband back to Dawson. They found it lodged among some rocks at the foot of a rapid. They also found pieces of the canoe, and my husband's pack."

"What become of the other fella—the one he went out with?"

"No one seems to know. The men found only the body of my husband."

"What fer lookin' was this other man?"

"I don't know. I never saw him. Then, just yesterday, Mr. Ingram came to see me. He had heard of my husband's death, and expressed deep sorrow. He told me he owed him ten thousand dollars, and had come to pay it. He asked me if I intended to remain here in Dawson, or return to the States."

IT THEN developed that the widow had told Ingram that she intended to take the first boat for the Outside. This was consistent with previous plans of her husband's—he had thought that as soon as he had collected his ten thousand dollars he would head back for Colorado and put the money in a hard-rock proposition.

From then on the story was somewhat confused. Ingram had pointed out to the engineer that if he were paid the ten thousand in gold, rather than cash, he could make a nice profit by cashing in the gold at the mint where it would bring twenty dollars and sixty-seven cents an ounce. In Dawson it was only worth sixteen dollars. The widow said her husband had jumped at the chance, figuring that the extra ounces would net him a clear profit of some twenty-nine hundred dollars.

Later on, after her husband's death—Ingram had told the woman that she could make even more by cashing in her deposited money for more gold dust, and she had agreed—without much hesitation, it seemed, though she did say something about having seen the royalty receipt issued by the policeman at detachment for the gold ounces she had received.

She had actually drawn fifteen thousand dollars out of the bank and paid the man after he had piled the gold in her tent from ten small sacks of nuggets.

"I found out that a steamboat was due upriver this afternoon," the widow continued, "so yesterday I sold the tent, and all my things, and carried the sacks to my room in the hotel. Then I went to the bank to draw what small balance I had left, and found that it amounted to only sixty dollars, which, with what I had realized from the sale of our belongings was not enough to pay our expenses back home. So I went to my room, and took some of the nuggets from one of the sacks, figuring to cash them at the bank for enough to meet our requirements." The woman paused, and again tears flooded her eyes. "It was then I found out that I had been swindled. The men at the bank examined the nuggets and told me they were iron pyrites—worthless rock, known as fool's gold.

"I hurried to the police detachment and reported the matter, and the young police man on duty there—the same one who had weighed in the nuggets and issued a gold royalty receipt for it—seemed rather cross about it—as though it were my fault, or something. He made some notes, and said the police would take the matter up, but, as the man had a day's start, it would probably be a long time before they could catch up with him."

BLACK JOHN nodded. "Yes, ma'm—it would be a long time before Rollo would catch up with him—a mighty long time. But I've got a hunch," he added grimly, "that when Downey comes back an' hears about this deal, it'll be a long time before anyone catches up with Rollo—the way he'll be goin'. No policeman with a brain in his head, but what would have known them sacks wasn't filled with gold, just by the weight of 'em."

"But," continued the woman, "you can see what a terrible position it places me in. Here we are, Freddie and I, stranded in Dawson, with no place to go, and only a few dollars to our name—and seemingly no chance for the police to get my money back from that swindler before the freeze-up." Her voice faltered and broke. "You said a while ago that things generally looked worse than they are—what could be worse than that?"

The big man smiled. "Now don't go losin' your nerve, ma'm. Things could be a lot worse. You've got your health. An' you've got your little boy. An' you've got them nuggets George Ingram gave you."

"Yes—but the men at the bank said they are worthless."

"Well, now—just because some men happens to work in a bank it don't necessarily mean that they know everything. In fact, I can rec'lect one banker that I had some dealin's with, not long ago, that proved to be plumb dumb about business matters. Them men at the bank might be wrong about them nuggets. An' maybe I was sort of malignin' Rollo, too. Maybe them nuggets are gold, after all. An' by the way, ma'm—what fer lookin' man is this George Ingram?"

"Why, he is a tall, dark man, with a sort of twitch in his eyes when he talks. But—I thought you said you knew him."

"Oh, shore, I know George, all right. I just wanted to make shore it was him that give you them nuggets for your husband's money."

"But of course—it must have been Mr. Ingram! Who else would give them to me? Who else would know about the deal?"

Black John nodded. "That's so, ma'm. Who would? You know I'd like to have a look at them nuggets, myself—not all of 'em—a handful would do. I've had quite a bit of experience with gold—prob'ly more than them clerks in the bank has. You said you packed 'em up to your room. Would you mind fetchin' a handful of 'em down here?"

"Why, certainly not! I'll go and get them, right now!"

As she disappeared, Cush, who had been an avid listener behind the newspaper that shielded his face, lowered the paper, and eyed Black John. "Quite a song an' dance she give you, wa'n't it? She's a damn good looker, too. By God, I'll bet you ten ounces, even money, she hooks you good an' proper! Any good-lookin' woman kin!"

"I'll take that bet."

"Huh—her claimin' George Ingram is a tall dark guy which his eyes twitches, when you know damn well George is short, an' light-haired an' them big blue eyes of his'n never twitched in their life!"

"That's so, Cush," Black John admitted. "Funny, I didn't rec'lect that. But—shut up! Here she comes!"

THE WOMAN resumed her seat, and laid a handful of metallic-looking lumps on the table. Black John examined them minutely, one by one as the woman watched him breathlessly. Presently he met her burning gaze with a smile. "You say the boat leaves for upriver today?"

"Yes, the *Hannah*. She is due to leave shortly after noon."

"Well, ma'm—you can catch her, if you want to. Them bank clerks was wrong. An' Rollo was right in collectin' the royalty an' issuin' that receipt. This is the real stuff, all right—an' I'll be glad to take it off your hands. I'm afraid you'll have to forget the profit you expected to make, because I can only pay you sixteen dollars an ounce—just what it's worth here. But that'll give you your twenty-five thousan'—just what George paid for the claim."

"You mean," cried the woman, her eyes wide with unbelief, "that this is really gold! And that you will pay me the money for it?"

Black John's smile widened. "I shore wouldn't pay no sech price for anything else but gold. I'll step over to the bank an' get the cash, an' you write out an assignment to me, John Smith, of the ten-thousan'-dollar balance George Ingram owed your husband."

"But—Mr. Ingram has already paid the debt, and I gave him a receipt in full."

"That's all right, ma'm. The assignment is only a matter of form. You can see for yourself that if George holds your receipt for the money, he shore ain't goin' to pay it again."

"That's so," the woman agreed. "I have a pen and paper in my room. I'll write out the assignment and have it ready when you get back from the bank." Gathering up the nuggets, she stepped from the room, followed by the little boy.

WHEN THEY had gone Cush frowned his disapproval. "Whilst yer over to the bank you better draw out them ten ounces, over an' above the twenty-five thousan'. My God—of all the damn fools I ever seen, you take the cake! Any good-lookin' woman kin take you fer anythin' she wants to. All she's got to do is look sad, an' jerk out a tear er two, an' tell some kind of a hard-luck story, an' you fall fer it, an' dig down an' shove her a bundle of bills! An' what the hell you gittin' out of it—with her hittin' fer the outside on the next boat?"

"Why, Cush, I'm gettin' the satisfaction of helpin' out a poor woman who was in trouble. Just think of her an' that little kid havin' to winter through in Dawson without no money to speak of. But about them ten ounces you mentioned. I ain't payin' that bet yet."

"Ain't payin' it! Say, ain't she jest took you fer twenty-five thousan'?"

Black John shook his head. "Not that I know of, she ain't. I won't know till I get an assay on them nuggets."

"An assay! Any damn fool kin see there ain't a grain of gold in a ton of that damn stuff!"

The big man grinned. "Yeah—but that's the trouble, Cush. I ain't a damn fool—so I can't see it like you do."

Proceeding to the bank, he drew out the cash, and returned to the hotel where he handed it to the woman in the lobby, and pocketed the assignment of the debt. Before accepting it, she glanced into his eyes. "But the gold—it's in my room. I'd rather you would step up there and see it, before I take the money."

"Oh, that's all right, ma'm. I know it'll be there when I want it. I know you wouldn't lie about it. Here—take the money—an' just remember what I told you—things generally look worse than they are."

"I'll certainly never forget that!" she beamed. "And—oh, just think—if you hadn't chanced upon me here and realized that I was in trouble, I might have believed those men in the bank, and thrown all that gold away!"

Black John nodded solemnly. "That's right, ma'm," he agreed. "You shore might. An' now, ma'm, if I was you, I'd take out what money you need for expenses, an' go over to the bank an' buy a draft on Seattle for the rest of it. It's a long trip outside, an' a rough one, an' twenty-five thousan' is quite a bit of cash for a woman to be packin'. There's too many doubtful characters scattered along the trail for you to take a chanct."

"I'll do just that," the woman replied, "and there are no words that will ever thank you enough for what you have done for me—and for Freddie. Only think of it, Mr. Smith—this morning I was in the very depths of despair. And now——"

"You don't owe me no thanks, ma'm. What I done ain't cost me a cent. You've got the cash, an' I've the gold. It's all the same." He paused and thrust out his hand. "Goodbye, ma'm—an' good luck to you—an' the little fella, too."

The woman took the hand and pressed it warmly. "Goodbye," she said. "I think you are a grand person." Drawing slightly closer she glanced toward Cush, who stood leaning against the desk apparently absorbed in studying the register. "Speaking of doubtful characters—if I were you I'd keep an eye on that man over there. He was seated at the next table during breakfast, and although he pretended to be absorbed in his newspaper, I got the impression that he was listening to every word I said. He may be waiting for a chance to make away with all that gold."

The big man followed her glance, and nodded solemnly. "Yes, ma'm," he agreed, in a voice that carried across the room, "he is a mighty doubtful-lookin' character, at that. Thanks for the tip. I'll keep an eye on him, all right. If anyone was to make off with that gold, they'll be sorry they done it—yes, ma'm—they shore will."

As the woman and little boy left the hotel and started for the bank, Black John sauntered over to the desk where Cush greeted him sourly. "So now yer a grand person, eh? Why the hell wouldn't you be? Anyone that was damn fool enough to fork over twenty-five thousan' in cash to me fer a hundred pound of purty colored rocks, I'd claim they was a grand person, too."

"She warned me against you, spotting you as a doubtful character, thus proving herself to be a young woman of extraordinary discernment and keen intuition in the analysis of human characteristics."

"Huh," Cush grunted, "if all them big words means she proved herself to be a damn slick article like all wimmin is, then I guess yer right. I gotta go over to the A.C. store, now an' git to work on them supplies. If I was you I'd hit over to the Tivoli an' set in a stud game an' try to git part of them twenty-five thousan' dollars back."

III

SHORTLY BEFORE THE noon hour Black John stepped into the Tivoli saloon and joined the little group of sourdoughs at the bar. "Fill 'em up," he invited, tossing a poke onto the bar. "Anyone seen George Ingram lately?"

Swiftwater Bill nodded. "Yeah. He's up the Klondike workin' a location he bought off 'n some minin' engineer that come in this spring an' hit it lucky on a feeder."

"He's the same fella Burr MacShane an' Henderson found floatin' around dead in that big eddy at the foot of them first rapids on Big Spruce," Bettles explained.

"If you want to see George," Swiftwater continued, "all you got to do is stick around a few days an' he'll be showin' up. He told me when I was up there, last month, that he had to come down in September an' pay this guy a ten-thousan'-dollar balance he owed on the location—an' when George promises a thing you kin bank on him makin' good."

"George'll have to pay the ten thousan' to the man's widder, now," Moosehide Charlie opined. "Her an' their little kid is livin' in a tent down a ways from the sawmill."

"That's kinda funny, too," Camillo Bill said. "I was down to the wharf when the *Hannah* pulled out a few minutes ago, an' I seen her an' the kid go aboard."

"Mebbe the bank give her the ten thousan' on George's say-so. He prob'ly give the guy a note, er somethin'."

Black John shook his head. "No, George didn't give him the scratch of a pen. He paid him fifteen thousan' down, an' promised to pay the rest in September. He checked up on George amongst some oldtimers, an' took his word. Fact is, I advanced the woman the ten thousan' this mornin', an' she give me an assignment of the debt. She was anxious to hit back to the States before the freeze-up, so I give her the money, an' she caught the boat."

"Kinda takin' a chanct, wasn't you?" Moosehide asked.

"Cripes, no! If George Ingram give his word, I'd take it, if it was a hundred thousan'."

"Not on George's word—on the woman's," Moosehide explained. "If she didn't have no note, or no promise wrote out an' signed, how'd you know George owed the ten thousan'?"

BLACK JOHN grinned. "Why, hell, Moosehide—don't you know that a woman as good-lookin' as her couldn't tell a lie no more'n George Washington could!"

"Huh," Moosehide grunted. "I've saw some damn good-lookin' wimmin' before now—an' I've heard 'em lie like hell. Fact is, I married one that could. That's why I'm up here. At that, though, she done me a good turn—not only I got shet of her, but I've done a damn sight better here than I'd ever done drivin' a dray, back home."

"Kinda funny about that guy gettin' drownded, at that," Bettles opined. "If he was jest stickin' around Dawson waitin' fer George to come down an' pay him—what was he doin' up Big Spruce, alone? Big Spruce is damn rough water fer anyone—let alone a *chechako*."

"It ain't no cinch he was alone," Moosehide said. "Three, four evenin's before they found this guy's body, I seen him talkin' to Bat Eye Cantrill over by the lumber piles."

"Bat Eye Cantrill!" Bettles exclaimed. "I didn't think he'd dare show up around here, what with Downey wantin' to question him about that Seth Brownley robbery over on Anvil Crick."

"That's right," Swiftwater Bill agreed. "But Bat Eye's cagey, all right. He don't show up around here, but at that, he slips in an' out of the Klondike Palace, now an' then. I figger mebbe Cuter Malone sort of tips him off to some dirty job he kin pull. Both Downey an' Peters are off up the McQuesten, an' Bat Eye could know that. It might be, too, that he know'd about George Ingram payin' that guy the fifteen thousan', an' got him to go along up Big Spruce on some kind of a proposition, an' then knocked him off, figgerin' he might have the fifteen thousan' on him."

Bettles shook his head. "I'd kinda doubt that. In the first place, how could he know about George payin' the guy the fifteen thousan'? An' even if he did, it was quite a while back, an' he wouldn't figger he'd be carryin' that much around in his pocket."

"Bat Eye could know all about George payin' over that money," Swiftwater Bill said, "an' he could know that he aimed to come down here this month an' pay him the balance, too. Because he worked fer George up there on the claim, ever sence George bought it—before that, even. He was workin' fer him on another location clost by, when George bought this one."

"Mebbe," Moosehide opined, "he thought George had already paid the ten thousan', an' he might git it."

"Who is this here Bat Eye Cantrill?" asked Black John, who had been an interested listener. "I don't seem to place him."

"Bat Eye, he's a bad actor," Camillo Bill replied. "He showed up this spring. He's suspected of pullin' off several robberies along the cricks. Downey jest about got the goods on him fer that Seth Brownley job."

"What fer lookin' is he?" Black John inquired. "Just in case he might take a notion to show up on Halfaday."

Bettles chuckled. "Oh, he'll be showin' up there when Downey begins crowdin' him. He's a tall, dark-complected guy that's always sort of battin' his eyes when he talks. An' you don't need to worry—he'll be showin' up, all right. A guy like him couldn't no more stay off'n Halfaday than a flea could stay off'n a dog."

"Thanks fer the compliment," Black John grinned. "Just for that, I'll buy another drink."

When the laughter had subsided, Camillo Bill scowled. "If Downey could corner Lafe Toms an' git him to talk, he could forgit the Seth Brownley case an' go after Bat Eye right. But Lafe won't talk. First place, he's afraid of what Bat Eye would do to him, if the case misfired an' some damn jury would turn him loose. An' agin, he's afraid that Bat Eye would lie the whole thing off on him, an' he'd git hung.

"It's like this—Lafe was workin' fer a guy name of Jake Tozzer, down on Birch Crick. He worked all winter fer him on a feeder, an' along this spring, Bat Eye shows up an' locates on another feeder up a little ways from Tozzer. Lafe says after they cleaned up the dump this spring Tozzer must of had damn clost to four thousan' ounces in his cache. Bat Eye, he wasn't doin' so good on his location. He goes down to Forty Mile an' comes back with five, six quarts of licker, an' he stops into Tozzer's an' the three of 'em starts in on it.

"Accordin' to Lafe, they all got pretty full, an' the more Tozzer an' Bat Eye drunk, the meaner they got. Lafe got kinda scairt, an' he told Tozzer he was goin' to quit, an' asks fer his pay, which he had sixty-three ounces comin'. Tozzer, he cussed him out, an' wound up by goin' out to his cache an' gittin' the dust. He says, Bat Eye slipped out of the cabin right after Tozzer did, an' come back in before Tozzer got back—so he figgers Bat Eye could of located the cache. Lafe had a couple more drinks an' then throws his stuff in his pack an' hit out fer Forty Mile. But it's damn near dark, an' he was pretty drunk by that time, so about a quarter of a mile down the crick he rolls up in his blankets an' hits the hay.

"There's a little crick comes in clost to where he camped in a spruce thicket fer the night, an' a big beaver dam on it that backs the water up in a deep pond. Along about daylight, next mornin', Lafe hears a noise, an' he peeks out an' sees Bat Eye had landed this canoe at the foot of the beaver dam on this side crick. He sees Bat Eye lift his pack out of the canoe, an' he says it's all he kin do to lift it—it was that heavy. Then he lifts out a long bundle rolled up in a blanket. He drags the canoe up over the dam. Then he carried the long bundle up to the top of the dam an' lays it down, an' hunts up a heavy rock, an ties it to the bundle, an' loads it in the canoe an' paddles out to the middle of the pond, an' throws it overboard. Then he comes back, drags the canoe back into the river, loads his pack in it, an' hits downstream.

"Lafe waits a while, an' then goes back to Tozzer's cabin. There ain't no one there, an' Tozzer's cache is empty. Out by the woodpile he finds a chunk of stovewood with some blood an' hairs stickin' to it. So he gits to hell outa there, pronto."

"Howcome you know this?" Black John asked.

"Lafe told me. He was hangin' around Fortymile, this summer, snipin' the bars, an' pannin' out jest about wages. I'd know'd him fer a long time, an' I camped alongside of him one night, an' seen there was somethin' on his mind, so I asked him what the trouble was, an' he told me. I advised him to go right to Downey with it, but he damn near throw'd a fit. 'Not by a damn sight!' he hollers. 'Bat Eye, he's smart, an' he'd lie out of it, shore as hell. He'd lie it onto me, claimin' I was the one that done it, what with workin' fer Tozzer all winter, I'd know where his cache was at, an' all. Or even if they arrested Bat Eye, they wouldn't have no hell of a good case an' if the jury turned him loose he'd hunt me up an' knock me off shore.'

"I seen how he was prob'ly right, so I never said nothin' to Downey, 'cause I'd shore hate to see Lafe hung fer somethin' that damn Bat Eye pulled off. Lafe ain't none too smart, an' some lawyer could git him all balled up, while Bat Eye could prob'ly lie out of it, an' have an iron-clad alibi worked out to boot. An' besides that old Jake wasn't no hell of a loss no way you'd look at him. Be'n in the country ever sence the Yukon wasn't nothin' but a crick. Ornery old cuss, what with peddlin' hooch to the Siwashes an' the like of that."

"Yeah," Bettles agreed, "an' there's plenty of us old-timers figgers it wasn't no one else but Jake that knocked off Tom Cole years ago on the Porcupine."

"Where's this Lafe at, now?" Black John asked.

"Oh, he's prob'ly still down around Fortymile. He hangs out down there most of the time."

LATE IN the afternoon Cush joined the party, more drinks were had, and shortly Bettles pointed toward a man who had just entered the room. "Speak of the devil, an' up he pops—there's George Ingram, now! Come on over here, George, an belly up!"

As the man joined them, Black John grinned.

"Yeah, belly up, George, an' shuck out that ten thousan' you owe me."

Ingram returned the smile. "Yeah—who says I owe you ten thousan'—an' what for?"

"This paper says so," the big man replied, laying the assignment signed by the woman on the bar. "The lady said you owed it to her husband, but bein' as he's dead, you owed it to her, an' as she was anxious to pull out on the *Hannah*, I shoved the ten thousan'."

Ingram glanced at the paper, and nodded. "Okay. I heard about 'em findin' his body on Big Spruce. Too bad. He was a good fella. Here's your ten thousan'," he added, counting the money onto the bar. "You took me for half what I draw'd out of the bank, figgerin' on settin' in a game, tonight."

"Oh, we'll set in a game, all right," Black John smiled, "an' I'll try to get the other ten thousan', on top of it."

"Even then you'd still be took," Cush said. "You better fork over them ten ounces."

"I ain't payin' that bet, yet," Black John said. "You wait till I'm through with this deal."

Bettles laughed. "Has someone be'n takin' Black John?" he asked.

"Oh, shore—any good-lookin' woman kin take him," Cush replied. "He jest got ten thousan' of it back off'n George—but she's still into him fer fifteen thousan'."

"How's that?" Swiftwater Bill asked.

"The transaction was a rather complicated one, which would take too long to explain," Black John replied.

"Complicated—hell!" Cush scoffed. "He give her twenty-five thousan', cash money, fer ten sacks of the damndest lookin' stuff you ever seen—fool's gold—that's what it was. I jest come from the *ho*tel, an' you'd ort to hear the clerk cussin' on account he had to carry the damn stuff outa her room an' throw it out back. I bet John ten ounces she'd take him, when I first seen him eyein' her there in the dinin' room—an' she done it—an' now the damn cuss won't pay his bet."

Bettles laughed. "How about it, John?"

"As I said, the transaction is so complicated that it is not yet concluded. When it's over with, the bet will be paid—Cush don't need to worry about that." He turned to Ingram. "By the way, George, did you have a fella workin' for you this summer, name of Bat Eye Cantrill?"

"Yeah, I hired him late in the spring. He jest quit a couple of weeks ago."

"Good man, was he?"

"No, I wouldn't call him a good man. Men were scarce up the river, or I'd never have hired him. He's no one I'd trust very far."

"Did he know about that deal you made with the *chechako* you bought the location from—that woman's husband?"

"Oh, shore. He knew about it. In fact, he was right there when I bought it. Why?"

"Oh, nothin'. I was just wonderin'. Come on, let's get supper over with, an' get that game goin'. I'm hungry."

IV

THE STUD GAME lasted till far into the night and as the two headed for the hotel Black John turned to Cush. "You about ready to hit out fer Halfaday?" he asked.

"Hell, no! It'll be four, five days yet, what with pickin' out all the stuff I need, an' then dickerin' to git it freighted up to the fort."

"Okay. Then I'll just slip out in the mornin' an' look over a proposition I heard about down Fortymile way. I'd ort to be back about the time you're ready to hit out fer Halfaday."

Cush slanted him a glance. "Is she good-lookin'?" he asked.

"Is who good-lookin'? What the hell you talkin' about?"

"This here proposition you heard about down to Fortymile. If she is, an' you'd pay up yer other bet, I'll go you ten more ounces you'll git took agin."

"Why, you damn fool! There's no woman mixed up in this. It's a proposition that might pay off pretty good."

"Huh, you know jest as well as I do there ain't nothin' doin' down around Fortymile, no more. All the good locations has be'n took up—like Sam Amery on Fortymile, an' old Jake Tozzer on Birch Crick. Fer's new propositions goes, Fortymile's dead."

"Jake Tozzer's dead, too, accordin' to the talk. Got murdered along in the spring."

"That's one good thing about the Fortymile country anyhow. Jake was as ornery as they make 'em."

"Howcome you knew Jake?"

"I never know'd him. Never even seen him. But that *klooch* of mine, she's told me about how old Jake used to sell hooch to the Siwashes. She claimed it was Jake's rotten hooch that killed her pa."

Black John nodded. "Yeah, accordin' to the talk, Jake ain't mourned none. The more of his kind that get knocked off, the better it is for the country. But in spite of you claimin' Fortymile's dead, I'm goin' down there an' look this proposition over. There might be somethin' in it."

"There better be fifteen thousan', an' ten ounces to boot in it, if you aim to break even on this trip," Cush replied, as they reached the hotel. "But don't be gone more'n four, five days. I shore don't want to hang around here waitin' on you."

INQUIRY AT Bergman's saloon in Forty Mile revealed that Lafe Toms was sniping the bars on a creek some ten miles up the river, where Black John found him the following day frying bacon over a little fire in front of his tent. "Your name Lafe Toms?" he asked, as the man looked up from forking over the bacon in the pan.

"Yeah. That's me."

"My name's John Smith—Black John, they call me, on account of my whiskers bein' that color."

"Black John Smith!" the man exclaimed. "So you're him, eh? The king of them outlaws that hangs out on Halfaday Crick! Glad to know you. I've heer'd about you. Bettles, an' Camillo Bill, an' Moosehide Charlie, an' Burr MacShane—all the sourdoughs claims to know you."

"Oh, shore. Fine bunch of men, them sourdoughs—providin' you don't set in a stud game with 'em. Fact is, it's on the word of Camillo Bill I come down here to hunt you up. You worked for Jake Tozzer all winter, an' on into the spring, didn't you?"

The man hesitated for a moment. "Yeah," he said, finally. "I was workin' fer Jake."

"Well, the talk is around Dawson amongst some of Jake's friends, that Jake got knocked off this spring, an' that you're the one that done it. Corporal Downey an' Constable Peters is off on a patrol way up the McQuesten, but when they come back these friends of Jake's are goin' to demand an investigation."

The man seemed to turn a shade paler. "It's a damn lie! I never done it!" he cried. "But if the police gits to nosin' around there, they might claim it was me—an' how the hell could I prove it worn't? It was Bat Eye Cantrill knocked him off! That's who done it!"

"Did you see him do it?"

"No, but I seen him sink Jake in a beaver dam, next mornin', an' make off with all the dust in Jake's cache—right around four thousan' ounces, it was! Bat Eye, he was workin' a claim above

Jake's, an' he wasn't doin' no good. He went down to Forty Mile, along in the spring, an' when he come back he fetched a lot of licker, an' he stopped into Jake's an' we started drinkin'. Jake an' Bat Eye got to quarrelin', an' the more they drunk, the ornerier they got. I got scairt an quit, an' Jake paid me off, an' I hit out fer Fortymile, but it was comin' on night, an' I was pretty well oiled, so I camped a little ways down the crick, an' in the mornin' I seen Bat Eye run his canoe ashore at the foot of a beaver dam that backs up the water of a little crick that runs in there—an' I seen him lift Jake's dust out, an' then carry Jake up to the top of the dam an' wire a rock to him, an' paddle out an' sink him. Then he drug his canoe back into Birch Crick an' loaded Jake's dust in it, an' hit off down the crick."

"You saw Jake, an' saw the dust, I s'pose?"

"Well, I seen him h'ist his pack outa the canoe, so damn heavy he couldn't hardly lift it. An' I seen him sink this here long bundle wropped up in some blankets. I went back to Jake's cabin after Bat Eye had went down the crick, an' Jake worn't there an' his cache was empty, an' I found a chunk of stovewood with blood an' hair—gray hair, like Jake's—stickin' to it. What I claim—if it worn't Jake an' his dust in that bundle an' that pack, what the hell was it? An' where the hell was they?"

"Your deduction seems logical."

"My which seems what?"

"I was goin' on to say that Camillo Bill slipped me the word that you told him the same story you just told me. He believes you've told the truth, an' so do I. But as you p'inted out, the police might not believe it. Especially, if Bat Eye would hear about the investigation, an' hunt Downey up, an' tell the story the other way around—that it was him laid in the brush an' watched you sink Jake in the beaver dam an' make off with the dust. I don't know this Bat Eye personally, but they tell me he's a pretty slick article."

"Yeah, he's smart, all right, Bat Eye is. Cripes—if he'd tell it like that to the police, I might even git hung!"

Black John nodded. "Yeah, that's what I figgered. That's why I come down here to find you. I've got the reputation of bein' an outlaw. But I've also got the reputation of sometimes helpin' someone out who's in trouble."

"That's right!" the man exclaimed eagerly. "That's what the sourdoughs all claim. Well, I'm in trouble, all right! An', by God, if Downey comes back, an' Bat Eye gits to him an' lies that murder off on me, I'll git hung—an' then it'll be too late to help me!"

"Your postulate seems tenable," Black John smiled.

"My which seems what, again? Yer allus sayin' that somethin' I don't even know I've got seems like somethin' I never heer'd tell of."

"Puttin' it another way, what I mean is, that you better hit for Halfaday Crick an' lay low there till this thing sort of blows over. You'll be safe there. The police hardly ever shows up on Halfaday, an' if one should, all you'll have to do is slip over acrost the line into Alaska, an' wait till he goes back."

"But where's this here Halfaday Crick at? How'll I git there?"

"You can handle a canoe, can't you?"

"Oh, shore. I'm good in a canoe."

"You're all set, then. It happens that Cush is in Dawson. He runs the tradin' post an' saloon on Halfaday. He'll be ready to go back about the time we hit Dawson. He ain't worth a damn in a canoe alone. We came down together, but I've got a little business to 'tend to before goin' back, so if you'll go back with Cush an' handle the canoe, it'll be a break for both of you."

"I'll say it will!" the man agreed heartily. "An' you come clean down here from Dawson jest to help me out of this here trouble—when you didn't even know me?"

"Oh, shore. Accordin' to Camillo Bill, you're a good sort of guy—an' I'd hate like hell to see an innocent man hung. What I claim—it never hurts to do a man a good turn. There may come a time when I'll need one myself."

"Well, if I git outs this here jam, an' you ever need a good turn, jest you holler, an' I'll come runnin'—even if it's clean down to Afriky!"

"Okay. We'll get busy now, an' throw your stuff together, an' hit out for Dawson. I wonder where this Bat Eye Cantrill hangs out? I'd sort of like to see what he looks like—just in case he'd ever take a notion to show up on Halfaday. We shore don't want no murderers like him living on the crick."

"I don't know where he's at. I ain't saw him sence that mornin' he shoved off down Birch Crick. But that night whilst we was drinkin' together in Jake's cabin, seems like he claimed he' had him a *klooch* he hid out with down to Moosehide. He kinda bragged that he'd pulled off some dust-stealin' jobs, an' then he'd go down an' hide out with this here *klooch* till things blow'd over. Claimed it was clost enough to Dawson so's he could sneak up there nights an' git the dope on how things was goin' from Cuter Malone."

V

ARRIVING IN DAWSON late the following evening, Black John swerved the canoe ashore at the abandoned sawmill. "You better camp here while I hunt Cush up an' find out when he's ready to hit for Halfaday. It's jest as well if no one sees you around here, 'specially with me or Cush. If there's a stink raised about Tozzer gettin' knocked off, an' someone told Downey he saw you with one of us, he'd hit right out for Halfaday. If everyone thinks you're somewheres on the Fortymile, Downey might fool around down there huntin' you till hell knows when."

Seated in the lobby of the hotel, Cush glanced up from his newspaper as Black John stepped into the room.

He eyed the big man over the top of his square-framed spectacles. "It's about time you was showin' up," he said. "I be'n over to the Tivoli three, four times sence supper, figgerin' you might go there instid of here when you got back. How much did she take you fer?"

Black John grinned. "Not much this time. I got off lucky. Fact is, Cush, I've got to stick around here for a day or so yet—"

"By Cripes!" Cush interrupted. "I ain't a-goin' to hang around here no longer! I finished up my business this mornin', an' if you'd of be'n here we'd of pulled out then. What with One Armed John runnin' things up there, I'll be damn lucky to have the fort left when I git back."

The big man's grin widened. "Oh, I don't know, Cush. Far's I can see, One Arm's as honest as men of his caliber are apt to be. His peculations would hardly amount to more than petty pilfering."

"I don't know a nothin' about his speculations—but give a man time an' he could petty pilfer the hull damn outfit! I'm hittin' out, come daylight, if I've got to hire me a paddler."

"I surmised that if your business was concluded, you'd be in a sweat to get goin', so I made an arrangement that will work out perfectly. This party that I went down to Fortymile to see, will be glad to accompany you to Halfaday and handle the canoe."

"Not by a damn sight! I ain't hittin' out with no woman no matter how good lookin' she is! I've be'n took three times a'ready—an' that's enough! The only one I ever married that was worth a damn, up an' died on me. An' when she done that, I says I'm through with wimmin from now on—an' I am! An' besides that, we don't want no wimmin of no kind on Halfaday. There ain't no one kin raise hell with a crick like a woman. You know that as well as I do—an' here yer tryin' to make me fetch one in!"

BLACK JOHN'S grin became an audible chuckle. "It has be'n my experience that a conclusion that was jumped at is rarely as tenable as one arrived at by logical deduction."

"Yeah, an' it's be'n my experience that all the big words you kin think up ain't a-goin' to make me hit out fer Halfaday with no woman—black, white, yaller, or red!"

"The party I referred to don't happen to be a woman. He's a man. Camillo Bill told me about him. Lafe Toms, his name is, an' he's a good guy—not too wide between the ears—but hard-workin' an' honest. He's in a jam on account of bein' suspected of knockin' off Jake Tozzer this spring—"

"Huh—if he done that I'd like him, even if he wasn't honest," Cush opined.

"That's ondoubtless the proper attitude, but as a matter of fact, he didn't murder Tozzer, but he's damn liable to swing for it on circumstantial evidence, bolstered up by the testimony of the damn cuss that pulled off the job. Downey's away an' it might be quite a while before he gets back. My idea is to slip Lafe up to Halfaday an' let him hole up in One Eyed John's cabin, while I sort of look around a little. After listenin' to Camillo's story, I sort of figgered that if I could locate Tozzer's murderer, I'd save Downey quite a lot of trouble, save an innocent man from the gallows, do society in general a good turn—an' just possible net some slight profit on the transaction."

Cush grunted. "Huh—this here slight profit you aim to make couldn't be the main reason, an' them other items a kind of a side-line, could it?"

"Again, I must p'int out that you're jumpin' to a conclusion."

"Yeah—well I'm a-goin' to jump to bed, too. I want to git goin' by daylight. Where's this here Lafe Toms at?"

"He's camped down to the sawmill. My canoe's there. Slip down there in the mornin', an' you'll find Lafe waitin'. I'll remain here for the present. But I'll reach Halfaday anon, as the poet would say. An' in the meantime, methinks I'll hie me to the Tivoli an' woo the gentle goddess of fortune."

"Huh, them goddesses down to Cuter Malone's Klondike Palace woos a damn sight easier'n what the cards does—'specially

174

with them sourdoughs settin' behind 'em. If I wasn't too sleepy to set up an' keep cases on you, I'd bet you ten ounces, daylight'll find you slippin' out of the Klondike Palace—an' not the Tivoli."

Black John frowned. "Why, my good man, do you mean to impugn my veracity?"

"I might if I knowed how," Cush retorted. "What I'm gittin' at is—you don't git down here so damn often—an' you kin play a hell of a lot of stud on Halfaday. Good night. I'm a-goin' to bed."

VI

BLACK JOHN PLAYED stud all night, and in the morning he slipped down to Moosehide, the Siwash village located on the river bank some four miles below Dawson, proceeding directly to the shack of Owl Man, an Indian he had once saved from drowning. When the door opened in answer to his knock, he stepped into the room and seated himself on a rude bench. "Long time no see," he said. "How they comin'?"

"I'm git 'long a'ri'. Ketch de feesh. Summer 'bout forty dog. Som'tam work 'roun—chop de wood—help wit the sluicin. How you be?"

"Oh, I manage to scrape along, somehow. Work my claim—a little of this—a little of that."

The Indian smiled. "Me, I'm t'ink dat more 'leetle dis, leetle dat' dan work de claim—eh?"

The big man scowled. "What the hell do you mean by that?"

The other shrugged. "Me—I'm wish I'm smart, lak you—I ain' got to work, nieder. W'at you want me do, now?"

"Just want to ask you a question—that's all. Do you know a man named Bat Eye Cantrill?"

The man hesitated, his glance fleeting swiftly from door to window. He shook his head. "No, me—I'm ain' know no one lak dat."

"You're a damn liar! Come across, now, an' tell me the truth, or I'll just drag you down to the rivet an' throw you in where I pulled you out, that time. You know Bat Eye—an' you know where he's at, right now. So do I. He's hidin' out with some *klooch*, right here in the village. You know what *klooch*. I don't. But you're goin' to tell me."

Again the man's eyes rolled furtively. "Dat Bat Eye—she dam' bad mans. She keel me sure lak hell, if I'm tell you w'ere she stay."

"No, he won't. Listen—did I ever lie to you?"

"No."

"Ain't you done a lot of things for me you didn't want to—an' didn't you always come out all right—an' get well paid, to boot?"

The Indian nodded.

"Okay then. You'll come out all right this time, too. An' I'll pay you five ounces. This Bat Eye might be tough—but you know damn well I'm tougher. You'd a damn sight better have Bat Eye on your tail than me.

"Here's what I want you to do. You go an' tell Bat Eye there's a guy in your shack from Cuter Malone's that wants to see him. Tell him it's important, an' to come right over here."

"Bat Eye, she no b'lieve dat. Cuter, she know w'ere Bat Eye hang out. He sen' de man to Minnie Claw house."

"Guess that's right," Black John agreed. "Well, you show me where this Minnie Claw lives, an' I'll give you the five ounces." The two stepped outside, and Owl Man pointed to a shack a short distance away. Smoke curled from the stovepipe. "Bat Eye, she dere, a'ri'. I'm see heem go een de house las' night."

Proceeding to the shack, Black John tapped on the door. Receiving no answer, he rapped louder, and presently the door opened a few inches and a young Indian woman peered out at him from between narrowed lids. "W'at you want?" she snapped.

"Tell Bat Eye there's a guy here from Cuter Malone's that wants to see him."

176

"Ain' no Bat Eye here. Me—I'm ain' know no Bat Eye."

"Don't lie to me! You're Minnie Claw, ain't you? Cuter knows where Bat Eye hangs out. He told me I'd find him here. I've got to see him."

The door slammed shut, and a few moments later was thrown open and Black John found himself face to face with a tall, dark man, whose amber-colored eyes peered sharply at him from between lids that opened and closed with a nervous twitch. "Who are you," the man growled, "an' what do you want?"

"Cuter tipped me off to where you was," the big man answered, noting that the other's right hand held a revolver half-concealed by his thigh. "You can put up the artillery. Smith, the name is—John Smith, better known in these parts as Black John."

The amber eyes suddenly widened and blinked rapidly. "You Black John Smith that runs that gang of outlaws up on Halfaday Crick? Well, come on inside. Glad to know you!"

Rummaging in a cupboard, the man produced a bottle, and two glasses which he placed on the table, seated himself, and indicated an empty chair. "Draw up, an' set, an' have a drink. What's on yer mind?"

BLACK JOHN seated himself, filled his glass from the bottle and glanced toward the *klooch* who stood near the stove eyeing the two sullenly. "She savvies English," he said. "Maybe we better go outside."

"To hell with goin' outside. Let her go." He turned to the woman. "Git out," he ordered. "Go on over to yer sister's an' stay there till I tell you to come back. I an' this guy's gonna make medicine."

Without a word the woman sidled from the room, and Bat Eye picked up his glass. "Here's lookin' at you," he said, as both downed the liquor. "Fill 'em up again," he invited. "It's your turn to talk."

"It's like this," Black John began, when the glasses were refilled. "A while back a guy shows up on Halfaday claimin' his name is Lafe Toms. He's a smallish sort of a guy without no more in under his hat than what it takes to get along. He locates on a feeder, an' shows up now an' then at Cush's—Cush he runs a saloon an' tradin' post on the crick—an' one evenin' him an' I an' Cush got to h'istin a few, an' Cush, he happens to say how he heard down to Dawson that some old fella down on Birch Crick, name of Jake Tozzer had disappeared along in the spring, an' some of his friends was aimin' to get the police to investigate.

"Well, Lafe, he sorts of gags on his licker, an' looks kind of scairt like, an' then he says that's why he hit for Halfaday. He heard the same talk down around Dawson, an' bein' as he was known to have be'n working for Tozzer, he was afraid the police would lay it onto him, if they figgered Tozzer had got knocked off. He claimed he never done it, but said he knows who did. Then he up an' tells us that one day this spring you came along with some hooch, an' the three of you got to hittin' her up, an' you an' Tozzer got ugly, an' he quit an' hit out for Fortymile. But bein' as it was late, an' he was pretty well loaded, he didn't get no more'n a quarter of a mile, an' camped in the bresh. In the mornin' he says he saw you come along in a canoe, lift a heavy pack out, which he figgers had Tozzer's dust in it, an' then he saw you lift out a long bundle wrapped in a blanket, carry it to the top of a beaver dam on a feeder that run in there, an' wire a rock to it, an' float it out onto the pond in the canoe, an' sink it. Then you dragged the canoe back into Birch Crick, an' hit out, takin' the heavy pack along with you. He says he went back to Tozzer's, but he wasn't there, an' his cache had be'n robbed."

As the big man talked, the other listened intently, as his eyes flikkered and twitched, and the scowl deepened on his face.

"He's a damn liar!" Bat Eye cried. "He told the story all right—only he told it wrong end to! What come off was like this—I stopped in to Jake's place, all right, an' I fetched along some licker, an' we drunk a lot of it, jest like Lafe claimed. Only it was him an' Jake got to augerin' about how much Lafe had comin'. Lafe, he wanted to quit, an' Jake wouldn't pay him. I seen there might be trouble, so I hit out fer my claim a little ways above Jake's. In the mornin' I got to wonderin' if everything was all right down there, so I slips down the crick. There ain't no one to Jake's, an' I hunted around an' found a place in the rocks where it looked like Jake's cache had be'n—but the hole was empty, an' then I found a chunk of firewood which it had blood an' gray hairs stickin' to it where Lafe had throw'd it after brainin' Jake. Well, it worn't none of my funeral, so I went back to my claim."

"Didn't go down to Fortymile an' report it, eh?"

"Not by a damn sight, I didn't! I didn't want the damn police snoopin' around there, 'cause there was quite a few in Bergman's saloon when I bought them six quarts, an' hit out fer Birch Crick. How'd I know the police wouldn't figger mebbe me an' Jake got to drinkin' an' I knocked him off? They might figger I knocked Lafe off, too—an' him not around there. The fewer police there is snoopin' around a place, the better I like it."

Black John nodded. "Yeah, we don't encourage police snoopin' on Halfaday, neither." He paused, downed his drink, and smiled. "Well, if that's the way of it, it looks like I've had my trip for nothin'."

"What do you mean—fer nothin'? Cripes, you tipped me off about what that damn Lafe Toms is blabbin' around, didn't you? I shore take it kind of you to come clean down here to tip me off. What I'd ort to do is hit fer Halfaday Crick an' blast that damn Lafe to hell, 'fore he goes ahead an' spills his guts to the police."

"The precaution would have its merits," Black John opined. "But what I meant about makin' this trip for nothin', is that I'm sorry to hear that you ain't the one that knocked Jake off. I must confess that I didn't come down here to tip you off to what Lafe was spreadin' around. Offhand, I wouldn't have deemed it any of my business. The reason I hunted you up is that the way Lafe told it, it looked to me like a damn smart piece of work. An' I figgered that a guy that could get away with a job of that kind would be a good man to have on Halfaday. You see, I run things up there, an' I'm always on the lookout for talent. We've got some damn good men in our gang, but we're always on the lookout for more." He paused and shoved his chair slightly back from the table. "Well—no harm done, I s'pose. Kind of sorry to hear it was Lafe, himself, pulled that job—because, from what I've seen of him, I don't figger he's smart enough to fill the bill."

BAT EYE cleared his throat roughly. "H-e-e-m, don't be in no hurry. Drink up, an' have another. Fact is, I've heard a lot about you boys up there on Halfaday Crick. An' how the police don't dast to show up there. An' how you pull off some big jobs, an' allus git away with it. An' how you hang anyone that tries to horn in on you." He paused and grinned. "Accordin' to Cuter Malone, you've took him fer plenty, a time er two—an' Cuter ain't no easy mark, at that."

"That's right," Black John admitted. "An' that's just why we've got to have smart guys in the gang."

"Tellin' you about me, I'd shore like to jine up with you, I've figgered on hittin' out fer Halfaday, one of these times, an' try to make a deal with you boys."

Black John shook his head. "It wouldn't hardly be worth yer while. We don't take on no one without he's had considerable experience along—well, along certain lines—if you get what I mean. We don't sign on no novices."

Bat Eye's thin lips twisted into a smile. "Let me tell you, brother—I ain't no novice. Not in no man's language, I ain't. Fact is, that damn Lafe Toms told you the truth—about how it was me knocked Jake Tozzer off an' got away with his dust. Four thousan' an six ounces is what I got—an' that ain't no chicken feed. But, at that, if I'd know'd Lafe was layin' in the bresh an' watchin' me sink Jake in that beaver pond, by God, I'd of knocked him off too—an' fed the both of 'em to the beavers."

Black John frowned. "Of course, you wantin' to join up with us, like you claim you do—it's easy to set there an' change yer tune."

"Hell—I'd be'n a damn fool to admit it, wouldn't I—when there wasn't no reason to?"

"Well, yes. Takin' it by an' large, as the sayin' goes, I s'pose a man wouldn't set around, offhand, an' brag about a murder."

"Yer damn right, he wouldn't—if he had all his buttons!"

"Talk's cheap, Bat Eye. I couldn't hardly set here an' take yer word for it, without I had some proof. What I'm huntin' for is a man that's got guts an' brains—not just a damn liar."

"I've got the proof, all right. I've got better'n three thousan', nine hundred of them ounces of Tozzer's cached, right now. Is that proof enough?"

Black John nodded. "Yes, I'd say that would be proof enough that you pulled off that job—provided you could produce the ounces. But I was just thinkin', even admittin' you pulled that job, maybe you're a one-job man. I don't like one-job men. Anyone might pull one job an' be lucky enough to get away with it—even a damn fool might do that. In my business I need men of experience. An' you can see for yourself that pullin' one job don't give a man no hell of a lot of experience, even if he got away with it."

"Oh, I've pulled other jobs—plenty of 'em. I robbed Seth Brownley on Anvil Crick, an' Jim Kirch on Hunker. An' only a couple of days ago I took a woman right there in Dawson fer fifteen thousan', cash money. Had to knock off her husban' to make the play. He sold a claim up the Klondike to a guy name of George Ingram. I was workin' fer George at the time. I know'd he had to make the final payment in September, so a couple of weeks ago I quit an' come on down to Dawson, where this guy was waitin' fer his money. He's a minin' engineer, so I gets him to go off up Big Spruce Crick to look over a hard-rock proposition, an' I knocks him off, makin' it look like he'd got drownded in a rapids, then I sacks up about a hundred pound of fool's gold, an' hits back to Dawson an' pays gold royalty on the damn stuff to a rookie policeman, an' then I hunts up this guy's widder, an' claimin' I'm George Ingram, which she hadn't never saw, I offers to pay her the balance in gold, which she kin cash in for more in the States. I not only pays off the balance George owed her, but I takes her fer the original payment he made, by sellin' her the rest of the fool's gold. How's that fer smart? Oh, I've got the experience, all right. I kin work on men er wimmin, either one."

"Pullin' off an intricate proposition like that shows you've got somethin', all right. But as the Good Book says, I'm from Missouri. I'd sort of like to see the proof of that deal."

"I kin prove it, all right," the man replied, as he removed a money-belt from beneath his shirt and tossed it onto the table. "The fifteen thousan' is in there along with the signed receipt. Count it."

BLACK JOHN counted the money, glanced at the receipt, and nodded slowly. "Okay, Bat Eye, I guess that proves it beyond any doubt. You're just the man I'm lookin' for. Yes, sir—just the kind of a guy I like to have show up on Halfaday. I sometimes have a hard time gettin' holt of the right man. A lot of 'em drifts in on us—but they drift on again."

"You don't need to worry about me. I know what side my bread's buttered on. By God, onct I git up there, I'll stay!"

The big man regarded him thoughtfully. "That's right, Bat Eye, I believe you will. Yes, sir, from what I've seen an' heard, I'd be willin' to bet that you'll be on Halfaday a long, long time. A lot of the boys has be'n there quite a while, already."

"I'll bet I'll stay there as long as any of 'em," the man boasted.

Black John nodded. "Somehow, I believe you're right. But there's one thing I forgot to tell you. You know, we've got a good gang up there on Halfaday. Well, while I'm generally credited with runnin' this gang, the fact is we all sort of run things to-gether. The rest of the boys have got just as much say as I have when it comes to takin' on new talent. An' they're just as hard-headed as I am when it comes to a man provin' what he's done—some of 'em's harder-headed, even. So when you get there, don't forget to fetch along all the proof you've got—all the cash an' all the dust saved off 'n them jobs you've pulled. I'd hate like hell to have the boys turn you down because they ain't satisfied—after all the trouble I've had locatin' you. If the boys okay you, you can stick all your dust in Cush's safe an' take a receipt for it. An' you can bet that once it gets in that safe it'll stay there."

"That's swell," the man agreed. "That's right where I'd want it to stay. 'Cause, like I said, I figure on bein' up there from now on, I'd want the stuff handy—an' it looks like the safe would beat a cache all to hell. I guess no one'll ever rob *that* safe, eh?"

"It ain't likely," Black John replied. "When can you start for Halfaday?"

"When you goin' back there?"

"Right now."

"Okay, I'll go along with you. The quicker we git up there, the quicker we kin git somethin' goin'."

"That's right, Bat Eye. In fact, I'm thinkin' of a play that I believe'll interest you from start to finish."

"An' you bet, the first damn thing I do when I git there will be to knock off that damn Lafe Toms before he blabs what he knows where the police kin git holt of it. Or better yet—I've heard how you boys hang damn cusses like him up there—how about it? How about hangin' him?"

Black John nodded. "Well—as a matter of fact, Bat Eye, it was a hangin' I had in mind, when I spoke. But come on—let's get goin'. Where's this cache you've got Tozzer's dust in?"

The man grinned, shoved the wood box aside, lifted several floorboards, and one at a time, removed forty-nine eighty-ounce sacks of dust which he placed in his pack sack. He glanced up with a grin. "The *klooch* made them sacks. Sewed 'em damn good an' stout. But she don't even know they're cached here—right in her own shack. I told her I cached the dust over there in the bresh on the sidehill. When she comes back an' I ain't here she'll think I'm off on some kind of a job. But when I don't show up after a while, I'll bet she'll dig that hull hill down an' throw it in the river huntin' fer the dust."

THE TRIP to Halfaday was made without incident, and the two went immediately to Black John's shack. "Jest stick the pack sack under the bunk, yonder," the big man advised. "We'll slip over to the saloon an' see Cush. There might be some characters hangin' around there that it would be just as well if they didn't spot a pack that heavy. None of the regular gang would make a play for it—but quite a lot of riff-raff drifts in on us, an' the way I figger, what they don't know won't hurt 'em. We can show the boys the proof, later."

The two proceeded to the saloon to find a dozen or more of the men of Halfaday, some at the bar, others at the stud tables. As they stepped into the room Bat Eye halted suddenly, glanced at Black John, and pointed to Lafe Toms who stood leaning against the bar. "There's the damn cuss, now! Why not go ahead an' hang him an' be done with it?"

The big man glanced about the room, as the eyes of all centered on the speaker. "Well, there seems to be a quorum present. All of 'em members in good standin'. Not a riff-raff amongst 'em. Guess we might's well git it over with, first as last." Striding to the bar he pounded loudly with his fist. "Miners' meetin' called to try one, Lafe Toms, fer murder, robbery, an' shootin' off his mouth. Five minutes will be allowed for cashin' in chips an' finishin' drinks."

Lafe Toms turned pale and his mouth sagged open, as all eyes centered on him. Drinks were downed, and chips cashed in.

Lafe eyed Black John. "What—what the hell do you mean—murder an' robbery? I never murdered no one—nor robbed 'em neither one!"

"Shut up!" the big man roared, scowling at the other. "I'll app'int Red John as custodian of the prisoner. Fetch him along, John—stand him right there." When the thoroughly terrified man was properly placed, Black John glanced into the faces of the men who had crowded about. "Boys," he began, "I have with me here, one Bat Eye Cantrill. Bat Eye claims to have heard of the gang of outlaws that hangs out here, an' he wants to become one of us. He claims to have a record behind him that includes murder, robbery, an' woman-swindlin'. I've listened to a recital of his activities, and am inclined to believe that he told the truth. 'Specially so, because one incident checks in with what I heard, not so long ago from the lips of the prisoner, Lafe Toms. I refer to the murder an' robbery, this spring, of Jake Tozzer, down on Birch Creek. Lafe claims he laid in the brush an' saw Bat Eye, here, sink Tozzer's body in a beaver dam, an' make off with his dust—facts which Bat Eye admits.

"Now bein' as it's customary for a new candidate that seeks to throw in with our gang, to prove himself worthy of our acceptance, I'll introduce, to wit, Bat Eye Cantrill, who will under oath, name over the jobs he pulled off here in the Yukon. Jobs that includes the robbery of Seth Brownley, on Anvil Crick, an' Jim Kirch, on Hunker. Likewise, as I said, he admits the Jake Tozzer job, an' also the murder of a minin' engineer on Big Spruce, an' the swindlin' of his widow, in Dawson. Gentlemen, I hereby introduce Bat Eye Cantrill, in person, who will describe these various jobs, in detail." He turned to the man. "Hold up your right or left hand. Do you swear to tell the truth, the hull truth, er any part of it, s'e'l'pe God?"

"Shore I do."

"Okay. Gentlemen—Mr. Bat Eye Cantrill!"

FOR AN hour the men of Halfaday stood and to their astonishment listened to a boasting recital of murder, robbery, and the swindling of a widow. When he finally finished, the voice of Black John boomed on the silence. "You've all heard what Bat Eye had to say—an' believe me, it was an earful! His complaint against the prisoner at the bar, to wit, Lafe Toms, is that the said Lafe did, in confidence, relate the Tozzer incident to me. His claim is that such act constitutes a hangable offense. Now I'll admit that under certain circumstances, tryin' to hang a murder an' robbery on a man would be hangable. But you have just heard from Bat Eye himself an admission, under oath, that he did, in fact, commit the said murder an' robbery, describin' the job in detail. It is evident, then, that Lafe's offense consisted merely in tellin' the truth—which is not a hangable offense on Halfaday."

"What the hell!" Bat Eye blurted, his eyes twitching as he glanced into the stony-eyed faces about him.

Black John turned to him. "Hold on, Bat Eye. I believe you expressed a desire to remain permanently on Halfaday, didn't you."

"Shore I did—but...."

"Then one of the first things you've got to learn is not to interrupt a miners' meetin'." He turned to the others. "We'll take the vote, now. All in favor of hangin' Lafe Toms for tellin' the truth, signify by sayin' 'Aye'." Silence greeted the words. "Contrary 'No.'" A thunder of "No"s followed, as Black John again pounded the bar with his fist. "Miners' meetin' reconvened to try one, to wit, alias Bat Eye Cantrill for numerous crimes committed on contiguous cricks, an' subtendin' territory—some of 'em more subtendin' an' contiguous than others, but all well within our jurisdiction. You heard the man's confession of these various revolting crimes under oath from his own lips. Therefore, the prosecution rests its case. I will observe, however, that you also heard from the prisoner's own lips his expressed determination to remain permanently here on the crick. I believe his wish, in this respect, should be granted. However, it's up to you men to say, whether such permanent sojourn shall be in the flesh, or only in the sperit. In other words do we want any such a self-confessed, cache-robbin', widow-swindlin', murderer livin' here amongst us—or do we not? Any one of the offenses he confessed to is hangable under our code. I will now put it to a vote. All in favor of hangin' the prisoner, to wit, alias Bat Eye Cantrill signify by sayin' 'Aye'." A deafening chorus of "Ayes" filled the room, and Pot-Gutted John, the official hangman of Halfaday stepped forward with a rope ready noosed.

After the body had been cut down, Black John ordered it carried into the storeroom. "We'll bury him in the mornin'," he said. "He expressed a wish to remain on Halfaday as long as anyone else does—an' from here, it looks like he will."

Later, when the others had departed, leaving him alone with Cush, Black John stepped into the storeroom and returning with a money-belt which he opened, and counted fifteen thousand dollars in bills onto the bar. "This is the money he got off the widow," he said. "Just shove it in the safe an' credit my account."

Cush frowned. "So—you got yer money back, after all."

The big man smiled. "That's right, Cush—an' some small profit, besides. Don't lock up, yet. I'll be back. Got to step over to my cabin a minute." He returned shortly, lugging the heavy pack sack. One by one he tossed the forty-nine moosehide sacks onto the bar. "Weigh 'em up, an' credit me with them, too."

One by one, Cush weighed the sacks, setting down the weight of each on a piece of paper, when he finished he added the figures. "An' you make a profit of thirty-nine hundred an' twenty ounces," he said, sourly, "on payin' that woman twenty-five thousan' dollars fer a hundred pounds of fool's gold!"

Black John's smile widened. "Thirty-nine hundred an' *thirty* ounces," he corrected. "Don't forget them ten ounces I win off'n you on that bet!"

WILLIE SHOWS UP
ON HALFADAY

LYME CUSHING, PROPRIETOR of Cushing's Fort, the combined trading post and saloon that served the little community of outlawed men that had sprung up on Halfaday Creek, close against the Yukon-Alaska border, eyed the stranger who stepped through the open doorway and crossed to the bar.

The pack the man swung from his shoulder thudded upon the floor at his feet as he met Cush's gaze through narrowed lids. "This is Halfaday Crick, ain't it?" he demanded. "An' this would be Cushing's Fort where this here Black John an' his gang of outlaws hangs out, ain't it?"

Cush nodded somberly as he set out a bottle and two glasses onto the bar. "Yeah, this is Halfaday Crick. An' this is Cushing's Fort. Cushing—that's me. Fill up. This un's on the house."

The man filled his glass and glanced about the room. "Where's this Black John at?"

"I couldn't say."

"An' where's all them outlaws I be'n hearin' about? Hell, it's quiet as a graveyard around here!"

" 'Tain't noisy."

"But—there is a bunch of outlaws hangs out here, ain't there?"

"I wouldn't know."

"You sure don't put out nothin', do you?"

"No."

"Well, listen here, bud—you can loosen up with me. I'm an outlaw, too, if anyone should ask you!"

"They ain't no one asked."

The man downed his drink, and tossed a bill onto the bar. "I'm buyin' one. An' like I said, you don't need to be afraid of me."

"I ain't."

"What I mean you don't need to be afraid I'll spill my guts. Listen—jest to show you I know the right kind of folks—do you remember a guy name of Simco Sam? An' another one name of Stiles? I ran acrost 'em in Frisco—an' a skirt name of Tacoma Kate, an' a guy they call the Chicago Kid."

Cush nodded. "Yeah. We run 'em off 'n the crick fer one thing an' another. We don't allow no crime on the crick. They was lucky they didn't git hung."

"That's where they claimed they made their mistake—tryin' to pull off somethin' on Halfaday. They claimed this here Black John won't stand fer no one pullin' off nothin' here on the crick. It ain't no bad idee, at that. Accordin' to them, if someone does pull somethin', Black John, he calls a miners' meetin' an' hangs 'em. But you don't need to be afraid I'll pull nothin' around here."

"I ain't."

"Yer damn right! I don't want to git hung!"

"None of 'em did."

"I done time in Atlanta. Draw'd a twenty-year stretch fer a mail-train robbery me an' a couple of other guys pulled off. Done ten years of it an got paroled. Fill 'em up agin. I'll buy another. Ain't had a drink sence I left Whitehorse. Might's well git acquainted." The man grinned and winked. "Bill Jones is my name. Good as any other, I guess. I'll bet none of the boys here on the crick is puttin' out their right name."

"I couldn't say."

"Like I told you a while back, you don't need to be so damn tight-mouthed with me. I don't run off at the head, no more'n you do—when I don't know who I'm talkin' to. I've kinda got it on you there—I know yer all outlaws up here, an' that I'm amongst friends. But you, don't know me. Fer all you know I might be some damn shamus that come snoopin' around fer to git him an eyeful. But listen—you never heard tell of no dick er hawkshaw carryin' around no sixty-thousan' dollars in cash money on him, did you?"

"No."

REACHING INTO his pack sack the man tossed a thick packet of currency onto the bar. "Count it!" he said.

Removing the rubber bands, Cush counted the money. "Fifty-eight thousan' three hundred an' sixty dollars," he announced.

"It was sixty thousan' when I drawed it outa the bank," he said. "I spent the difference comin' up here. An' I didn't draw it out with no check, neither. Draw'd it at night with a nice electric drill an' a couple of horse blankets an' a little soup. You see, back there in stir I palled up with a couple of yeggs—post offices, an' hick banks was their line—an' they give me the the low-down on how to work it. They even put me wise to a hideout they had over in Tennessee, an' when I got me a parole I slipped over an' picked up the drill an' a bottle of soup they had hid there. Then I slipped out into the mountains to a town near where I come from.

"My pa, he was a preacher back there in the hills, an' along with his preachin' he done a little farmin' on a sidehill forty. I figgers on goin' back to the farm fer a spell till I could kinda look around fer a job to pull. But when I got there the cabin was empty. I figgered mebbe pa had died an' no one had wrote me about it. So I started walkin' to town, an' I met up with a neighbor—an old fella name of Ross Sergeant, I'd know'd when I was a kid. I ask him if the parson that usta live back there was dead, and I seen right away that he didn't know me from Adam's off ox. He give a kind of a cacklin' laugh an' thumped the ground with his cane, an' set down on a rock alongside the road, an' I set down on another one, an' he says 'No sir, the parson ain't dead by a dang sight!' He called him by name, but I ain't namin' him, bein' as already told you my name is Bill Jones.

"The old man goes on to say how Pa was about to lose the farm on a mortgage the bank held on it, when along comes a stranger an' give Pa the money to pay off the bank, an' then he buys the farm off'n Pa. He not only give Pa some cash money, but he throw'd in a house in town, an' a horse an' a red-wheeled rig, an' some kind of insurance where the company's got to pay Pa a hundred dollars a month as long as he lives. Everyone in the hills was laughin' about what a damn fool this here stranger was, makin' a deal like that, fer a woreout hillside forty. Then the old man claimed, this stranger begun depositin' gold in the bank till he'd deposited sixteen thousan' dollars' worth in about a month.

"Seems like the banker, Jud Grimm, had figgered all along there was gold somewhere in the hills on account of old Nate Bascome showin' him some samples a few years back. So when this stranger claimed he was goin' to New York an' start a company to mine this gold, Jud Grimm talked him out of it, an' offered to buy a partnership in the mine. The stranger, he took Jud up on it, an' Jud he forked over two hundred thousan' in cash fer a half interest in the mine—an' that's the last he ever seen of the stranger, er his two hundred thousan' neither.

"This here mine was s'posed to be in a cave at the back end of Pa's farm. But hell there worn't no more gold in there than there is right here in this floor—not so much, 'cause I've got fourteen, fifteen pound of it there in my pack.

"Where the stranger got the gold he deposited, er who he was no one ever found out. All Pa could tell 'em, he claimed his name was John Smith—but hell, anyone could claim their name was that, couldn't they?"

"Quite a few does."

"Well, seein' I'd changed enough so old Ross Sergeant didn't know me, an' him our next-door neighbor you might say, I figgered no one else would, neither—an' mebbe even Pa wouldn't. So I walks on to town, packin' my drill an' the soup in my keister. I gits there around suppertime an' finds board an lodgin' with a widder name of Sloan, down by the gristmill, tellin' her I was a house painter out of a job. I'd learnt paintin' whilst I was in stir, bein' on the repair gang.

"I'd spotted the bank as I come along—a one-story brick buildin', with one of them there hick burglar alarms consistin' of a brass gong high up over the door, an' that night I got a big grin out of figgerin' how I'd take this here Jud Grimm over the jumps agin, like the stranger done.

"Next mornin' I'm walkin' down the street, figgerin' on kinda casin' the joint, when I comes face to face with Pa. He's jest stepped outa his house, which it's next door to Clem Whipple's store, an' he looks square at me, an' I seen he didn't know me, so I stops an' kinda points to his house. 'Mister,' I says, 'yer house needs paintin'. It'll be rottin' down on you 'fore long, the way the paint's wore off in spots. I'm a good painter,' I says, 'an' I'm lookin' fer a job.'

"Well, Pa he turns around an' gives the house a good look. 'Couple of coats of paint wouldn't hurt none,' he says. 'How much would it cost?' I measures her up an' give him a figger, an' he told me to go ahead. So I got a ladder an' paint an' brushes off'n Clem Whipple an' went to work. I worked all day. At noon I slipped over to the bank an' changed a ten-dollar bill, an' cased the place, an' that night I slips out about midnight an' give her the works. I carries my ladder over an' clogs up the burglar alarm with an old gunny sack, an' swipes a couple of horse blankets outa Pa's barn, an' shoots the safe without wakin' a soul in town. Then I hits fer the hills, with sixty thousan' in my keister.

"There couldn't no one ketch me in them hills—I know'd 'em fer miles around. I finally gets to Nashville, an' on to Cincinnati, an' St. Louey, an' Frisco, an' whilst I'm there I connect up with them folks I mentioned an' they told me about this here Halfaday Crick, an' how if I could hook up with this here Black John, I'd be all jake. 'But you've got to be good—damn good in yer line, er Black John won't have nothin' to do with you,' they said. An' I'm tellin' you, brother, I am good. Do you think I'm a damn dick, now?"

"Nope."

"AN' THAT ain't all—comin' up here, jest below Selkirk, on the Yukon, I run onto a couple of fellas headin' back to the States. They was campin' there on the bank, an' I landed, an' I seen how they kinda glanced at a pack layin' there, so I pulls a gun on 'em an' reaches fer the pack. One of 'em took to the bresh, but the other reached fer his gun er a rock, an' I let him have it. Then I throw'd their pack into my canoe an' hit on downriver—there was fourteen, fifteen pound of fine gold, kinda like sand in the pack. So now—do you figger this Black John will be interested in me?"

"Yeah," Cush replied a bit grimly. "I figger he shore will."

"When can I connect up with him?"

"When he gits back."

"When'll that be?"

"I couldn't say."

"You mean I've got to hang around here fer God knows how long waitin' fer him to show up?"

"Nope. You don't got to. You kin keep on goin', er go back the way you come. It's all the same to me."

"You keep lodgers, here?"

"Nope."

"Where the hell can I stay?"

"One-Eyed John's shack. First cabin down the crick."

"But—where's this One-Eyed John?"

"Out back."

"Out back?"

"Yup. In the graveyard. We hung him."

"What did you hang him fer?"

"We didn't want him around no more."

The man scowled. "Well, I'm goin' to connect up with Black John if I've got to wait a month! Give me a bottle of licker an' I'll go hunt up this cabin. Damn if I wouldn't ruther stand around an' talk to a rock than you!"

"An' I'd ruther you would."

Picking up the bottle and the packet of bills from the bar, the man stowed them in his pack and crossed to the doorway where he paused. "I'll be back fer some grub when I figger what I'll be needin'," he said, and disappeared.

II

ONE MORNING, SEVERAL days later, Black John stepped into the room and crossed to the bar as Cush set out a bottle, two glasses, and the leather dice box. The big man picked up the box and cast the dice. "I feel lucky, this mornin'," he said. "I'm leavin' them three fours in one."

Cush rolled out three aces, and came back with four fives, which Black John failed to beat. He smiled and filled his glass as Cush made the proper entry in his day book. "Guess I ain't as lucky as I thought," he said.

"I know damn well you ain't," Cush replied. Filling his own glass, he shoved the square-framed steel-rimmed spectacles from nose to forehead, and eyed the other somberly. "No, sir," he repeated, "you shore ain't."

"Oh, cheer up, Cush. Things are never so bad they can't get worse."

"The hell they can't!"

"What are you drivin' at? Has some on toward circumstance arisen to disturb the tranquility of our crick?"

"Whatever that means, accordin to your angle, this here's worst. A stranger come amongst us. That is, he's a stranger to me. I got a hunch mebbe you won't figger he's so damn strange."

"*Chechako?*"

"Yeah, he's a *chechako*, all right."

"Is he a promisin'-lookin' prospect? Does he seem fairly well heeled?"

"He's about as promisin' lookin' as a rattlesnake. An' he fetched in a little better'n fifty-eight thousan' in bills, an' right around two hundred an fifty ounces of dust."

"The proceeds, no doubt, of some crime, or series of crimes?"

"He bragged that he blow'd them bills out of a safe, back in the States, an' got the dust off'n a couple of prospectors that was headin' outside with it, on the river jest below Selkirk. Claims he shot one, an' the other tuk to the bresh."

BLACK JOHN nodded. "Yeah, Downey told me about that stick-up jest before I left Dawson. Couple of lads name of Townley an' Emerson hittin' outside with two hundred an' forty ounces. Emerson's the one that got shot. Townley got a good look at the robber, an' he's hangin' around Dawson to identify him if the police pick him up. Where is this enterprisin' stranger domiciled?"

"Where's he which?"

"Where's he holed up at?"

"He's in One-Eyed John's shack."

"H-u-u-m. The amount—the fifty-eight thousan', I mean, is worth contemplatin'. The dust, of course, should find its way back into the hands of its rightful owners. I trust that this miscreant has been, able to locate the cache hidden in the wall of One-Eyed's cabin."

"Oh, shore—he'd find that all right. The string that pulls out that there section of log was stickin' out jest enough so's he'd see it when he'd go to hang up his hat er coat on them nails. But hell, John—if he don't pull nothin'—like some kind of skullduggery, er somethin', here on the crick, we can't do nothin' about them bills."

"Yer in error. The p'int of law that would automatically place those bills in our custody might seem slightly involved, to the average layman, inasmuch as the crime by which they were obtained was ondoubtless committed outside our jurisdiction. However, when viewed in its larger aspect, the problem becomes exceedingly simple. You see, the holdup there on the big river by which the dust in this criminal's possession was obtained, was committed well within our jurisdiction, which I have frequently held to include Halfaday Creek, its surroundin' an' contiguous territory, an' all subtendin' an connectin' waters.

"All we have to do is to send down to Dawson, as get this Townley up here, let Townley identify the robber, an' then turn over the dust to him. An' bang the culprit.

"If, in locatin' this dust, we should inadvertently happen upon some bills, that would be a matter entirely aside an' extraneous to the case in p'int, an' wouldn't be even mentioned durin' the course of the proceedin'."

Cush grunted and shrugged. "I know'd damn well you'd figger out we had jewishdiction in the case—an' I'm remindin' you, right now, if you grab off that there fifty-eight thousan', I git my half of it."

Black John grinned. "Yer choice of one little word is amusin', Cush. You know very well that I have repeatedly maintained that the surest wok of teachin' a criminal that crime don't pay, is to deprive him of the emolument of his crime. Under the circumstances, you should have said *when* I grab off that fifty-eight thousan'—not *if*."

CUSH DELIBERATELY refilled his glass and shoved the bottle across the bar. "Fill up, John," he said. "I'm buyin' this un. An' I didn't make no mistake in choosin' my words, neither. I said *if*—an' by God, I mean *if*—'cause I ain't so shore you'll be grabbin' off that fifty-eight thousan'."

The big man regarded him with a puzzled frown. "What do you mean?" he asked. "It was the proceeds of a crime, wasn't it? It wasn't obtained from a poor man, or a needy one? You said it was a bank job."

Cush nodded. "Yeah—that's what the guy claimed. Accordin' to his tell, it was got off'n a man which you, yerself, told me was as mean an' graspin' a coot as ever lived."

The big man's yes widened. "I told you! What the hell are you talkin' about?"

"It's a kind of a special case, John," Cush replied. "An' it's goin' to be interestin' to see how it comes out. Seems like fer onct, yer goin' to find yerself right plumb in the middle of one of these here damn draymas that yer allus puttin' me in the middle of. Yes, sir—seems like, fer onct, there's a drayma comin' up that I kin set back an' enjoy."

"What in the devil are you drivin' at?"

"Well, this here stranger, he sort of run off at the head. An' some of the things he said reminded me of certain things I'd heard before. From your angle, John, I'd say the worst has happened. The way I figger it, this here stranger ain't no one else than Willie. Now—let's see you figger yer way out of that one!"

"Willie? Willie who?"

"He claims he's Bill Jones. But Cripes—his hind name ain't no more Jones than what yourn's Smith. You'd know what it is—but I wouldn't."

"What do you mean—I'd know what it is?"

"By God, you'd ort to! He's yer own brother!"

"What!"

"Yup. That there brother Willie you was tellin' about bein' in the Atlanta pen. He's showed up here on Halfaday, like all the other damn crooks does."

"Did he say he's my brother?"

"No. He don't even know it."

"How do you know it?"

"Sort of figgered it out from things he said that checked up with things you told me when you come back from the outside last year. Like about his pa bein' a preacher back there in the hills an' ownin' a hillside forty with a cave on the back end of it, an' he told how some guy name of John Smith come along there an' paid off the old man's mortgage, an' traded him a horse an' red-wheeled rig, an' a house in town, an' that there insurance thing that gives him a hundred dollars a month long as he lives. Then he told how all the hill folks was laughin' about how the parson skun this guy ontil they found out about him onloadin' that cave onto that there banker, Jud Grimm, fer two hundred thousan' in cash. Then they begun laughin' at Jud."

"An' he figgers I'm the John Smith that pulled off that deal?"

"Nope. He don't even suspicion that."

"How'd he get out of the pen? An' how come he told all that—about Pa, an' Jud Grimm, an' all—if he ain't huntin' me?"

"He's huntin' you, all right, but he don't suspicion you're either that John Smith—nor yet his brother. He says he got paroled. Then he hit fer home, aimin' to hole up with the old man till he figgered out some play. But there wasn't no one around the farm, an' he asks some old guy name of Rass somethin' er other, if his pa was dead, an' this Rass, he told him all about what come off.

"So Willie, he goes on to town, an' he meets his pa, an' the old man don't recognize him, an' Willie offers to paint his house, an' that noon he cases the bank, an' that night he blows the safe an' gits away with sixty thousan' in cash.

"He winds up in Frisco, where he meets up with Simco Sam, an' Tacoma Kate, an' Stiles, an' some more of the riffraff we run off the crick, an they tell him about Halfaday, an' how he could hook up with you, he'd be all set. So he come on up here.

"The reason he run off at the head to me, was to prove he's an outlaw instead of a cop er a marshal. He's got better'n fifty-eight thousan' in cash on him, which is more than any police would have. Besides that he claims he's got fourteen, fifteen pound of dust. He said it like that—in pounds like a damn *cheechako* would—instid of ounces. An' I guess he had it, all right. His pack hit the floor with about a two hundred an' fifty ounce tunk."

"This fifty-eight thousan' Willie claims to have? If all you've got is his word for that, you might as well forget it. Because along with numerous other moral laxities Willie's the damndest liar I ever run acrost."

"I don't know nothin' about no mortal laxitives. But he's got the fifty-eight thousan', all right, in good cash money. He was so damn anxious I wouldn't figger him fer no police of no kind that he tossed the money onto the bar here, an' let me count it."

BLACK JOHN tossed off his drink and refilled his glass. "H-u-u-m," he said. "The situation does seem a might involved, at that. Let's recapitulate—we'll assume that Willie's here on Halfaday. That in itself is a catastrophe, in any man's language. He is possessed of certain funds dishonestly come by. He's seekin' to connect with me, not suspectin' that I'm his brother, or that I'm the John Smith that took Jud Grimm over the jumps, but because them damn riffraff down in Frisco told him I'm the leader of a gang of outlaws that hangs out here on the crick. Others have done the same an' failed to discover their error till it was too late. If Willie had be'n content to show up with merely the fifty-eight thousan' he got out of the bank, there's nothin' we could have done about it, except wait till he committed some crime here on the crick. However, steeped in original sin as he is, he couldn't refrain from pullin' off that robbery down on the Yukon, an' thus place himself squarely within our jurisdiction. It is plainly our duty, Cush, to send to Dawson for Townley an' then call a miners' meetin' an' bring this miscreant to trial."

"Yeah—but, hell, John—after all, he's yer brother. I never had no brother. But seems like, if I had, I somehow wouldn't like to hang him."

"Yer p'int is well taken, an' I'm inclined to agree with you that, as a pastime, brother-hangin' ortn't to be condoned."

"Does that mean you ain't goin' to hang him? If it does, it kinda puts us in a spot, too. 'Cause, if we don't hang him, how the hell are we goin' to git hold of them fifty-eight thousan'? We can't jest go ahead an' rob his cache, much as we'd like to. Even if we went ahead an' give Townley the dust back it don't somehow seem legal. On the other hand, they can't no one blame you fer not likin' to hang yer own brother. An', on top of that, you've got to make the trip back to Dawson an' fetch

Townley back yerself. 'Cause if you was to send someone else, an' you hung around here, Willie would reco'nize you shore as hell. I rec'lect you told me you went down to the Atlanta pen an' seen him last year."

"The case has complications enough without draggin' in any more."

"Yer damn right it has. An' fer onct you've got ketched right plumb in the middle of one of yer damn draymas instid of me. The shoe's on the other foot this time—an' it's goin' to be fun to lay back an' watch you try to wiggle out of it."

"At least, we can eliminate the probability of Willie's recog-nizing me. It's true, I went down to Atlanta an' had a short visit with Willie, strivin' durin' the interview to p'int out to him the error of his ways, an' impress upon him that crime don't pay. But before I ventured to appear anywhere in public after my business deal with Jud Grimm, I took the precaution of shaving off my beard an' mustache. If I do say it, myself, the transforma-tion was effective and gratifying in the extreme. I wasn't a bad-lookin' fella—smooth-shaved. Guess I'll go hunt up Red John an send him down to Dawson to fetch Townley back. You see, I want to give Willie all the breaks he's got comin'—like if it was someone else that committed that robbery, Townley could exonerate Willie."

III

AN HOUR LATER when Black John returned to the saloon, Cush introduced him to the stranger who stood, glass in hand, before the bar. "This here's the guy I was tellin' you about that's be'n hangin' around fer to connect up with you. Claims his name's Bill Jones." He turned to the other. "An', Jones, that there's Black John."

Jones eyed the big man appraisingly: "So you're the one I be'n hearin' so much about, eh? Fill up. I'm buyin' one. It's about time you got back. Hell, I be'n hangin' around here fer a couple of weeks an things is so damn quiet I feel like I was in a grave-yard."

"Yeah? Well, quite a few of the boys feels the same way—layin' in under them slabs, out back."

"Oh, you don't need to be afraid I'll try to pull off nothin' here on the crick. Simco Sam an' them others down to Frisco, they told me how you hang folks up here that tries to git away with somethin. But now I'm here an' you're back, I crave action."

Black John filled his glass from the bottle the other shoved toward him. "You crave action, eh? Well, I reckon me an' Cush can satisfy yer cravin'. How about shakin' a game of dice fer the drinks?"

"Shake fer the drinks—hell! What I mean, ain't you got no job figgered out we kin go ahead an' pull? Accordin' to them ones down to Frisco, you're the damndest outlaw they is, an' I come clean up here to throw in with you—an' you want to shake dice fer the drinks!"

"You an outlaw, too?"

"Outlaw! Who—me? I'll tell the world I'm an outlaw—an' a damn good one, too! Cripes, man, I done time in Atlanta!" he added boastfully. "Yes, sir—draw'd a twenty-year stretch fer a train robbery me an' a couple other guys pulled off."

Black John grinned. "Done all right, eh? Be'n me I'm afraid I might of botched the job an' draw'd only a five, er ten-year stretch."

"How?" the man asked, regarding the speaker with a puzzled frown.

"Oh, there's several ways a job like that could be botched."

"Yeah. We didn't work it right, neither. That's how come we got ketched."

"You must have be'n middlin' young when you pulled the train job, if you done a twenty-year stretch for it."

"I only served ten years an' got paroled fer good behavior. I'm out on parole, now."

"I trust yet reformation is more er less permanent."

"How?"

"I mean, I assume that yer moral regeneration percludes any possibility of yer reversion to type."

"God A'mighty! You talk like some damn lawyer, er jedge, er preacher, er someone like that. That time I got convicted there in court, I heard more big words spoke than I know'd there was. My pa, he's a preacher—but he don't know no big words. He's jest a common mountain preacher that goes by the Book. When he comes to a big word, er one of them funny names, he jest makes a stab at it an' keeps right on a-goin'.

"But I got a brother that's one of these here eggicated preachers. An' he talks jest like you—" Cush gulped his drink and emitted a peculiar choking cough. The speaker eyed him. "What's the matter—swaller a tonsil er somethin'?"

"No, they was a fly in my licker, an' he tickled goin' down."

The man resumed. "Pa, he wanted my brother should be a preacher like him, only better. So he sent him to one of these here preachin' cemeteries where they learn 'em how to preach to beat hell. He was in there when I got sent up. An' then, last year, he come down to Atlanta pen to see me. Big cuss, like you, he is—only smooth-shaved. An' he stud there an' run off at the head about the errors of my ways, an' how crime don't pay, an' all that tripe. You bet I cussed him out good an' proper, an' if it hadn't be'n fer them iron bars between us, I'd of give him a damn good sock in the jaw!"

BLACK JOHN grinned. "But at that, Jones, you've got to admit that if you'd heeded them early teachin's of yer pa, you might of turned out to be the same sterlin' character that yer brother is."

Again Cush gagged audibly over his drink.

"If you'd spit out them flies instead of swallerin' 'em, you'd git along better," Jones advised.

"It wasn't no fly this time," Cush explained. "I jest sucked a little licker down my wrong throat."

Jones turned to Black John. "Now yer back, you got anythin' lined up we kin go out an' pull?"

"W-e-e-l-l, just at present I can't say that I have."

"Hell's fire! I figgered you was prob'ly off somewheres casin' some job. Tellin' you about me, I crave action! I've already pulled off two jobs sence I got paroled. What I claim, the world owes me a damn good livin'—an' I aim to git it."

"Why would the world owe you a livin'?" Black John asked.

"I never asked to be born into it, did I? Well, I was. An' now it owes me a livin', don't it?"

The big man grinned. "Yeah, but look at it from the world's angle—it never asked you to be born into it, neither. In a good many respects it's a foolish old world—but not that foolish. Damned if I can see why the world should have to pay for an onfortunate biological accident."

"More big words! Hell, you give me a pain in the neck!"

"Well, we've give quite a few hombres a pain in the neck, jest above where you're standin'."

"What do you mean—above where I'm standin'?"

"Oh—two, three feet, straight up—between you an' that rafter."

The other scowled. "Then you don't aim to pull nothin' off right soon, eh?"

"W-e-e-l-l, I wouldn't go so far as to say that. The fact is, Jones, the only specific qualification you've give so far as to your ability as an outlaw, is the fact that you done time for a botched job of train robbin'. I rec'lect that you made casual reference to a couple of jobs you pulled off sence you was paroled. Was they successful in a financial way?"

"You mean—did I git away with 'em?"

"That's the p'int I was strivin' to bring out."

"I'll tell the world I did! I blowed a bank safe, back home, an' got away with sixty thousan' in bills, an' then, comin' down the Yukon River 'tween here an' Selkirk I run onto a couple of fellas campin' there on the bank. It was gittin' along toward night, so I landed there, an' when I seen 'em lookin' at one of their pack sacks sort of oneasy like, I swings my rifle on 'em. One tuk to the bresh, an' the other reached fer his gun, er a rock, er somethin', so I let him have it. Then I throwed the pack sack in my canoe an' got to hell outa there. I run down the river till plumb into the dark an' then camped on the other side, an' jest like I figgered, they was gold in that pack—fourteen—fifteen pound of it."

"This man you shot—did you kill him?"

"How the hell do I know? I didn't hang around to find out. What if I did? I got the gold, didn't I? An' that proves I'm an outlaw, don't it? What I mean—am I good enough to throw in with youse guys—er ain't I? Like I says—I crave action!"

"Okay, Jonesy. Just stick around an' be patient. I wouldn't be surprised if somethin' would pop up that will satisfy yer cravin' for action. Somethin' generally does when a fella like you shows up on the crick."

IV

TOWARD THE MIDDLE of the afternoon, a couple of days later, Black John stepped into the saloon to find Jones shaking dice with Cush for the drinks.

"Ain't you got nothin' doped out, yet?" Jones asked, as the big man joined them at the bar.

"Well, I've got a proposition in mind that I figger you'll be interested in. All the details ain't worked out yet, but it won't be long. Here, shove me the box, an' I'll beat one of you fellas out of a drink."

Several drinks were had when, at the sound of voices, all three faced the door just as Corporal Downey stepped into the room closely followed by a man who, at the sight of Jones, leaped forward excitedly, "There he is! That's the fellow that robbed me an' Emerson—standin' right there!"

Jones stood as though petrified as his glance shifted from the man's face to the uniformed officer. "My God," he muttered thickly, "it's—it's the Law."

"That's right," Downey said, "yer under arrest. An' it's my duty to warn you that anything you say may be used against you."

"Good gosh!" Black John exclaimed, and headed for the door. "That worshin' of mine! I left them clothes in the b'iler an' only a little water on 'em an' a good fire goin', whilst I stepped over fer a drink! Cripes, they'll be burnt to a frazzle!"

"It's murder," Jones mumbled, clutching at the bar. "Oh my God—an' now I'll git hung!"

Black John disappeared, to return some ten minutes later. "Got there just in time," he said. "Five minutes longer an' the b'iler'd be'n dry an' them clothes would have be'n ruined. They'll b'ile all right, now. I got her filled damn near to the top."

Jones sat slumped in a chair at one of the card tables, his gaze centered on his manacled wrists, as Black John edged close to Downey at the bar. "How is he—the one that got shot?" he asked in an undertone.

"He's all right," Downey whispered. "Got it in the shoulder. Doc says it ain't bad. Jones thinks he killed him. We didn't tell him no different. A little worryin' won't hurt him none."

The big man nodded. "Ondoubtless be good for his soul. A damn miscreant like him had ort to worry." He turned to the prisoner. "Step up, Jones, an' j'ine us. I guess Downey won't object to you havin' a little drink to sort of steady yer nerves. Hell, settin' there all slunched down in that chair, you don't look like no tough outlaw, like you bragged you was. Cripes, what I claim—if a man sets up to be an outlaw he'd ort to look the part."

"By God, I'll git hung!" the man whimpered. "You wouldn't look like no tough outlaw neither, if you was goin' to git hung! Yer a hell of an outlaw, anyhow," he cried, in a sudden outburst of fury, "lettin' one lone cop come up here an' arrest a pal, right in yer own hangout!"

Black John scowled. "Listen—just because you come up here on the recommendation of as ornery a bunch as ever disgraced a crick, don't make you a pal of mine—by a damn sight. Yer attitude is wrong, not to say totally depraved. All you think about is gittin' hung. You ain't expressed no contrition, nor no sorrow over shootin' that poor cuss down there on the river."

"I'm sorry, all right," the man snarled, "sorry I didn't knock off that other guy standin' there—then I'd be'n in the clear. I'd of got him, too, if the damn coward hadn't took to the bresh! The way it is, with him swearin' the rope around my neck, I ain't got a show."

"Tch, tch, tch, yer depravity is astoundin'. But just remember this, my good man, whatever the law does to you is for yer own good."

"Fer my own good! How the hell is it fer my own good if I git hung?"

"That," replied Black John, "is a problem each man must work out for himself. Anyway, it should teach you that gettin' caught don't pay."

"Where's he be'n holin' up at?" Downey asked. "Accordin' to Townley, here, he got away with two hundred an' forty ounces. We better go dig it out."

"Dig an' be damned!" the prisoner cried. "You kin dig the hull damn country up, an' you won't never find that gold! I got it hid where you won't never git hold of it. An' that ain't all—I got better'n fifty-eight thousan' in bills hid along with it."

"Where'd you get the fifty-eight thousan'?" Downey asked. "Rob someone else along the river?"

"No. I blow'd a safe in a bank, back home. That's where I got it—sixty thousan' dollars. An' listen here, Copper, I'll make a deal—I'll split them bills even with you, if you turn me loose. Think of that—twenty-nine thousan' dollars you kin shove in yer pocket—an' no one knows the difference jest except us. Black John an' Cush won't never blow their top, an' I'm bettin' this guy won't neither—'cause on top of that I'll give him back his gold—every damn pound of it. Hell—that's fair enough, ain't it?"

Black John grinned. "There you are, Downey. That seems like a good forthright proposition. You make a profit of twenty-nine thousan', Townley gets his dust back, an' Jones gets turned loose."

"That's right, Copper," Jones agreed eagerly. "How about it? Are you takin' me up?"

"Nope," Downey grinned. "Taking you down—down to Dawson to stand trial." He turned to Black John. "Where'd you say he holed up? We better try to locate that dust an' them bills."

"He's be'n sojournin' in One-Eyed John's shack."

"Yeah," the prisoner taunted, "go dig fer that stuff! Dig wide an' deep—but you'll never find it."

Downey chuckled. "It couldn't be, perchanct, that you cached it in the wall—where you pull out a section of log with a piece of cord that sticks out beside them nails where a man would hang up his hat an' coat?"

The man's jaw dropped as he glared into the officer's face. Then he whirled on Black John and Cush. "By God, it's a frame-up! Yer a hell of a gang, claimin' to be outlaws, an' all the time throwin' in with the cops!"

"Yer in error," Black John replied. "I must inform you that on Halfaday we neither help nor hinder the police. It just so happens that a year or so back, Downey had occasion to arrest another damn thief who had holed up there, an' in doin' so, he inadvertently discovered this cache. It's a trivial matter—just one of them little things a good policeman don't fergit. I must also inform you that we do not claim to be outlaws. We are a simple minin' folk, tendin' to our business, an' enjoyin' our harmless pleasures in our own placid way. If, as happens now an' then, some onregenerate an' sin-blistered soul drifts in amongst us, an' momentarily disturbs the tranquility of—"

"Shet up!" cried the man. "You'll drive me nuts—you an' yer big words! Yer worst than that damn' preachin' brother of mine. If I ever see him again, I'll give him a sock in the jaw—an' you, too, if it worn't fer these damn handcuffs!"

TAKING THE prisoner with them, the three proceeded to One-Eyed John's cabin, leaving Cush alone in the saloon. Stepping to the opposite wall, Downey pulled the cord, removed the section of log, and thrusting his arm into the aperture withdrew, one at a time, three eighty-ounce moosehide sacks of dust, which Townley immediately identified as the property of himself and Emerson.

Again Downey thrust his arm into the cache, his brows drawing into a frown as his groping fingers explored every inch of the box-like enclosure. Withdrawing his hand, he eyed the prisoner. "I guess you was dreamin' about that fifty-eight thousan'," he said. "There ain't no bills in there—nothin' only them three sacks of dust."

"You lie!" the man cried, his eyes blazing. "No wonder you wouldn't take me up on that deal—splittin' that fifty-eight thousan' with you to turn me loose! You know'd all the time where the stuff was hid, an' you figgered on leavin' them bills in there an' hoggin' 'em all!"

Downey shrugged, and stepping to the man's side, unlocked a cuff, freeing his hand. He nodded toward the cache. "Go ahead an' feel fer yerself. You seen what I pulled out of there—them three sacks. An' you seen me pull my hand out empty when I went in after them bills. If you put 'em in there, they must be there, now. I shore as hell didn't get 'em."

As his fingers explored the enclosure, the man's eyes glared at the three onlookers. "By God, I put them bills in there," he shouted. "They sure as hell ain't there now! Someone got 'em!"

Black John grinned as Downey relocked the manacle about the prisoner's wrist. "You ondoubtless lied about them fifty-eight thousan'," he said. "I ain't surprised none. A man who would stoop to murder an' robbery wouldn't hesitate to lie. An' besides that, my good man, it's plain to see that a sixty thousan' dollar bank robbery would be a bigger job than a man of your calibre could handle."

"Is that so!" cried the man. "By God, I kin prove I had that money—fifty-eight thousan' three hundred an' sixty dollars! I showed them bills to Cush—an' he counted 'em right there on the bar!"

Returning to the saloon, the four lined up at the bar. "Hey, Cush," Black John said. "Jonesy, here, claims there's a rift in his loot."

Cush scowled as he set out bottle and glasses. "A what in his which? Why the hell can't you say somethin' onct in a while that means somethin'?"

"By God, them bills is gone!" the prisoner cried.

Cush eyed the man coldly. "What bills?" he asked.

"You know what bills! Them fifty-eight thousan' three hundred an' sixty dollars! You counted 'em yerself—right here on the bar the first day I come!"

Cush shook his head slowly. "It's a while back. I disremember."

"Disremember—hell! You know damn well you stud right there an' counted 'em!"

Cush stared blankly into the man's outraged eyes. "Like I says—it's a while back. A lot of loose change goes back an' forth acrost the bar every day, what with the boys buyin' drinks, an' supplies, an' cashin' in chips. No one could rec'lect all them items. An' besides that, I ketched a dost of the gout onct, a long while back, an I don't remember good ever sence."

As the others poured their drinks, Downey edged close to Black John near the end of the bar. "Admittin', fer the sake of argument, that Jones did have them fifty-eight thousan'—it's kind of queer, ain't it, that the money stole from a bank should disappear completely, while the dust stole from a couple of prospectors should find its way back to the rightful owners?"

The big man eyed the officer guilelessly. "Why, yes, Downey, sence you mentioned it—it is a kind of coincidence, at that."

"A-h-e-m, about them clothes of yours in yer wash boiler, John—are you shore you put water enough on 'em so they won't burn, this time? They've be'n on the stove quite a while."

"Oh, shore, Downey—don't you go worryin' about them clothes. I filled the b'iler damn near full—an' anyhow, the fire's prob'ly out by now."

AFTER DOWNEY, Townley and the prisoner had departed down the creek, Black John stepped from the room to return a few minutes later and toss a huge packet of bills onto the bar. Cush counted them, credited Black John's account with twenty-nine thousand, one hundred and eighty dollars, and shoved the bottle toward him across the bar. "Fill up," he invited. "I'm buyin' this un. But at that, John, by God, if it was me, I couldn't of went ahead an' let my own brother git arrested when I know'd damn well he'd git hung. I ain't that hard!"

The big man grinned. "Don't go worryin' about Willie. He ain't goin' to get hung. Downey told me about that stick-up when I was down to Dawson. Then today he slipped me the word that this Emerson wasn't hurt bad. Willie thought he'd killed him because he prob'ly laid still after gettin' nicked in the shoulder so Willie'd think he was dead, an' wouldn't shoot again. Likewise, I knew that Downey an' Townley was on their way up here, because Downey told me he'd be hittin' for Halfday in a couple of days an' fetch Townley with him just in case the robber had hit for here. I was jest kiddin' about sendin' Red John down for him.

"Such bein' the case I just set back an' let nature take her course. In the first place I saw to it that not one penny of that fifty-eight thousan' would ever get returned to Jud Grimm, whose record of widow-foreclosin' an' orphan-cheatin' is enough to turn an honest man's stomach. Willie will draw a good long stretch in the pen for armed robbery. An that's a damn good place for him. His moral status is such that he's a damn sight better off in than out—an' so's society, in general. An' besides," he added, with a grin, "I don't want him runnin' around loose fer fear that sometime he might run onto that moral an' high-minded brother of his an' give him a sock in the jaw."

THE
HALFADAY
CREEK
LIBRARY

JAMES B. HENDRYX

James B. Hendryx's classic series returns to print! The author of more than 50 novels and anthologies, he's best known for his characters set around the outlaw community of Halfaday Creek in the Yukon. Set during the Gold Rush of the late 1890s, Hendryx penned over a hundred stories featuring these characters over the span of 25 years for a variety of pulp magazines.

Now, Altus Press has committed to return these to print. Using the original pulp magazines as the source material, along with the illustrations from their original pulp magazine appearances, and augmented with rare material.

Leelanau Historical Society

Celebrating 150 Years of Leelanau History

Leelanau County was officially established in 1863 when the State of Michigan was a young 26 years old. People were attracted to the natural resources from the beginning—first as a way to earn a living and build a home, and later to enjoy recreation away from the cities. Early settlers arrived on the islands beginning in 1839, while Native Americans populated the Leelanau peninsula until pioneers began exploring the area in 1847. For the next 45 years, the villages known today—and some that are abandoned—were settled. North and South Manitou Islands and the Fox Islands officially joined the county in 1895.

The Leelanau Historical Society was launched in 1957 by a group of residents dedicated to collecting and preserving Leelanau's history. Leland, first established in 1853 and later the county seat, seemed the natural location for the Society. When the old county jail became available in 1959, the museum found its first home. Through generous donations and grants, a new museum was built in 1985 and later expanded.

Today, the collections and archives contain more than 11,000 items. Visitors to the museum learn about Leelanau life and maritime history from exhibits, educational programs and publications. The Society continues to collect, document and preserve items relating to Leelanau history.

203 East Cedar Street, Leland, MI 49654

Tel. (231) 256-7475

info@LeelanauHistory.org

http://www.leelanauhistory.org/